CLAUDINE

BARBARA PALMER

THE BERKLEY PUBLISHING GROUP
Published by the Penguin Group
Penguin Group (USA) LLC
375 Hudson Street, New York, New York 10014

USA • Canada • UK • Ireland • Australia • New Zealand • India • South Africa • China

penguin.com

A Penguin Random House Company

This book is an original publication of The Berkley Publishing Group.

Library of Congress Cataloging-in-Publication Data

Palmer, Barbara (Novelist)
Claudine / Barbara Palmer.—Berkley trade paperback edition.
pages cm
ISBN 978-0-425-27672-3 (paperback)
1. Escort services—Fiction. 2. Murder—Fiction. 3. Erotic fiction. 4. Suspense fiction. I. Title.
PR9199.4.P344C58 2014
813'.6—dc23
2014015808

PUBLISHING HISTORY
Berkley trade paperback edition / September 2014

PRINTED IN THE UNITED STATES OF AMERICA

10 9 8 7 6 5 4 3 2 1

Cover images: Satin © Alexpi/Shutterstock; Feathers © Roman Malyshev/Shutterstock.
Cover design by Diana Kolsky.
Interior text design by Kristin del Rosario.

In memory of author
Joseph Kessel

For his masterpiece,
Belle de Jour,
one of the great literary classics

ACKNOWLEDGMENTS

I'm most grateful to my publishers: Leslie Gelbman (Berkley), and Nicole Winstanley (Penguin Canada), for the opportunity to write *Claudine*. It's been an exciting journey and one I couldn't have managed without the guidance of my very talented editors, Cindy Hwang and Adrienne Kerr.

No book is an island; it's the product of the foresight and hard work of a whole team of people in copyedit, sales, publicity and marketing. I'm so thankful to work with the expert staff at Penguin U.S. and Penguin Canada. Kudos as well to my North American and international literary agents.

Thank you to a former escort who helped me enormously to shape the novel's content and hats off to my friends and family for their sage advice.

CHAPTER 1

Claudine's appointment was for eight P.M., and by design, she arrived precisely two minutes late. She stood between two elaborate topiaries under a portico at one of the residences making up the grand flank of white stucco town houses in London's Grosvenor Square, Belgravia. It was a pleasant evening, if overwarm for April. She fanned herself and pressed a tentative finger to the bell. Chimes echoed inside. She smoothed the plain gray skirt that reached just below her knees, adjusted her glasses and pulled in her stomach. She fought back a flurry of nerves at the sound of steps approaching the entrance.

The door opened. A housemaid in stark black shirt and slacks gave her a quick, appraising glance and beckoned her inside, accepting the business card Claudine presented as she passed through a wide rotunda. "This way, please," the maid said without warmth, leading her to a room on the right. "The earl will be with you presently." The door closed behind her with a soft click.

The room had all the trappings of a male den, with bronze leather wingback chairs, somber oil paintings, an Oushak rug on the glossy parquet floor and a bar. Heavy damask drapes across the front window hid the room from prying eyes out on the street. Silver-framed photographs of a woman and three boys cluttered an antique davenport desk, and glass-fronted mahogany cases filled with books stretched across two walls. This wouldn't be the earl's main library, she surmised, but it was an impressive display.

She sat in one of the deep leather chairs, kept her spine ramrod straight and crossed her legs primly. Her oversized faded leather bag lay across her lap; she noticed with dismay the fraying straps, tucked them inside the bag and took a deep, steadying breath. Had she dressed appropriately? Was she too dowdy? Or would her severe apparel give just the right impression of a young librarian applying for access to the earl's substantial book collection? She took out her compact and gave herself a quick once-over. Her naturally long lashes required no mascara but she wondered if she should have softened her features with nude lipstick and a little blush.

Claudine waited; checked her watch. It had been over fifteen minutes. She got up from the chair with the intention of surveying the volumes in the nearest case. She'd just plucked a handsome calfskin folio from the shelf when the door opened and the earl strode into the room.

"Ah, there you are," he said with a posh accent that hinted of exclusive clubs. "How do you do?" He gave her a friendly nod. "I've kept you waiting. I appreciate your promptness."

Claudine inclined her head in greeting and returned the book to its place. "Very pleased to meet you, sir."

He gave her a long look. "Splendid. Let's have a drink, shall we?"

Since it was the evening hour and she wanted to appear collegial she obliged. "Yes. That would be fine, thank you."

A quick smile lit up the earl's features, and he went over to the bar. She took in his large blue eyes, thick hair—blond generously sprinkled with gray—and a ruddy complexion that made him look athletic and outdoorsy. Quite handsome, in an affluent, imposing kind of way. His smart burgundy smoking jacket with silken lapels was securely belted around his waist over dark trousers. He wore oxblood leather loafers.

He held up a bottle of Campari, the bitter ruby red liquid sloshing a little as he did. "An Americano, in honor of your native country?"

"Perfect," she replied. In truth, she hated the taste of the sweet vermouth he added to the drink.

He shot the drink with soda from a seltzer bottle, then fixed a whiskey, neat, for himself. He handed her the glass, took a seat in a leather wingback and motioned for her to settle in its mate.

"I didn't expect a librarian to actually look like one." He surveyed her modest skirt and glasses with approval.

She risked a cheeky comeback. "Occupational hazard. Does that mean you've decided to grant me access to your collection?"

He relaxed, crossed his legs. Claudine got a whiff of his sweet, smoky cologne. "Let's not jump to conclusions just yet. Tell me, why should I trust you with my very valuable books?"

"I believe you've already reviewed my résumé but just in

case, I brought a copy with me." As she bent to retrieve the papers from her purse, he waved his hand in the air.

"That won't be necessary. In your own words, please."

"Well," she began, "I've always loved books. As a child I . . ."

"And you spent your childhood where?" he interrupted.

"Boston. My parents were high school teachers who encouraged my love of reading. I studied English at Wellesley and took my masters in library science."

"Wellesley, did you?" He swirled the whiskey in his glass. "They must pay high school teachers very generously in America."

"Scholarships," she answered a tad too sharply, hoping he wouldn't detect the lie in her words. "Is your full collection housed here?"

"Goodness, no. It's a library of over twenty thousand volumes. The bulk of the collection, natural history and English letters, is kept at our family estate in Cheshire. This is only a small, eclectic selection." He finished his whiskey and rose to pour another. She had barely taken a sip of her drink. "My wife and sons are settled there now," he said, with his back to her.

"I see. It must be quite lovely, especially as summer comes on."

"Excuse me, my dear," the earl said, settling down once more in his chair. "I'm a touch nearsighted and wonder if you'd consider removing those glasses. I want to take your measure."

"My measure?"

"Look you square in the eyes. Examine your character."

Claudine folded her glasses and tucked them carefully into her purse. She had a way of widening her eyes that had a hypnotic effect. It worked its magic on the earl.

"That's better. You can tell much from a face, you know. And

I see your eyes are . . . dazzling. A most remarkable green." He threw back a generous slug of his drink.

"Getting back to my suitability, I graduated summa cum . . ."

"Yes, yes," the earl said, his voice clipped and impatient, "your credentials are excellent. Yet few references. Why is that?"

"Discretion is essential to my work. Clients are understandably concerned about their private affairs becoming public. Though you might be surprised by *how* secretive some are about their collections."

He stared her down.

She'd worn a fine-gauge knit cardigan over her crisp white blouse and sweat trickled down her spine. She shifted uncomfortably in the chair.

"I warrant this room is a trifle hot," the earl continued. "I'm sure that sweater is making you warm. Please don't stand on ceremony. Feel free to breathe a little."

"Thank you. I am a bit overheated." She took a quick sip of her drink, recoiled inwardly from the tangy taste and set it down again. She fumbled with the tiny buttons and shrugged off the sweater, arching her back slightly, which caused her breasts to press against the thin cotton of her blouse. The earl's gaze fastened on her chest. She quickly rounded her shoulders to mitigate the effect. "As I was saying, the private collectors I've worked for don't wish to be contacted; however, I forwarded a very good reference from the New York Public Library."

"Where you worked as a summer intern. That's neither a satisfactory nor sufficient reference in my view. But let's leave that topic for now. What brings you to London?"

"I'm surprised at your question, sir. For anyone who admires books as much as I do, London is the center of the universe. The hours I've spent at the Bodleian have been pure paradise! I planned a year's stay in the city. Unfortunately I miscalculated the cost and will be forced to return sooner than I wanted to. That's the reason for the urgency of my request."

"The Bodleian's in Oxford."

"Only a quick train ride from London."

He tossed back the rest of his drink. "Well"—he slapped his thigh—"I find I'm ready for another glass. And look—you've barely touched yours." As he stood up, she noticed his jacket fall open, revealing a prominent bulge at his crotch. She quickly averted her eyes.

While he busied himself once more behind the bar, Claudine tried to collect herself. The interview was progressing reasonably well, though she was growing uncomfortable under his scrutiny.

When he returned with a freshened drink, she saw his belt had come loose and the smoking jacket was still open. He flopped back into his chair. "It is damn hot in here. Young lady, please forgive my brusque manner. You don't take umbrage, I hope?"

She gave him a tentative smile and shook her head.

"Excellent. One must have a strong character to impress me. I've been told I have a tendency to steamroll over people. If it's any consolation, I might add that so far your answers have been admirable—except, of course, the lack of suitable references."

His words boosted her confidence. "I'm glad you find them so. I think you'll learn I can be quite assertive if the occasion calls for it. And I prefer frankness to subterfuge."

His blue eyes twinkled. "Well, then. In the spirit of directness, I have a request. I'd like to see what lies beneath that blouse you're wearing. It's buttoned right up to your neck. Very constricting, especially in this heat. And if you venture to whet a man's appetite, you must not leave him hungry."

She scrambled to her feet, indignation causing her color to rise. "You're implying I'm deliberately tantalizing you? That's in your imagination, sir. What you're suggesting is totally improper. And offensive. I'm beginning to think you agreed to see me under false pretenses."

"All the same, I must insist."

"But this is the twenty-first century," she protested. "Men can't take that sort of advantage anymore—no matter what their station in life."

"You see I remain seated in my chair," he said. "I'm not intimidating you or threatening you in any way. It is a request only. Whether or not you choose to comply is entirely up to you. You're of age. What harm can there be in that?"

She paused as though weighing the pros and cons and sighed. "Very well, then." She slowly undid each button and her blouse fell open, revealing a pretty white lace bra. She had big breasts; her nipples poked against the thin white fabric. "There," she said. "I trust that's satisfactory." A tiny smile tugged at the corner of her lips.

As she began to rebutton her blouse, the earl held up his hand. "Come, come. Now you *are* being deliberately provocative. The brassiere must come off."

Her full lips parted slightly. He caught a glimpse of her small white teeth. "No, sir. That is going too far. I'm afraid the interview is over." She plucked her bag from the carpet.

"Do you expect me to beg for it? I will, you know." His smile faded and he caught and held her eyes. "You're a total stunner, Claudine. Worth every penny."

She gave a little huff, half-exasperated, half-amused. She tossed her bag to the floor and shrugged the blouse from her shoulders. It fell around her heels. She reached for the catch at the front of her bra and flicked it open to reveal perfectly round breasts with rosy nipples. The earl's eyes narrowed.

She walked toward him, her breasts swaying hypnotically above her narrow waist and slim skirt. "This is too unfair," she teased. "You have the upper hand, and I don't care for that at all. I have just as much right to judge as you." She stood in front of him, her breasts level with his eyes. His nostrils flared, and she knew he could smell her perfume rising with the heat of her skin, a scent of roses in bloom with a peppery undertone. He tried to rise but she pushed him down. His large hands reached for her breasts and she brushed them away. She squatted, stretching the fabric of her skirt taut over her thighs, and ran her forefinger over the bulge in his trousers.

"What have you hidden in there?" She looked up at him through her long lashes with an expression of mock surprise. He took her hand and pressed it against his cock.

She felt for the zipper and found only a placket, an open seam. She reached in and gently exposed his prick: thick, humid and engorged. She regarded his cock quizzically, as if she'd never seen one before. Kneeling before him, she spread his legs apart and ran her fingertips over the skin of his shaft. He placed his hands on the pearly skin of her shoulders to bring her closer. She could smell the whiskey on his breath.

She brought the head of his cock to her lips and gave it a

chaste kiss. Rubbed it against her closed lips and across her cheek. She pouted her mouth and let the silky skin of her inner lip wet the tip of his penis. Opening her mouth wider, she sucked in the whole head of it, pushed her tongue wetly at him, gobbling him up, bit by bit.

Claudine let her mouth fill with saliva, and locked her throat. She took all of him in; let him thrust in and out. Her saliva pooled in his blondish pubic hair when one of his thrusts broke the seal of her lips. His eyes were slits of pleasure. "God, I'm not going to last. Take off your skirt."

Delighted with his response, she pulled away and smiled. "Not yet." She drew his cock up, freeing his balls, and lapped at them with her pink tongue.

He watched her ministrations for as long as he could, then let his head fall back against the chair with a groan.

She stood up and moved just out of reach and undid her skirt. It fell in gray folds to the floor. She had a narrow waist that blossomed into full hips and long legs. Her silken panty hose made her legs and pelvis gleam as if her skin had a coat of satin. Underneath the hose she wore tiny white lace panties with a long slit that revealed her shaved cunt. The earl could easily view the pink blush of her vulva.

He sighed on seeing her genitals thus exposed. "Not the innocent you made yourself out to be, Claudine. How delightful." He rose, dropped his pants and moved toward her, his penis a stiff soldier. She gripped his shoulders. He bent his head to her breasts and sucked and nibbled at her nipples, sending rich tingles deep into her belly. He tucked his fingers into the waistband of her panty hose and slowly peeled them down, squatting lower as he went. As she raised a delicate foot for him to pull the stockings off, he took his opportunity and buried his nose in her cleft. He parted her with his tongue and licked at her hungrily. She braced herself against the davenport desk, spread herself wide with one hand and guided him into her notch. He thrust deeply and grasped her buttocks with greedy fingers, knocking over the silver photo frames. After a few moments of vigorous pumping, he came in an electric rush.

CHAPTER 2

As she always did after a performance, Maria Lantos changed into street clothes, using the Edwardian powder room the maid directed her to. In the restroom she disposed of the female condom she wore. Many of the commercial varieties were clumsy, off-putting contraptions, but she had hers custom-made by a Munich firm and fashioned from a material as soft as her own skin. They fit her perfectly.

After tidying her wig and refreshing her makeup, she stepped out of the town house door wearing a sleek black dress, her eyes hidden by a pair of large sunglasses. Her black leather, red-soled Christian Louboutin stilettos clicked on the short flight of steps, and she crossed the sidewalk to a sedan idling by the curb. She slid into the passenger seat. Beside her, Andrei Baranov checked his mirror before swinging smoothly into the road.

She gave herself a shake. "I'm still sweaty. You'd think with all his billions the guy could turn up the air-conditioning."

"You're finished early," Andrei said, accelerating past a black London taxi.

She buckled up and pulled down the visor. She lifted her sunglasses, yanked off her brown wig, tossed it on the dash and shook out her own naturally blond locks.

"I tried everything but he was only good for one go. Big drinker. We spent the rest of the time talking about his book collection. It surprised him I actually knew something about literature—though, apparently, I do make a very convincing librarian. He wants me back tomorrow night. Wouldn't take no for an answer."

"Of course he does. What did you say?"

"Said I'd make an exception for him."

Andrei frowned. Maria laughed wickedly and cuffed his shoulder. His disapproval had no weight with her, though he'd proven fundamental to her success. He was her guard and business manager all rolled into one. She and Andrei were close, but he was her employee, not her pimp. *She* ran the show.

She glanced at her business cards in the divider pocket. On simple black stock embossed in silver were the words: UNIQUE EVENTS—ONE NIGHT ONLY. Underneath that, her stage name, CLAUDINE, and below it a website address and cell phone number.

"They never take it seriously, do they?" Andrei said. "Those men are so used to everyone doing their bidding, they can't conceive of anything different." Concern made tiny wrinkles at the corners of his deep hazel eyes. "One of these days, Maria, it's going to backfire on you."

"It hasn't yet," she said brightly, paying his caution no heed.

"I haven't eaten anything since breakfast. Will the Grill Room still be open?"

Andrei checked the time on the dash. "Should be." He took his eyes off the road for a moment to look at her. "You don't want to go clubbing tonight?" He straightened his tie in the rearview mirror. He was dressed immaculately in an English-tailored navy suit. Claudine glanced at him approvingly. His suit fit perfectly, just hugging his broad shoulders, and like his other gear, always the height of fashion.

"No, not tonight. I'm not feeling up to it. Just a quiet dinner—the two of us. Sound good?"

"Fine by me."

"Where are we tomorrow?"

Andrei took his cell phone from its holder and used his right hand to scroll through a menu while keeping his left on the wheel.

She looked at the screen when he handed her the phone. "Oh yes, Frankfurt. We have a transition day there and then next night I see my client. Who is it? Remind me."

Andrei was forced into a crawl behind a line of backed-up vehicles. He shook his head in irritation. "Gridlock even at this time of night. It's the one thing I hate about London."

"You should be used to it. New York is worse."

"I'll never get used to it. Your client's a businessman—Hirsch. Imports electronics. But the appointment is for his son. The father's worried because the young man's turning twenty and still doesn't show much interest—in either sex. Spends all his time gaming."

"Oh, that's right. I'm the birthday present and I'm playing

his favorite female avatar. Commander Shepard, I think. From something called Mass Effect 3. Should be fun.

"Mass Effect 3? I have no idea what you're talking about."

She laughed. "Neither do I. And the politician in Milan is two days after that—right?"

"Yes. A party at a villa just outside the city."

"And then Rome at the end of the week?"

"He canceled."

"Andrei, no! Any chance of making it up this close to the appointment?"

"Sure. There's a waiting list. But I won't have time to do a proper background check."

"See what you can do. You know we need it to offset the cost of the hotel and the flights."

"It's not the only consideration. You've got to think about your security."

"That's what I have you for." She snuck a glance at his handsome profile. He was smiling.

Maria walked into her London hotel room and pecked Lillian on the cheek. "Thanks for waiting up, sweetie. We stopped off at the Grill Room." She stripped off her clothes as she headed for the bathroom, "Did you have a good night?"

"Not bad. I watched *Britain's Got Talent* on TV. You're back early."

"I know! Lucky break, huh? Because I'm exhausted."

She emerged from the shower ten minutes later, her skin damp and steaming.

Lillian had the bedsheets turned down, a second cover thrown over to protect the sheets from the oils. Maria flopped onto the bed and turned facedown on her stomach. Lillian tucked a pillow underneath her lower legs and squirted citrus-scented oil on her hands.

"Not too long tonight, Lil. I'm not feeling great."

"You aren't coming down with something, are you?"

"Just tired, I expect."

"I'm not surprised. You've been keeping an insane pace. You need a holiday."

A muffled sound came from her mouth and she lifted her head. "I have time for holidays?"

"That's *exactly* what I mean!"

Lillian was the only person who dared to boss Maria around. A petite Filipino woman who barely topped five feet three inches, she was, nevertheless, a bulldog. An affectionate bulldog. A former movie makeup artist and hair stylist, she came recommended by another courtesan, a French film star who occasionally plied the trade.

Lillian knew how to exert just the right amount of pressure to untie the knots in Maria's muscles without causing pain. She ran her strong brown fingers down Maria's spine, worked on her shoulders and neck and along the pale, beautiful skin that glowed with an inner radiance. It was completely unblemished except for the small scar on the inside of Maria's right wrist. She'd had the scarification etched into her skin in the shape of a nightingale feather to hide the only blemish on her body: a discoloration caused when, as a child, her right hand had been tied to her crib railing.

"Your skin is getting really dry," Lillian said disapprovingly, applying more oil. "You should drink more water."

"It's the flights. The air is parched."

Lillian's strong hands kneaded Maria's plump buttocks and finished with her lower legs, the arches of her feet and her toes. Then she tapped Maria's shoulder to turn over. After oiling and massaging her upper body, Lillian noticed several blond hairs on her pubis.

"Some hairs are growing back. You'll have to get another laser treatment when we get home."

Maria groaned. Her skin was sensitive and her whole pubic area had been tender and red for several days after the last treatment. It stung horribly when she urinated. She hadn't been able to work for a week. Yet the laser produced wonders; the hairs pulled out as easily as clumps of dead grass. She had to have a treatment every six weeks; this time she'd gone for seven. "Can you wax me instead? The laser treatment hurts too much."

Lillian tutted, pushing one side of her black bob behind her ear. She massaged Maria's arms. "Yes, but now is time for sleep."

Maria rolled off the cover. Lillian swept it away and tucked the bedsheets over Maria's legs while she sat up. She got a glass and a cold bottle of Iceland Spring from the half fridge and handed them to Maria along with her sleeping pill.

"That's too mild. Don't I have any Benadryl?"

"It's too strong. You shouldn't be taking that just to sleep."

Maria closed her eyes.

"Is there anything else you want?" Lillian asked a little more affectionately.

"No, that's all, thanks."

Maria opened her eyes again in time to intercept Lillian's worried glance. Maria had been relying on sleeping pills too much and had started taking Xanax during the day as well to keep herself on an even keel. Even that hadn't been enough to produce a good night's rest.

"How was it tonight?"

"Just fine, Lillian. Not to worry. He was a perfect gentleman."

Lillian harrumphed and turned off the lamps, leaving only the bathroom light on because Maria was unable to sleep in total dark. After bidding her good night, Lillian went to the adjoining room. Andrei had a separate suite across the hall.

Maria waited until the sound of her companion's movements next door ceased—once Lillian fell asleep, not even a bomb could wake her—and then slipped out of bed. She always packed two cases: one held lube, extra condoms and sex toys, the other cosmetics, nail polish, and hair and body care essentials. She rooted through both. No Benadryl. Nor could she find anything tucked away in the bathroom cabinets. Damn. Lillian was keeping it all in her room, to dispense as she saw fit. Maria grew annoyed, although part of her knew Lillian was right. Loading her body with drugs was a bad idea.

In addition to the sleeping aids and Xanax, she took Lybrel to stop her periods. In her profession, they meant too much time away from work. She wondered if it was taking a toll on her body. She took a long look in the bathroom mirror. No one would guess she was twenty-six. But there were small signs. She ran her fingers over the tender skin underneath her eyes. A line or two. Almost imperceptible, but there. And she'd found a gray hair at her temple the other day. Just one, yet even that alarmed her. Her breasts were still full and perky—how long would that last? She didn't have implants, and that set her apart. Most of her clients preferred real to silicone, and a number of them actually asked before they booked her. She'd steadily built her business over five years and was now at the top of her form, in demand around the world and able to command the highest prices. She'd always known her career would be short, like a professional athlete's. One didn't last in this game for very long. Her feelings about that were ambivalent: some days she wanted to be a courtesan forever—loving the fame, sexuality and power—other days she never wanted to have sex again.

There were additional considerations too. Maria hadn't had a boyfriend in months; in the past, they'd either become jealous when they found out what she did, or they wanted to watch. As for women friends, it had become too complicated to avoid the intimate confessions of friendship to hide her double life, to explain her frequent absences from New York and the comfortable lifestyle she enjoyed. Many interesting and intelligent women in her grad program at Yale had made overtures of friendship: invitations to coffee, art house films, drinks at the campus bar. She turned them all down. Who among them would understand her lifestyle? How many would befriend her if they knew the truth? She refused to justify her choices or be judged by puritanical standards. No, casual friendships were out of the question. The risk of discovery was too great and she didn't want to lose what she'd earned through hard work. She was close to paying off her apartment, and if all went well with her thesis on early erotic literature, she was practically assured of a faculty position. Besides, she had two of the truest friends in Andrei and Lillian. They protected her, took care of her. They were her family and all she needed.

Sleep wouldn't come easily tonight. She was tired, but keyed up. She felt aroused—inexplicably so. She hadn't found the earl particularly hot. Still, the sexual tension lingered. She rarely climaxed with clients. It happened spontaneously sometimes, or if she used a sexual aide. But the missionary position did nothing for her. She knew how to simulate orgasm convincingly; it was all part of her performance. Few of her clients ever detected the truth, and those who did probably didn't care. On nights like tonight, when peace eluded her, an orgasm was the quickest route to a restful sleep.

She shut the bathroom door and sat on the rim of the tub, her back to the tiled wall. She took her nipple between her thumb and forefinger and caressed it. Her vagina responded, contracting, growing moist. She closed her eyes, imagined a naked man, his face indistinct but his arms, his shoulders and his hands muscular and well-defined. His cock was ready for her. She put the flat of her palm on her sex and rubbed gently, and then more emphatically, imagining it was the man's hand there, not hers. Fantasized his tongue tasting her tang, his fingers pleasuring her. She could sense the buildup now, warm sensations at her core, and fondled her clit, coaxing her body to climax. Felt the softening, got ready for the rush. She cried out as she came, an exultant tremble running through her. It was over too soon, followed by a curious flat feeling, as if the world had suddenly lost its color.

Afterward, tucked into the big hotel bed, she fell into a dream-filled sleep. In her dream, she lay, cold and frightened, on a dirty cot in a pitch-black room, a cell. She tried to find the paler outline of the window, high up on the wall, but the darkness was too deep. When her eyes adjusted to the light, she made out a giant blackbird on the sill, with a long black beak and hunched neck—the kind that stole the young from other birds' nests.

The door creaked open and a vertical bar of light spread across the bare floor. A shadowy bulk in silhouette shuffled toward her. She heard raspy whispering, saw glittering blackbird eyes, felt the brush of wings on her bare stomach. She struggled against the pillow flattened against her mouth to stop her screams. The nightmare of her youth had come again.

CHAPTER 3

NEW YORK CITY

Two weeks later, Maria sipped a cup of coffee while she lazed in bed, the midmorning sun pouring through the open window. She heard a knock, then the sound of Lillian's voice in the hallway. Something in her tone made Maria sit up, alert. It was the clipped cold edge of fear. She jumped out of bed, ran her fingers through her messy hair, belted a pretty floral silk robe around her body and ran out of her bedroom in bare feet.

"Who's there, Lillian?"

She heard Lillian pronounce loudly, as if in warning, "Please come into the living room. I will bring Ms. Lantos." Lillian's quick steps were followed by louder, slower ones, the heavy tread of shoes on the hardwood floor. She snuck back into her bedroom. Lillian rushed in, her bright expressive face tinged with anxiety.

"What's wrong, Lillian? Who is it?"

"The police," she hissed. "They want to see you."

Her eyes widened. "Me? What for?" She grew pale, and without waiting for an answer, slipped her feet into flats and hurried out the bedroom door. Lillian hovered behind her.

Two plainclothes officers rose from the sofa when she entered the living room. Both darted glances at her cleavage, blinking when they did so, as if to give the impression they were not really eyeing her bosom. The taller one, who had close-cut auburn hair graying at the temples, held out his hand in greeting.

"Detective Steve Trainor and Detective Julio da Silva, 110th Precinct, Queens." Trainor wore a sharp suit that emphasized his muscles and height; da Silva looked small, rumpled and unkempt in contrast. "Your assistant, Lillian Flores, tells me you are Maria Lantos. Is that your legal name?"

Maria took his hand, gave it a quick shake and stepped back, gathering her robe tighter at the neck. "Yes. What's the problem, Detective?" She gave him just enough of a smile to appear welcoming. Smiles came easily to her even if they bore no relation to her real mood.

"Can you show us some ID?"

"Of course." She retrieved her vintage Louis Vuitton wallet from the marble-topped credenza where she'd tossed it last night, extracted her driver's license and handed it to him.

He checked it and gave it back. "I'd like to see everything. Your birth certificate too, if you have it handy."

"Okay, but can you tell me what this is all about?"

"We're investigating a homicide. The victim, a young woman, was found with ID for Maria Lantos that listed her residence as this address. Including a birth certificate. Any idea how she got it?"

"No, of course not. You said she died?"

"We're investigating a *murder*, Ms. Lantos." Trainor spoke slowly, as if to a small child. "So you have no idea how someone got their hands on your ID? Your purse wasn't recently lost or stolen?"

She shook her head. "No."

Da Silva took a small spiral-bound notebook from his inside breast pocket and began jotting down notes.

"Well, fake IDs are a big business. Maybe someone with access to your things had it reproduced and sold it." He gave Lillian a suggestive look.

Behind her, Lillian gasped. Maria turned around and said gently, "It's okay, Lil. I'll deal with this. Why don't you let me discuss it with the detectives?"

White-faced, Lillian hurried out of the room.

Maria turned back to Trainor. "If you're implying my assistant's involved, I don't think that's the case here, Detective."

"Can't be too careful, Ms. Lantos." Trainor thumbed through her credit cards while she took her birth certificate from the credenza drawer and handed it to him.

"You're Romanian?" Trainor asked after he'd glanced at it and handed it to da Silva.

"Yes. Born in Romania and adopted by my American mother when I was six."

"You were adopted but you kept your birth surname?"

"I went back to it later. When I turned eighteen."

"Hmmm. The deceased was using a New York driver's license with your name and address," he said, handing the paper back to her, "and she looks a lot like you. Do you have a sister? A cousin, maybe?"

A current of fear ran through Maria's body. For a few seconds she was silent, trying to pull herself together. "I don't have any blood relatives alive that I know of."

Da Silva had small eyes with overlarge whites bulging out from underneath thick, fleshy lids. He swept his gaze around the room. Took in the chamois leather sectional sofa, the Chinese Ninghsia rug, the Frederick Cooper lamps, noted how costly they were. His gaze settled on her left hand.

"Are you married, Ms. Lantos?" da Silva said.

"No. It's just Lillian and me here."

"What do you do for a living?" he asked, eyebrows raised.

She imagined answering him truthfully. *I fuck men for a living. Fathers, brothers, uncles, sons. Men who want to be sucked, groped, squeezed. Fat men whose stomachs have grown so pendulous they can no longer see their dicks when they stand up. Young men who think their cocks are gifts. High rollers, doctors, sports heroes, senators, actors. Lonely men who've lost their wives or sweethearts. Cheaters. Old men who've discovered the little blue pill and whose wives, thinking they'd been released from sex, turn away from them in dismay. Bachelors, husbands, men whose girlfriends say they want to watch but really don't. Rich men. So many that they blur together in an infinitely repeating refrain you can never get out of your head.*

"I'm a postgrad student at Yale."

Da Silva looked up, alert. "Fancy place for a student. Mind telling me how you afford it?"

"My mother helps me out." Maria mentioned her adoptive mother's name, a well-known New York lawyer. Da Silva recognized it immediately. His jaw twitched and he glanced over at Trainor. "I'm sorry for the intrusion," he said, "We have to ask, you know."

"I understand."

Trainor reached inside a breast pocket for a thin, fake alligator-skin case. He unzipped it and took out two pieces of paper enclosed in a cheap transparent plastic folder. He held them up. "Do you know this girl?" He handed her the photos. There were two shots, front and back of a thin blond woman. She lay on a stainless steel gurney under bright lights. Her body was rigid and naked. No sheet had been draped over her to protect her dignity.

She examined the frontal first. The murdered girl had the thin hips of a teenager just beginning to mature into womanly roundness; her parched blond hair splayed just below her shoulder was the same length as Maria's. Her pouty childish lips were the only feature still recognizable in a battered face. Her overlarge breasts looked incongruous on the teenager's body. Implants, clearly. But the worst sight of all was a jagged open wound on her pelvis, the skin and underlying tissue split apart all the way to her pubis.

She gagged and looked away. She felt a pain in her womb—a pang of sympathy. She looked at the other photo—the back shot. Nestled on the underside of the girl's right wrist was a raised scar in the shape of a nightingale feather.

CHAPTER 4

"I've never seen her before in my life," Maria whispered, handing the photos back to Trainor.

"You sure?"

"Positive."

For an instant, his flinty gray eyes took in her curves, then his face became unreadable again. "Okay. Here, take my card. If you can think of anywhere you might have seen this girl, or someone who might have copied your ID, give me a call."

"I will. Thank you, Detectives."

They shook hands again, and Maria was just about to lock the dead bolt behind them, when she changed her mind and yanked the door back open.

Trainor and da Silva turned around when they heard the door open and she motioned for them to come back. "Do you have a suspect?"

Trainor eyed her. "No. Not yet."

"He's still out there, then," she said, more to herself than to them.

"Yes, ma'am," da Silva replied. He blinked like a reptile. "We don't know if there's any connection to you besides the ID, but you should be cautious. We'll be in touch if there are any developments you need to know about."

Maria smiled her thanks, closed the door again and sagged against it; her heart flipped around like a bird with a broken wing. She didn't recognize the girl. That was true enough. But she couldn't tell Trainor or da Silva about the identical scar; the thought of the police digging into her personal life momentarily paralyzed her. If they discovered her secret, she'd be thrown in prison. She wrapped herself tightly in her robe and called for Lillian. There was no answer.

She found Lillian huddled in her bedroom, her shoulders heaving with the effort to suppress her sobs. Maria put her arms around her, hugging her like a hurt child. "Lillian dear, it's okay. I don't believe for one second you took my ID."

"*They* do."

"When they ask questions like that, they're . . . It's probably just a kind of test. They're judging your reactions. They're likely narrowing things down trying to sift out the truth."

"No, Maria. Because I'm Filipina they think I'm an illegal. It's bullshit and I should be used to it. But that doesn't matter now. How did the dead girl get your ID? Past the doorman, and into the apartment? This is a safe building. That kind of thing shouldn't happen here."

"I don't know, Lil." Only she, Lillian and Andrei had apartment keys. "No place is one hundred percent secure. I'm less worried about *how*; I want to know *why* and *who*." Maria dried

Lillian's tears with the edge of her robe. "Listen to me. While you were in the bedroom, the police told me the dead girl looked exactly like me. They showed me photos."

"Oh my God!" Lillian cried, jumping to her feet. "What does this mean? Do they think you were the intended victim? We've got to do something." She began to pace. The bulldog was back.

Maria got up. "No. They didn't say that. I have to phone Andrei."

Her stomach churned as she dialed his number. He answered after two rings. She gave him a detailed account of the police interview.

He listened without saying anything but sounded grim when he did speak. "I'm coming over, Maria. Right now. Don't open your door for anyone."

His order made her bristle. "Absolutely not, Andrei. I'm going to Yale today. I've got research to do and it can't wait. I've been too busy with clients lately. I won't end up being a prisoner in my own home."

"For God's sake, Maria. A girl who looks like you, carrying your ID, was killed. Doesn't that suggest something to you? I'm coming over."

"Fine. And when you get here, I'll be gone. So do whatever you need to—install security cameras, extra locks, whatever. But I'm not going to wait for you."

Andrei was silent for a moment. Maria could hear him breathing heavily and knew how upset he was. When he spoke it was with resignation. "I've got some contacts at the NYPD. I'll keep tabs on the investigation. Give me the detectives' names again."

Maria took a deep breath. "Trainor and da Silva." While Andrei jotted down the information, Maria promised she'd stay in touch by phone while she was on campus. She clicked off, reassured that she could count on him.

She washed down the toast and eggs Lillian made with another cup of coffee, then took a shower. Fear the police would discover her after-hours profession rattled her more deeply than her worries over the murdered girl. And though she chastised herself for it, self-preservation won out over empathy. She gave herself a shake and tried to calm down. She'd planned to spend the entire day at Yale and that was exactly what she was going to do. And later, she was meeting her old drama professor, who'd asked her to stop by.

Ironically, her scholarly ambitions—for it was her goal to become a professor—prompted her life as a courtesan. Like many teenagers, she'd once dreamed of becoming an actor. She possessed the fine bone structure and radiant skin the camera loved. That, and a few good connections, landed her a few small parts in movies. She also worked as an extra and took commercial assignments. But her dream of breaking into serious film roles eventually vanished along with her meager funds. She'd decided to switch majors from theater to literature in her sophomore year. Then she'd happened to pick up a copy of an Anaïs Nin novel. The world of the sexual professional caught her interest. She'd known other girls who'd ventured into the escort trade and made fabulous money at it. Why not her? She found the notion of a woman's value declining as she grew sexually experienced hopelessly outdated and offensive, and resolved never to buy into the chauvinism that lay behind it.

The challenge was to find a unique niche in the sex trade.

Something to separate herself from the pack. She came up with the role-playing idea and put a one-night limit on any man's access. It was a complete reversal of the usual practice of high-end escorts who established a stable of regular clients. It proved to be a stroke of genius. Maria understood early on that what was rare and hard to get would always command a higher price. She hired a top New York fashion photographer, sent her portfolio to the largest-circulation men's magazine and landed the centerfold spot. That sealed the deal. She could barely keep up with the demand even at her inflated prices. Her value was not so much in how she performed, but in the men's eyes, her celebrity status.

Few women around the world belonged to this elite group, and she had climbed her way to the top with nothing but her wits and her allure.

To keep up the appearance of legality, she cloaked her business as an event management enterprise—an added layer of protection for both her and her clients. Maria used the good taste and social graces drummed into her by her adoptive mother to create events around her performances—parties or elaborate dinners—harking back to the famous courtesans who entertained their "guests." She named herself after Claudine Alexandrine Guérin de Tencin, a sixteenth-century French courtesan famous for her salons. The heroine of Colette's novels—her favorite French novelist—also inspired her choice. In no time at all, she gained an international reputation.

Dressed in boot-cut jeans and a faded red T-shirt, Maria wore little makeup and looked no different from the end-of-term students strolling about the lawns. The heat, unusual for late April and so cloying in the city, was mitigated by the shade of the elm and cherry trees on the Connecticut campus. The cooler air carried the heavy perfume of spring flowers filling the beds. She took a deep breath. Here in the small world of the campus she could truly relax. No one to impress, no one to seduce. Because of its massive collection of volumes in all aspects of the arts, she spent most of her time at the Robert B. Haas Family Arts Library. Given the season, she had no problem finding an empty carrel. She took her tablet out of her satchel, set it in front of her and booted up her digital copy of *Fanny Hill: Memoirs of a Woman of Pleasure.* Of all the so-called pornographic works, it was her favorite. She loved the carefree, bawdy, comic undertones of the story—little more than a string of explicit, sexually rambunctious episodes. John Cleland had written it out of boredom while incarcerated in debtors' prison. He bet a friend that he could write a pornographic book without using any common, lewd words, and it became the most banned book in history.

She took a swig from her water bottle, remembering Lillian's admonition to keep hydrated, and scrolled through the text to find the section she'd intended to highlight: an account of a gathering at Mrs. Cole's establishment where Fanny was initiated into group sex.

Immersed in the book, she didn't hear the footfalls approaching from behind or see the hand reaching for her shoulder. She jumped at the warm pressure on her skin, and whipped around in her chair.

Reed Whitman raised his hands in mock surrender.

"Hey, hey. Take it easy! You didn't remember, did you?" Her old drama professor flashed a dazzling dimpled smile to show the missed appointment wasn't a big deal.

"I'm *so* sorry, Reed," she said. "I lost track of time."

"Didn't mean to startle you. You were on another planet."

"Yes, catching up on some reading. How'd you know where I was?" She began packing her tablet into her satchel.

"It wasn't hard to figure out where to find you, Maria. You're a creature of habit. It's after two—have you eaten? How about some lunch?"

She could feel her empty stomach complaining. "Sounds good."

"I'm not up to student fare today, so let's give that a pass. I thought Jade would be fun. You know it, right—on Chapel Street?"

"Pretty fancy."

"Glad to make it my treat. I'm guessing you've been cracking the books pretty strenuously, from the looks of those shadows under your eyes. Consider it a reward for your hard work."

Maria didn't really want to take the time for an extended lunch, but after missing their appointment she didn't feel like she had a choice. And she knew Reed could well afford it. It was rumored he owned a couple of commercial buildings in Manhattan and a large summer home on the coast somewhere east of New York State. Still, what she had expected would be a quick meeting was turning into something resembling a date. She pushed down her annoyance.

He took her to an intimate private room on the second floor of the restaurant. Their balcony table overlooked a flagstone patio, shaded by an enormous aged tree. Ivy had grown around its trunk to such an extent that the bark was no longer visible.

"I'd forgotten how fabulous it was here," she said as they took their seats.

"Pleasure's all mine," Reed said, taking the credit. He reached over and squeezed her hand. "The food's incredible here. They have a top-notch chef."

Maria eyed his hand upon hers. An adjunct professor who taught a few drama classes, Reed had been one of her favorite teachers; his charisma and wit made students flock to his lectures. He was wealthy aside from any teaching income and also owned an off-Broadway theater. And when you were a bit groggy and hungover from a long night at the clubs or hitting the books, seeing his handsome face at the front of the lecture hall didn't hurt. He had a well-defined Roman nose over sensual lips, an olive complexion, heavy brows and well-cut salt-and-pepper hair. Late forties, she guessed. No wedding ring. He fit her client profile to a tee.

Their drinks arrived. Perrier and ice with a twist for her and chilled Chablis for him.

"As I said in my message, I think your work shows great promise, and I wanted to see you to offer my help. Is there anything you'd like me to assist with? If so, fire away."

She withdrew her hand, the warmth of his touch still on her fingers. "I've written an outline and the first few chapters of my thesis—but that's all. Would you consider looking at it? I'd love your opinion on whether or not I'm on the right track. My supervisor is great on feedback. Still, it's always useful to have another pair of eyes."

"Sure. Tell me more about it. Erotic literature—what's your approach?"

"It's titled *Forbidden Texts: Eighteenth-Century Erotic Narratives.*"

"Hmmm. Pretty big range there, everything from *Fanny Hill* to *Justine*."

Whenever she told someone her thesis topic, they responded predictably with a smartass comeback. She appreciated Reed taking the subject seriously and warmed to her topic.

"That's right. I'm comparing *Fanny Hill: Memoirs of a Woman of Pleasure* with de Sade's *The Misfortunes of Virtue* and Richardson's *Pamela: Or, Virtue Rewarded.*"

"No Henry Fielding?"

"Fielding differs too much from the others."

"Still—quite a range. But here's to virtue, an antiquated notion these days—present company excepted." He grinned devilishly and they clinked glasses.

She considered, naughtily, of toasting to vice as well, but thought better of it, not wanting to give Reed the wrong idea. "Actually, I find de Sade excruciating to read. The brutal boarding school scene he described is horrific. I suggested dropping him from my thesis. I don't think his work is genuinely erotic. More of a torture manifesto."

"What did your supervisor say?"

"She said no. To keep it in. That the three books have parallels even though they seem so different on the surface. They're all firsthand confessions from women who started out as innocents and became entangled in a life of vice. Women oppressed by sadistic males."

Reed crossed his legs. He wore chinos, which she would have dismissed as nerdy but on him they looked good, displaying sinewy thigh muscles. She bet he played squash.

"I agree with your advisor. You can't ignore de Sade just because he offends you. You have to challenge those notions of propriety head-on in your thesis—otherwise, what's the point? I'm very interested in hearing your take on the ingénue. The simple country girl who is forced by circumstances into a life of sin. Quaint notion these days when college kids tweet their favorite sexual positions and upload twerking videos. They could teach us forty-somethings a few things, no doubt." He cocked his eye. "I was referring to myself, of course. You can't be much over twenty."

She didn't take the bait. "You think innocent young women caught in a vice trap is a thing of the past? No way."

"Well, maybe if you're talking about girls hooked on crack or something."

"I don't think so. Massage parlors are full of them. Women from Eastern Europe, Asia—country girls promised jobs as nannies—come to the States and are screwed remorselessly by their traffickers to get them ready for the men they'll service. When they finally end up in the bordello or massage parlor, or wherever, they don't even try to escape. By then they're too psychologically damaged."

Reed colored slightly. "Of course. Didn't think of that."

Maria wondered if she'd sounded too shrill. She hadn't meant to pontificate. Fortunately the waiter arrived with their order, giving her the space to switch tracks.

Reed had suggested an assortment of appetizers to share and they ended up ordering one of each from the menu. The waiter deposited the small plates in the center of the table, each dish garnished so artfully it almost seemed a shame to spoil them. Maria helped herself to hummus on toasted pita and popped it into her mouth. Other dishes held fat popcorn shrimp, steak tartare perfectly spiced and something called Flammkuchen, an Alsatian thin-crust pizza with bacon, onion and sour cream.

"This is delicious," she said between bites. "I was really hungry."

Reed swallowed and wiped his mouth with his napkin. "Very reliable here, no? Let's come back for dinner—tomorrow night. I'd love to see you again." He lolled back in his chair, and leveled her with his eyes. "In fact, I insist."

She set her water glass down on the white tablecloth, so crisp it seemed to actually gleam, and wished now she'd ordered something stronger to drink. No question, the thought of spending time with him was appealing. And it certainly wouldn't hurt her scholastic goals. But right now her after-hours work trumped everything else. "That's a nice thought, Reed. Thank you. The problem is I have a really tight schedule these days. I'm rushing hard to get more work done now because I'm going to be away a lot over the rest of the spring and summer. How about I take a rain check for the fall when school's back in session?"

Reed couldn't hide his look of irritation but he covered it up quickly. "Much sooner than that, I hope. I'm not letting you off the hook so easily." He pushed his plate away, then dangled the lure: "You're not teaching yet are you? Do you take any tutorials?"

She shook her head. "No. I don't have time. I bulked up on courses last winter so I could get through faster." Even to her it sounded like an awkward lie. Her other profession barely left time to write. "I hope to start teaching next year."

"You should reconsider. Taking on a tutorial or two is essential if you eventually want an academic post." He took her hand.

"I'm happy to organize something. I'm on pretty good terms with the administration, you know."

That was an understatement. He was a prized staff member. But the implication was unmistakable. Play nice and you'll move up. She had a feeling he'd find a way to do it without breaching any of Yale's strict guidelines.

On the other hand, Reed was a perfect choice for a mentor: distinguished, influential. Even though she got on well with her supervisor, another point of view would only enrich her work. It would be foolish to decline his offer. She gave him a slow smile that she knew had a distracting effect. "I'd love your help, Reed. Thank you."

"Excellent. I hope you don't mind me asking, but without teaching income, how do you manage? Postgrad studies don't come cheap. Mom and dad still helping out?"

"A small inheritance," Maria said. "It's hard to make ends meet. I'm pretty frugal. I'm hoping that will see me through. I haven't exchanged more than a few words with my adoptive mother in years."

"Oh. Pardon me. I didn't mean to pry. I have a bad habit that way."

Maria had perfected the narrative of her life story and practiced it on others until it became watertight and utterly convincing. The secret to credibility was to stick close to the truth. She'd been caught off guard by the detectives that morning, and had deviated from her usual script. She'd had to tell the truth about the age she was adopted—she wasn't sure if Romanian adoptions were sealed and she didn't want to raise their suspicions by lying. "Not at all. I was born in Romania," she explained. "My birth parents were killed by Ceausescu's secret police. I ended up in one of those horrible orphanages you hear about. Lucky for me, an American woman adopted me as a baby. Plucked me out of all those mistreated kids, horribly imprisoned in their dirty cots, and brought me over here." Reed's eyes followed her fingers as she smoothed her hair. "My adoptive mother wanted a fair-haired child."

"Wow. That's quite a story. Do you have any memories of Romania?"

"I was too young. I wasn't yet two when I came here. I did go back once. By then, the government had shut down the orphanage." Her mind went back to the trip she'd taken several years ago when she'd learned the truth about her parents.

"Must have been terrible for you," he said sympathetically.

"Once Ceausescu was gone, conditions in the orphanages improved—so I'm told. I don't remember it." She smiled pleasantly and changed the subject. "Enough about me! Your theater's in SoHo, right? What are you working on?"

Reed's face lit up. "*The Balcony* by Jean Genet. An incredibly important work. Set the stage for postmodern drama. I'll take you to a rehearsal. Are you familiar with the story?"

She tried to hide her dismay at how once again the conversation was touching sensitively on the private side of her life. "I know of it. It's set in a brothel."

"Trust the French to have a particularly intriguing term for a cathouse—'the house of illusions.' A madam runs a fantasy establishment, a place of mirrors and dark chambers. The set designer is really going to town on that. The brothel clients include a judge, a bishop and prominent local officials. Outside, a brutal revolution is taking place in the city. The director's even recruited real-life hookers for the walk-ons. That will be a total shot in the arm for marketing when we publicize it."

"The other actors don't mind rubbing shoulders with them, then?" Maria asked.

He laughed. He'd completely missed her acid undertone. "No, of course not. They think it's fun. The women are very interesting. Well-endowed to say the least, and I haven't seen that much bling in a jewelry store. I suspect one of the male actors has been practicing his lines pretty hard—off hours." He pushed his chair back, got up. "Come with me." He took her hand again and led her over to the edge of the balcony. "Knockout view from here."

He slid his arm around her and held her tightly so that her left breast pressed against his chest. "I intend to see a lot more of you, Maria." He turned his dark eyes on her. He had a way of drawing her in that she found hard to resist—in spite of his references to prostitutes and his elitist attitude.

"What if I don't have the time to date?" She pulled away slightly and gave him a flirtatious smile.

"Make the time." He leaned over and pressed his lips to her cheek. When she didn't move away, he kissed her. She parted her lips and met his caress. She rarely kissed her clients; it had been a long time since she'd felt a man's tongue explore hers.

He pulled back and his gaze traveled up and down her body. "Student clothes don't suit you. I bet you look fabulous all dressed up." Or wearing nothing on at all, he seemed to imply.

"I'll think about it," she said, placing a hand upon his chest. "Right now I have to get back. Do you mind?"

"I mind very much." He kissed her again. "But I won't press

my luck." He walked over to their table and left a pile of cash for the bill and tip.

Reed talked animatedly on the way back to the library, mostly about the staging of the Genet play. Maria answered his questions perfunctorily, her mind elsewhere. Was it pure coincidence he mentioned a play featuring prostitutes? Maybe the topic arose naturally from their discussion of her thesis. Or did he know who she really was? She never took pains to hide her face at her performances and her New York clients no doubt traveled in the same circles as he. Then again, maybe she was just being paranoid.

"Thanks again for lunch," she said as he bid her good-bye at the library door.

"Send me those chapters. I'd love to take a look." She felt the brush of his fingers on the nape of her neck. "I mean to see you again. Very soon."

When she entered the building, a student librarian she recognized was sitting at the front desk. "Hi, Claire."

"Have a good time? I saw you with Whitman through the window."

"Terrific, thanks."

"A word to the wise. Whitman's got quite a rep."

"What do you mean?" She knew perfectly well what Claire was getting at but wanted to hear the gossip.

"He's high on romance but short on sticking around. If you look hard enough, you'll see a string of broken hearts around here."

"No worries. Mine won't be one of them. But thanks for the tip."

Maria settled back into her carrel to concentrate on *Fanny*

Hill. Almost immediately she shut off her tablet in frustration. The conversation at lunch had been too unsettling. She didn't like Reed's insinuation that she'd get a teaching post if she played nice, although it was an enticing offer. She was suspicious that Reed knew about her after-hours activities and even more unnerved by the memories of Romania their conversation raised. The conditions at Spital Neuropshici di Copii, the death camp euphemistically called an orphanage, hidden away in Romania's desolate countryside, plagued her mind now. She'd lied when she told Reed she remembered none of it. She'd lived there for five months at the age of six when her parents were declared enemies of the state. A harrowing place. Babies packed like battery hens into filthy cribs, lying in their own waste, older children kept in basements for years on end, drugged and chained to their cots, never allowed into the fresh air and sunlight.

One night she'd woken to find the young boy named Lani curled up beside her, his skin like fine marble, bluish white and cold to the touch, his eyes open, unblinking. She'd screamed until her throat bled. But no one came.

CHAPTER 5

Maria walked from Grand Central Terminal back to her West Side co-op overlooking Central Park. She liked to wander along the park's green verge, especially on fine, warm days. Just last week she'd seen Pale Male, one of the park's red-tailed hawks, perched with his new mate on a tree branch, casting his yellow raptor's eye on the dog walkers' teacup poodles and Chihuahuas. Today, the pleasures of the park eluded her. Despite all the people on the walkways, she glanced over her shoulder checking for anyone who seemed suspicious. She felt a warm rush of relief at seeing the doorman and she passed through the marble foyer.

Two women, both a little older than Maria and very stylish, waited for the elevator. They carried shopping bags from Armani and Chloé. She recognized them as residents, although she didn't know their names.

She entered the elevator behind them. They exchanged a

glance when they saw her. The older of the two arched a perfectly threaded eyebrow but said nothing.

She nodded to them in greeting. "I'm Maria Lantos. I moved into the building six months ago."

The woman standing to the right, slim boned with fashionably tangled hair, glanced at her friend and smirked. "We know who you are, Claudine. Word gets around. Some of your clients have been boastful."

Maria's cheeks burned.

They reached her floor and the doors whooshed open. She stepped out. Behind her the woman spoke again. "Don't even think about bringing your johns here. The board will throw you out if you do. We'll see to it."

She stopped in her tracks and turned to face them with a smile that blazed. "That won't be necessary. Your husband's only a couple of floors up." She tossed her satchel over her shoulder as the elevator doors pinged closed behind her.

In spite of herself, the woman's remark cut her like a razor. It also took her by surprise. The careful separation she'd built between her two lives was collapsing like a blown-out tire.

Still shaken from the harsh words with her neighbors, Maria threw her satchel on the kitchen island and poured herself a vodka and soda over ice. She was sitting on one of the tall kitchen stools with her drink on the island in front of her when Andrei appeared in the doorway. He'd come over as he'd said he would.

"I can't believe you went out by yourself today after everything you learned this morning," he said quietly.

"Andrei, please don't start with me. I've had a very tiring day." She tossed back her hair and stared into her tumbler.

"Well, there's something I've got to tell you and you're not going to want to hear it." His look commanded her attention and she waited for him to speak.

"There's been a breach. Your secret is out. Someone has made the connection between Maria Lantos and Claudine. I don't know how it happened—only that it has."

She sighed. "Yes, I know."

"You know! How? Have you been checking the messages?" He walked over to where she sat at the island and placed two hands on the granite surface.

"No, Andrei. I didn't need to. Some snotty bitch in the penthouse just outed me in the elevator. She referred to me as Claudine. I don't know how she figured it out, but I think she's going to go to the condo board and try to have me evicted." She shook her head. "I really don't need this right now."

"Maria, it's worse than you think. We have a bigger problem than your neighbor."

"What?" She looked up sharply.

"There have been text messages. Threatening ones. Calling you a whore. Saying you'd regret not living up to your promises. I received them a couple of days ago but I dismissed them, not wanting to upset you. Now this—this murder and your stolen ID—" He paused. "I should have told you sooner. I'm sorry. We have to assume that the threats and this murdered girl are linked."

She fought her rising panic; to acknowledge it would be to go to a very dark place. "We don't know that. Maybe the threat's from a disgruntled client, and it's got nothing to do with the murder. I mean, it wouldn't be the first time someone's gotten pissed off. But back up a bit. What makes you think this guy's made the connection between Claudine and me?"

"The text was addressed to 'Miss Lantos.'"

Her face fell.

"I've done everything possible to check the origin. It's a dead end. I can't trace it."

"Do you think it was someone I've seen recently?"

"That's my guess. You know I check them all out. Someone's fallen through the cracks. I'm sorry." His taut shoulders stretched the fabric of his well-cut jacket as he leaned toward her. Andrei's mood was often cool, at times even detached. The anxiety on his face was something new and she didn't like it.

"It's probably someone in New York, don't you think? Maybe a guy who's seen me on the street, or followed me home?"

Andrei was scrupulously careful—it was a point of pride with him. When a performance was requested, he went first on Apollo, a clandestine website with restricted membership that a group of high-end escorts put together to warn each other about dangerous johns. If someone turned out to be a problem, the details would be posted anonymously. Once a client passed the Apollo test, Andrei did a further background check.

"I'm not sure. You remember London?" he asked. "You promised the earl to show up the next night—and you didn't."

"One night. That's the deal. We tell them that up front."

"It doesn't mean they have to like it."

Strangely, the mention of the earl brought her some relief. "You think it's the earl? He didn't seem the type at all."

Andrei shrugged. "It could be anyone. What concerns me is that I'm not always around to watch out for you. Someone has made the connection between you and Claudine. That means he might make a move when you're studying at the library or out shopping."

She squirmed on her stool. "Well, I can hardly take you to the library with me. How would I explain it? And you'd be bored out of your mind."

A faint flush tinged his cheeks and he drew back. "What? You think I don't read? I may surprise you."

"Okay," she said, rising to the challenge. "Who's your favorite author? And don't say Dostoyevsky."

"Tolstoy." He grinned.

Maria made a face. "C'mon, that's the same."

"George Orwell."

She picked up her drink and tilted it toward him. "Good choice."

Andrei grabbed a tumbler from the cupboard and poured a generous hit of vodka. He grew serious again. "Coming on top of this murder, these new threats against you seem really bad. Could be the same man, or maybe someone different. Who knows? You need to lie low for a while. You don't want to be playing the starring role in this guy's sick fantasies."

Maria had to reach back in her memory to find a time when Andrei had been this forceful with her and still she came up short. Endearing though his concern was, he had no business telling her what to do. The alcohol loosened her tongue and she let her irritation show.

"No way. I've got an important performance tomorrow night. The client's already paid for it. If I let this . . . stalker, whoever he is, get in my way, my business is finished. Don't even try to suggest it."

"You pay me to look after you. That's what I'm doing."

"Did he mention any of those fantasies in his texts, or are you just speculating?"

"No, he didn't. But I want you to think hard about this. If anything happened to you . . ."

His fingers trembled slightly as he grasped the glass. His apprehension seemed to have jumped the bounds of a business relationship and taken on the possessive tone of a boyfriend. Something about the softness in his eyes when he looked at her, the depth of emotion in his voice was new. Maybe. Or perhaps in her troubled state of mind she was reading too much into it all.

"I'm not going to run and hide, Andrei, but I do need your help. We need to step up security and find out who this guy is."

"I'll keep working on it."

"You know how much I appreciate everything you do for me. I feel safe having you to count on."

He threw back a slug of his drink and set his glass down on the counter. "I can't be there all the time, Maria. Don't forget that."

CHAPTER 6

Claudine lay on the spotless white sheet covering the raised table while Lillian worked on her. The bathroom in her condo, enlarged to accommodate the table, also contained a cupboard filled with the specialized tools and cosmetic aids needed to fashion her fantasy personas. Tonight's performance required an elaborate costume and makeup, so Lillian had started her preparations early.

Claudine was scheduled to appear at a small, private party at the Aqua Club where guests were required to wear Victorian evening dress. The host, who owned a sizeable stock portfolio, had paid her to stage a Victorian dinner and play the role of his consort. She'd hired a first-rate party organizer and approved all the arrangements.

After carefully cleaning, exfoliating and buffing Maria's skin, Lillian was in the process of applying a lightly frosted, gold-tinted body powder to every inch of her, except around her eyes. The powder enhanced her skin's natural luminosity. A few pounds had crept on during her trip to Europe, so for the last week she'd taken an appetite suppressant and gone on a partial fast. Better than the bulimia practiced by so many movie stars. She was still regretting her lunch with Reed.

Lillian grasped her left foot, lifted it and held it to apply the tint to her sole with a soft brush. Claudine winced.

"Did I hurt you?"

"No. It's all right. Just my baby toe again. It's been bothering me lately." She'd had her baby toes surgically shortened to make the five-inch stilettos she frequently wore fit more comfortably on her feet. She knew a few women in the business who had had their baby toes removed altogether. She wasn't prepared to go to those lengths.

She'd sought other professional treatments too—an injection of chemical filler to create pouty bee-stung lips that Lillian augmented with a topical gloss before performances, porcelain veneers applied to her teeth to keep them a pure white. She'd never opted for butt implants or other bodyscaping alterations that were so widespread now; she often wondered whether she'd ever have resorted to this surgery if her natural curves hadn't been enough. Yes, probably. A newly wealthy crop of Middle Eastern men were pushing rates into the stratosphere, and top-tier escorts like her could now command upward of forty thousand dollars per night. A modest amount compared to some profligate expenditures. She knew of one businessman who hired several women at a time at those prices and then didn't bother to even show up to sample the wares. Her fees provided an irresistible amount of money, and if surgeries could defy gravity for a few more years, she wouldn't begrudge any woman the option.

"Okay, we're finished with this." Lillian gently set her foot back down, and golden sprinkles fell on the white sheet. "Let's dress you now. It's going to take ages. How on earth did court ladies move? Even going for a walk in all those layers of stuff would be hard. Imagine what it felt like on a sweltering summer day. And no antiperspirant—yech."

Claudine laughed. "At least I get to do it in air-conditioning."

After painstakingly lacing her stays, Lillian fastened the overdress, a fabulous creation in gold silk. Claudine rented many of her "costumes" from a talented New York couturier who also designed opera gowns.

She sat at her bedroom dressing table, swimming in yards of gold silk, while Lillian pinned her shoulder-length hair tightly to her head. She dipped her finger in a dark brown coloring agent, applying it to the perimeter of Claudine's hairline, and then fitted the wig. They'd settled on brunette; the best color to enhance the gold dress. Flat across her crown, the wig had a center part with long, heavy ringlets falling on both sides of her head. Lillian fixed delicate pearl earrings into her earlobes.

"Okay. Up," commanded Lillian.

She stood, and the waves of silk shimmered to the floor. Lillian fiddled with the dress, tugging and arranging it to make sure it fit perfectly. She stood back. "There! You look like a princess. Let me get you a drink before we do your makeup."

"That would be great. Can you mix up one of those energy drinks? I already feel faint from these stays. It's like my ribs have been pushed into my throat. I can hardly breathe. When they called stays 'tight-laced,' they sure as hell meant it."

Lillian disappeared for a moment, then popped back into the

room. "Here," she said, handing her the drink. "Be careful not to spill any."

When Claudine finished it, Lillian made her sit again, covered her dress with a hairdresser's wrap and applied her makeup. To add more mystique, Lillian applied tiny gold particles in a mask shape around her eyes and extending out to her temples with a skin-friendly adhesive. The effect was the same as a mask but more alluring. A misting of perfume provided the last touch. Although she changed her roles constantly, Claudine always wore the same rose-based fragrance. It was enhanced with pheromones to augment sexual attraction. A Paris perfumer had designed it especially for her as a signature scent.

Lillian helped her on with kid leather boots and folded a hooded, floor-length cape around her. "Be back by twelve, Cinderella."

Her black BMW 760Li wasn't roomy enough to accommodate her elaborate costume, so Andrei had rented an SUV. He pulled the front passenger seat as far forward as possible to fit her wide, hooped skirt. Even with that, she maneuvered into the back with difficulty. She let her hood fall away once she was seated and parted her cloak. "What do you think, Andrei?"

He looked over his shoulder and his hazel eyes lingered on her face. "Very beautiful. Here—I brought you something." He reached down beside him and handed her a golden rose in full bloom, fitted artfully into a hair clip.

"How nice!" she exclaimed, genuinely surprised. She didn't think Andrei had a sentimental side. Life for him always seemed a deadly serious proposition.

She'd met him at an Atlantic City all-night sex party, a

birthday celebration for one of the Russian mafia kingpins. They'd flown porno queens in from Hollywood for the event, and Claudine was the starring attraction. She'd noticed Andrei right away: a roughly handsome man who stood apart, watchful, but not lascivious. She could tell he wasn't a bodyguard. They were obvious. Men who looked like they'd just stepped out of Rikers, thugs with weapons visibly bulging underneath their jackets. Andrei was more sophisticated than the others, but no less powerful. As the night wore on, the party got out of hand. One of the waitresses was cornered in a back room and gang-raped. With a nod to her client, Andrei appeared behind Claudine, placed a protective hand on her elbow and smoothly ushered her to a dark sedan. At her request, he saw her home, and waited until she disappeared in the elevator before pulling away. She called the client the next day for Andrei's contact information and when she reached Andrei, asked him to work for her. She knew basic details about him like his age—he was thirty-six—but otherwise he told her little about his life and she didn't press him on it. She knew he had a license to carry a concealed weapon, not something easy to get in New York State. Even better, he was discreet and loyal. One of a kind.

"Andrei—thank you. I love it." She fastened the rose just above her ringlets. "I'm guessing Lillian suggested this—didn't she?"

He glanced at her in the rearview mirror. "You don't think I can admire a lovely woman—even if she is a browbeating boss?"

"Browbeating? I'll dock your pay for that."

He smiled and started the car.

The Aqua Club was located in a former hotel—a Greek Revival sandstone building near the Village renovated into offices and galleries. A luxury spa was housed on the first floor, a bar on the second floor and private party rooms above. The bar was noted for its fine tapas, superb jazz and upstairs rooms for swingers and others interested in discreet sex-oriented entertainment.

She pulled the hood and cape around her once more. Andrei waved as she climbed out. "I'll park and wait for you downstairs," he said. She presented her card to the club doorman, who called up to her client and escorted her past the spa entrance to the elevator. On the third floor, she stepped into a small lobby where her host, Claude Ferrer, waited for her. He was of medium height, slim, with gray hair, and Andrei's research disclosed that Ferrer was in his late fifties and unmarried. He was dressed in black trousers and a tailcoat, open to reveal a rich brocade waistcoat and white silk ascot pierced with a diamond stickpin. He doffed his hat fully enjoying the fantasy. "Good evening, my lady," he intoned dramatically. "You are a vision."

He raised her hand to his lips and murmured against her skin, "I thank you for your efforts. The dinner arrangements are impeccable. And I have no doubt that you've taken as much care with the entertainment."

"Thank you, sir, for your delightful invitation." She gave him her most winning smile, dipping slightly in a mock curtsey. She parted her cape to reveal the tops of her round breasts, dusted with gold.

He took the folds of the cape from her hands and pressed them closed against her bosom. His fingertips ran lightly over her throat. "Please leave your cape on. My guests are looking forward to the reveal." He playfully tweaked her chin.

She didn't care for the gesture, which she found condescending and over-familiar, but she took pains to hide her displeasure.

Ferrer turned to press a button on the walnut paneling behind him. The doors swung open to reveal an intimate Victorian dining room. Wine-colored velvet drapes covered the windows and old oil portraits in gilt frames gleamed in the candlelight. Maroon divans trimmed in black flanked the walls, on which flickering sconces were mounted. Two ornate candelabras upon the table cast an ambient glow over crystal stemware. Vintage Victorian china laden with fresh oysters on the half shell, partridge beautifully garnished, lobster with lettuce wedges in an egg and oil dressing, broiled lamb kidneys and assorted side dishes promised a sumptuous dinner. Claudine admired the presentation, gratified the arrangements had turned out so well.

"Ladies and gentlemen, may I present Claudine."

Ferrer's guests, two men and three women seated around the table, turned to regard her. The men's features lit up in admiration. The women, a blonde and two redheads, regarded her with cool but not unkind appraisal. She guessed they were escorts. While not yet a legend, she had earned an impressive reputation; the men were fascinated and the women had a professional interest.

Ferrer stood behind her, and with long tapered fingers, pulled the hood from her hair and the cloak from her shoulders with a flourish. An off-the-shoulder swath of lace and ruffles beaded with pearls exposed her shoulders and deep cleavage. The bodice dipped to a marked V at her tiny waist and billowed out to a very wide skirt sweeping to the floor in tiers of embroidered, lace-edged ruffles.

The women scrutinized every inch of her gown, imagining what it must have cost. The blonde, wearing a red velvet gown with a bodice trimmed in transparent voile so that the rouged nipples of her breasts showed through, smiled at her wantonly. The other two, dressed identically in green satin with copper-colored wigs, looked at each other and whispered behind their hands. Their gowns were attractive but came from a standard costume house.

Ferrer made introductions. The two men—Clayton, middle-aged, and Haines, in his thirties, both well-groomed—kissed her hand. "I'm delighted to make your acquaintance, gentlemen." When it was their turn, the matching redheads pecked her cheeks demurely. The blonde, more brazen than her counterparts, brushed her breasts against Claudine's and kissed the corner of her mouth in full view of the men.

"Charmed, I'm sure," whispered the blonde.

Once they were seated, a waiter dressed as a footman emerged from the shadows to pour wine into Ferrer's goblet. He tasted the vintage and nodded to the waiter, who filled the guests' glasses.

"It is a wonderful occasion that brings us together, gentlemen. The celebration of a business deal that will make us all very wealthy. The contracts are signed, the press releases prepared. All that's left for us to do is seal the deal. These beautiful women"—he raised his glass to the redheads, the blonde and lastly to Claudine—"are for your delectation. You've earned them, and I have no doubt that they will make sure we never forget this night."

Ferrer clinked glasses with Claudine, while Haines toasted the blonde. Clayton sipped from the goblet of the redhead on his right, then from the redhead's on his left. They giggled again when Clayton's hands moved beneath the table to stroke their thighs. A package deal, she thought. Two for the price of one?

The waiter served the oysters to start. Claudine nibbled at her food, still feeling half-suffocated by the stays. Across from her, the blonde sucked her oyster from its shell while staring intently into Claudine's eyes. It was a brazen signal, and one Ferrer immediately noticed approvingly. He motioned for Haines to fully expose the breasts of the blonde. Clayton pulled down the voile, and the blonde's rouged nipples hardened at once. She let the juice from the oyster trace a glistening trail between her jutting breasts, all the while keeping her eyes latched onto Claudine's. She let the empty shell clatter to her plate and plucked another from the dish, sucking it noisily.

Ferrer's hand rested on Claudine's thigh. He began to stroke it through the delicate fabric. Taking his cue, her hand stole to his groin and fondled his penis, fully hard in his trousers.

He pushed her hand away delicately and cleared his throat. "Tell me, Clayton, how are you finding the entertainment so far?"

Clayton fondled the breasts of the redheads on either side of him. He had his tongue in the ear of the redhead on his right. "No complaints here." He laughed loudly, bending his head to suckle her nipple.

Puzzled by Ferrer's behavior, Claudine wondered if he was displeased. He signaled for more wine and watched delightedly as Haines took the bottle from the footman, poured it directly into the open mouth of the blonde. She offered her crimson lips to him in thanks, kissing him passionately on the mouth.

The wine flowed liberally and soon Clayton had a redhead in his lap. A scattering of freckles dusted the tops of her breasts.

Her friend leaned over, captured her breast, ran her tongue around the pale areola, drawing it delicately into her mouth. Clayton took her other breast between his lips. The redhead on his lap giggled and held both her breasts aloft so the other guests could see their mouths working hungrily at her.

Ferrer gazed appreciatively at the sight, then signaled for the plates to be cleared. After the waiter left, he rose. "Gentlemen and ladies, I'll keep you waiting no longer. Before dessert is served, I'm pleased to offer a very special treat. My sugarplum fairy." He took up his wineglass and inclined his head toward Claudine. "To a lady of unsurpassed sweetness." The guests raised their glasses and toasted her.

"Why, thank you," she said with a hint of coquettishness. She felt a tingle rush through her body. The performance was about to begin in earnest.

With an enigmatic smile, she got up and walked over to a small dais. It was only a step high and when she slipped off her kid boots, her skirts billowed over it, hiding it from view. Ferrer circled her. "The Victorians, ladies and gentlemen, liked their women demure, obedient and modest. So do I."

Haines laughed out loud, and then looked around embarrassed when no one joined in. Ferrer continued, "But from time to time, a man needs more than the pleasures a virtuous wife can provide. Beneath her lovely accoutrements, Claudine is a wanton woman. Do you believe me?"

Haines wasn't risking another misstep, so Clayton spoke up. "Ferrer, I think we must see for ourselves."

"Quite right, Clayton, quite right!"

Ferrer positioned himself behind Claudine and slowly untied the laces of her gown. The bodice fell open and the gown slipped in a crumpled golden heap to the floor. She stood in her underclothing, the hoops of her crinoline like a delicate cage. Ferrer helped her step out of the stiff garment, and began to undo her stays. She considered playfully resisting him, but the serious look upon his face gave her pause. The petticoat came next. He tugged it down to her feet and left her standing in her short muslin shift. Squatting at her feet, he reached up, pushed down a garter and rolled down the silk stocking. He repeated the process on the other leg, then, like a magician producing a rabbit, swept her shift over her head with a flourish.

Silence reigned. All eyes were transfixed upon Claudine's naked body.

Her skin shone with a golden glow in the candlelight. Her hair tumbled over her delicate collarbones, and her breasts rose and fell with each breath. Her nipples and belly button had been tipped with the same gold particles Lillian used for her mask. Ferrer watched his guests take in the full, delicious view.

He offered her his hand and she stepped down from the podium. He led her back to the table, where he gestured for her to stand upon her chair. She obeyed, and then, following his direction, lay down upon the table. Her dark ringlets cascaded over the white tablecloth, and her round, full breasts sloped gently to the side. Her long thighs and calves stretched on forever, and her delicate feet rested at Ferrer's place at the head of the table. Bowing over her, he ran his hands over her body as if she were a prized sculpture. He smoothed her hair in opulent waves, teased her nipples erect, and tested the heft of her breasts for the men to see. Then he traced the line of her ribs down to her soft flat belly and finally to her mound, which he stroked gently, for a moment or two, while she held her breath.

"Who will taste the sugarplum first—gentlemen?"

The men, engrossed by the vision of Claudine lying before them on the table, didn't speak. It was the blonde who broke the silence.

"I will."

All eyes turned to her. The blonde stood and removed her gown, her corset and her stays. Except for her delicate buttoned boots, she was nude. She took the hand of Ferrer, who, obviously delighted by this turn of events, escorted her around the table to Claudine's feet. She knelt upon the table, delicately parted the gold-dusted thighs of the courtesan, and began to kiss and nuzzle Claudine's mound. The blonde raised her ass and spread her hips so Ferrer had a tantalizing glimpse of her from behind. He grasped the globes of the blonde's rump and spread them. He looked hungrily at the blonde before teasing her with his finger. With his other hand, he reached between her thighs and patted her plump labia.

"And who will be the first to taste this split peach?"

The blonde pushed her bottom out further. She focused her attention on Claudine's pussy, pushing her thighs up and apart so that the guests still seated around the table could see the pink folds of the courtesan's slit and the tiny bud of her clitoris. Her genitals shone with moisture in the candlelight, and the blonde gazed at her rapturously. The blonde was an expert. She lowered her mouth and pushed her wet tongue to Claudine's inner folds softly and with a gentle rhythm. The dinner guests could hear the clicks of moisture as the blonde lapped. Once Claudine was soaking and emitting tiny moans, the blonde moved higher to her clit. She circled it with her tongue gently, over and over, and then when Claudine began to buck and arch her back, the blonde slid her tongue inside her. Claudine's body shuddered as her orgasm came in undulating waves.

Ferrer remained behind the blonde, squeezing the cheeks of her bottom. He motioned for one of the redheads to come over. He supervised as the redhead grasped the blonde's ass, lowered her head, and licked her. Once she had a good rhythm going on the blonde, he gave Clayton permission to fuck the redhead from behind. His cock already sheathed with a condom, Clayton quivered with excitement as he grabbed the redhead's bottom, pushed into her and pumped energetically.

The other redhead had removed her gown. Wearing only her garter belt, stockings and delicate high-heeled shoes, she was being energetically humped by Haines over a chair.

Ferrer looked appreciatively as the tableau he'd created. But his eyes returned again and again to Claudine, lying serenely upon the table, her cheeks flushed from her orgasm.

"Claudine, my dear," he called softly. "The night is still young."

The wine had gone to her head, but she accepted the flute of champagne Ferrer produced. She raised herself up on one elbow, careful not to bump the blonde, still straddling her on all fours.

"Come, my love."

Ferrer helped her off the table and put his arm around her, fondling one of her nipples. In spite of herself, Claudine felt a new, delightful shiver spread from her breast to her groin. The hand on her waist trailed over her buttocks and reached behind her. He slid his middle finger into her slit and moved it in slow circles. Her knees buckled a little, so he guided her gently to one of the divans. He sat upon it and arranged her so she was kneeling in front of him. He pushed his cock into her mouth.

She breathed deeply, willing herself to relax, and ran her

tongue along along his stalk. "That's my girl," he murmured encouragingly. Clearly on fire now, he quickly maneuvered Claudine onto the divan. She knelt with her face to the wall, her back arched, her bottom enticingly splayed. She felt him guide his cock into her. Her pussy, still dripping from the blonde's agile tongue-fucking, opened to him.

"My girl has a nice, tight little cunt." His hands gripped her hard now and he grunted with effort. She tightened her muscles in tandem with his strenuous thrusts. To help him along she let little cries escape her lips. He rode her and pulled on her nipples as if they were the reins of a horse. The tugging on her breasts hurt, but it was a delicious pain. The grip of her pussy pushed him over the edge. He shuddered as he came.

She looked up to see Clayton watching them. *My turn*, his smile seemed to say.

By midnight the ladies had been excused. In keeping with the Victorian tone, the men dressed, drank port and talked business. Maria flung her cloak around her nude body, slipped into her boots and gathered her dress and undergarments in her arms.

Her reflection in the mirror showed a face still flushed from her performance, as if her color had been heightened not only by the thrill but also by the tinge of depravity it beckoned to. A mistress of desire, Ferrer had called her as she bid him good-bye. She liked that. She pulled a simple shift from an inside pocket of her cloak, put it on, ran a towel over her face, removed her wig, wiped traces of brown dye from the skin near her hairline and combed her hair. Then she wrapped the apparel in her cloak and went down to the spa lobby where Andrei waited patiently, leaning against a column in his dark blue suit and crisp white shirt.

"Should we find something to eat?" he asked as he took the bundle from her and opened the door to the street. She often wanted to dine or go to a club after a performance, as much to wind down as anything; she liked never having to be "on" with Andrei. If she wanted to sit through a meal without saying much, she did, knowing he wouldn't take offence.

"Yes, please." She smiled. "With no performance tomorrow I can splurge a little."

Her favorite spot had always been Elaine's—a late-night watering hole for New York's movers and shakers in the entertainment business. After Elaine had died and her legendary establishment closed, Maria had been upset for weeks.

Their new favorite spot was on the East Side, a place named The Limelight after the famous nightclub. An intimate, upscale dining establishment, it stayed open past normal hours to service late-night customers. The owner greeted Maria with a double kiss. "Ravishing as always, darling."

She ordered red wine; Andrei his usual vodka. They split an antipasto plate and added a salad for her and steak for him. When their drinks arrived, Andrei sat back in his chair and gazed across the room. While he was thus distracted, she took a long look at him. He was quite sexy in his own way. She wondered if he had a woman in his life. She'd asked him once and he'd dismissed her question with a vague response. It seemed odd. He took things a bit too seriously, but when he was in a good mood his laughter was infectious. She found she could easily read his emotions in his eyes. Right now they still carried a hint of worry.

"You don't have more bad news, do you?" She toyed with the artichokes in her salad.

"I talked to a guy I know, like I said I would. A top informer for the cops. He told me the murdered girl with your ID was a Romanian prostitute. Illegal. Only been here six months. Worked out of a slimy massage parlor in the Bronx. She was fifteen years old. Had a couple of regular clients. Of course, no one's saying who they were. They're all bastards in that business."

She dropped her fork. "A prostitute? How could she possibly end up with a duplicate of my ID?"

"It gets worse. The cards didn't have any fingerprints. Not even the girl's. That means probably whoever murdered her stuck your ID into her purse." He reached over and gently squeezed her hand. "I don't want to upset you any more, but it seems clear your stalker must have copied your ID somehow, maybe during one of your performances, and put it back in your purse. It's not easy to create new cards like that. And it's expensive. You know what that means? This guy's willing to go to great lengths. The point of the murder was all about you."

Her mind raced. "Maybe he did get my ID at a performance, but what about my birth certificate? How did he get that? Break into my apartment?"

Andrei shook his head. "He could have applied to Romania for a new copy. Easy enough to pull off. No need to go near your apartment."

It was a small consolation. She pushed her plate away, feeling suddenly deflated. "This is a nightmare. Let's just go home."

Andrei took care of the bill. He put his arm around her as they walked to the car. She leaned against him, feeling comforted by his strong body close to her.

He buckled her in the passenger seat and walked around to the driver's side. When he got inside, he held her hand again and looked into her eyes. "You might as well know all of it. According to my inside guy, you'll be hearing from Trainor again. He thinks you're going to be the next target."

CHAPTER 7

Maria said little in the car on the way home. The butchery inflicted on the Romanian prostitute and the connection to Maria burrowed into her brain like a parasite. And Trainor believed she'd be the next one on the slab. She could no longer deny that the threats against her were deadly serious. All of the pains she'd taken to be discreet, professional and safe had been in vain. She felt exposed and targeted by both her stalker and the police. She'd always thought the choice of when to retire from performing would be hers to make. Now she wasn't so sure.

The next morning, she relented and let Andrei drive her to the university. She'd tossed and turned all night and was in no mood to put up a fight. He parked as close to the library as possible. Claire looked up from her paperwork as they passed the library reception desk and gave Andrei the once-over before reaching for her phone.

"Don't hover," Maria said testily when they reached her

study carrel. “Nothing’s going to happen in here. In fact, how about getting us some coffees?” She gave him directions to the café and booted up her tablet. He reminded her of a faithful Labrador as he walked away. Sometimes she wished he’d challenge her more.

With the memory of Andrei’s words about the dead girl still ringing in her ears, de Sade was the last author she wanted to read. Still, she’d put off opening those pages too long already. She was deep into his description of the cruel aristocrat Antonin, who required his young female charges to line up every morning and lift their skirts for his inspection, when faint laughter from the front desk made her look up. Reed Whitman stood next to Claire. He carried an oversized bouquet neatly tied with a raffia bow.

Through the cellophane wrapping Maria saw roses. The flowers’ pink centers made it look as if each bloom were blushing. Reed caught her eye and strode confidently toward her.

“Just happened to have these sitting on my desk,” he said, “and I thought of a lady who might like them.”

“They’re gorgeous.” She felt her color rise, a little taken aback by the unexpected gift. “Thank you. How did you know to find me here?”

“My informant.” He winked, at Claire who immediately buried her nose in a file.

Betrayer, thought Maria. Really, whose side was she on? She spotted Andrei returning, two paper cups stuck into cardboard sleeves in his hands. When Andrei took in Reed and the mass of flowers in her arms he stopped short. From the look in his eyes she could see a storm brewing. Thunder and lightning weren’t far off.

"Reed, one sec—okay?" She set the bouquet down and rushed over to intercept Andrei.

"Who's he?" Andrei said suspiciously.

"Just one of my former professors. No need to be concerned."

"Your old professors usually bring you flowers?"

"Andrei," she said without bothering to hide her irritation. "Do I need to share every microscopic detail of my life with you? Listen, I'm going to be here awhile. A good couple of hours, probably more. Why don't you take a walk around campus, get some lunch? Or just drive back to the city. I can find my own way home."

"I'll wait," Andrei said stubbornly.

"Suit yourself, but please don't hang around. I can't concentrate knowing you're looking over my shoulder."

Andrei cast another glance over to Reed, who was patiently waiting with a half smile on his face as if he knew exactly what was being said between them. "Doesn't look like you've been concentrating all that hard."

"I'll call you when I'm ready to be picked up. Can I have my coffee?" She snatched the paper cup. Without saying another word, she turned on her heel and went back to Reed.

"I have a competitor, I see." Reed turned his lips up in a smile but Maria got the distinct impression he wasn't pleased. "Kind of a formal dresser for campus, I'd say." He was clearly referring to Andrei's tailored suit.

"Just an old family friend who gave me a lift here. And I didn't know there was any competition." She pinned her remark with a quick laugh, then glanced back, relieved to see that Andrei had left.

"Well, look. I have two tickets for the Met. Box seats at Verdi's

Rigoletto. I'd love to take you. It's a rare chance to hear Nancy Herrera sing." He leaned over and whispered in her ear, "Frankly I'm dying to see you all dressed up."

Reed was in fine form today, and quite gallant. He was a little tanned already from the spring sun, which made his dark eyes sparkle. He showed his teeth too much when he grinned, but that was a tiny imperfection in an otherwise perfect face.

In spite of herself, Maria was flattered. When was the last time she'd been wooed or attended a concert or play off the clock? She needed a little fun to take her mind off her troubles.

"Sounds wonderful."

"Great. Pick you up around seven?"

"Is seven thirty okay? I have a lot to cover here today."

"Well then, don't let me keep you. I'll pick you up at seven thirty." He leaned over and briefly touched his lips to her cheek. She felt a tingle of pleasure, and after watching him pass by Claire's desk, she turned back to her book.

From time to time she opened the cellophane and pressed her nose deep into a bloom, surrounding herself with scent that transported her far away from the marquis's grotesque scenes. It wasn't until much later when Andrei returned to pick her up that she realized Reed hadn't asked for her address.

CHAPTER 8

"It's about time you got a boyfriend." Lillian raised her voice over the blow-dryer. The rush of hot air and pull of the brush felt good on Maria's scalp. She closed her eyes. "You have all those men, night after night, but really, when it comes to love, you might as well be a nun."

Maria smiled, glad to see Lillian back to her bossy, outspoken self.

"I'd make a good nun, Lil. I say my Hail Marys often enough."

Lillian shut off the dryer and set down the brush, plumped up Maria's blond tresses with her fingers and used a comb to smooth the strays. Maria stood. "What should I wear—black? I can't make up my mind."

"Black is too severe. White, for spring. That one with those tiny straps."

"White's intimidating. The red Christian Lacroix cocktail dress maybe. Red is more passionate."

Lillian helped her into the red dress, which hugged her body without looking vulgar. She patted Maria's tummy. "Don't eat too much or the seams will stretch."

"Thanks. The one time I'm taken out for dinner and you tell me not to eat!"

"You dine almost every night with Andrei." She cast a critical eye over the dress. "Wear a different bra. That one looks like it's pinching you."

"With Andrei, it's work," she said, shrugging the straps down and unfastening her bra. "That's different. Half the time I just have salad anyway. Tonight, I'm going to indulge." She selected an ivory silk bra, put it on and pulled up her dress. Lillian nodded appreciatively and went to straighten the closet.

Maria opened one of the drawers in her dressing table and brought out a pink box. Designed as a little girl's traveling case and decorated with princesses wearing Cinderella gowns, it had solid brass hinges and a leather handle. Her nanny had given it to her for her first Christmas in America. Inside, she kept a few treasures from her childhood in Providence. Three stones she'd gathered from the seashore and painted with her secret lucky symbols, her first ballet shoes, pink satin with the toes and soles marked and stubbed, a necklace of tiny fake gold links with a heart pendant from her first "boyfriend" in fourth grade, and a box containing vials of little girl's perfume in scents of lavender, rose, lilac and lily of the valley. Last, a little golden cage that held a small porcelain nightingale on a perch. To make the nightingale sing, you turned the key at the bottom of the cage. A present from a neighbor of her parents' in Romania, an old woman who kept a real nightingale. As a girl, she'd loved to feed the bird and listen to it sing. She dabbed some of the lily of the valley perfume behind each ear. It was a silly superstition but on special nights, she liked to use a little of the scent for good luck. The rose fragrance was strictly for work nights.

She'd just slipped on her heels when the doorman phoned up to announce Reed's arrival. She took her silk shawl and called over her shoulder on her way out the door, "Tell him I'll come down, Lil. There's no need for him to traipse all the way up here."

For a man who was always on a charm offensive, firmly in control of any social situation, Reed seemed at a loss for words when he set eyes on her. "You look lovely, Maria."

A taxi waited outside. He opened the door for her and slid in beside her. "Great building," he said as they pulled away, straightening his crisp white cuffs. He wore a custom-made gray suit, diamond cuff links and gray silk tie.

"I'm bunking with a friend for the time being. I'm in between apartments." The lie slipped easily from her lips. Lies were easy to tell to mere acquaintances or the men she serviced. She tailored them to fit the roles she found herself playing at any given time. But they became messy in longer-term relationships, which was precisely why she rarely allowed those entanglements to form in the first place. It got so she couldn't always remember the first lie she'd told, making the second and third much riskier.

"By the way," she said, "how did you know my address? You never asked for it."

"I asked your thesis supervisor—hope you don't mind."

"Oh, no. Just curious."

Golden light poured through the five massive contemporary arches at the front of the Lincoln Center. Her excitement mounted as she climbed the steps hand in hand with Reed. The lobby hummed with people and she was pleased when Reed stopped to introduce her to some of his distinguished acquaintances. For the first time since the detectives had walked in her door, her fears slipped away and she was able to enjoy herself. As she sat in the plush expanse of the Met with the lights dimmed, a thrill raced through her body when Reed's warm hand caressed her hip.

Maria never drank alcohol before her performances, but that night at dinner she made up for it and consumed more than she had in a long time. Amused by Reed's jokes, she felt the anxiety of the last few days tumble away. Reed insisted on ordering champagne, a sublime Veuve Clicquot, to celebrate their renewed acquaintance. Their talk turned to contemporary erotica and she confessed she'd been unable to finish *Story of O*, it had chilled her so. She far preferred Joseph Kessel's *Belle de Jour*.

"You're very sensitive," Reed said, laughing. "There's very little actual description of sex in *Belle de Jour*. I'm beginning to think you've chosen the wrong field of study."

"But it's all stunningly inferred. You get such a vivid picture. To me that's more erotic."

When he leaned forward to emphasize his next point, she got a sudden flash, a mental picture of him in a board room or lecture hall, all eyes trained on him, hanging on his every word. It had been Maria's good fortune that he offered to be her mentor. And if it led to a more permanent relationship, it was hard to see how she could find a better match. He was cultured, attractive and fit for a man in his late forties. They were definitely on the same wavelength.

After they ordered double espressos to help them sober up before heading home, Reed leaned back in his chair and gave her a long look.

"What?" She giggled. The champagne bubbles had gone to her head.

"I have a proposition to make." One look from those eyes, she thought, would have you panting for him or quaking in your boots. "I seem to remember from your undergrad years that you liked to perform—right?"

"Excuse me?" Suddenly she felt very sober and she squirmed uncomfortably in her chair.

"You remember the play I mentioned that will run at my theater—the Genet?

"Yes, of course. The one you hired the hookers for."

Reed grinned. "I should never have told you that. The show's shaping up wonderfully and I want you to see a rehearsal. I'd be interested in your opinion."

As if a freezing wind had suddenly blown up, she tugged her silk shawl off the back of her chair and wrapped it around her shoulders.

"The central role is the madam, an older woman," Reed continued. "We've got a top-notch actor for that part. All the same, the scene needs more heat. It takes place in a brothel, after all. A fresh pair of eyes would help immeasurably."

Her blood pounded in her ears. Did he know? Did he think a professional's take on prostitutes would help the production? The whole evening suddenly turned to ashes. She blurted out the first thought that came into her head, "I couldn't possibly do it. I don't have time."

He gave her hand a squeeze. "You have no worries on the academic front, I can assure you. And I won't take no for an answer."

She wouldn't budge, but he carried on relentlessly. "Frankly, Maria, I'm surprised at you. I thought you'd jump at the chance. It dovetails so beautifully with your interests."

"Which are?" she said, barely suppressing her temper.

"Theater and the erotic canon, of course. What's gotten into you?"

She threw back the rest of the champagne in her glass. It tasted yeasty on her tongue. "Let me think about it," she said flatly. "I'll let you know."

"I'll consider that a yes."

Maria forced a smile. "Well, that might leave you disappointed." Of course, I'd be the perfect choice to give advice, she thought.

The restaurant wasn't far from her home so they decided to walk back through the park. Other couples sauntered past, hand in hand or arm in arm. Reed folded his arm around her and diverted her along a small path secluded by high shrubs and bushes. He pulled her to him and gave her a deep kiss, his tongue wetting her lips, moving inside, probing her mouth. He pulled down the wide strap of her dress and slipped his hand underneath the fabric, felt for the silk cups of her bra, ran his fingers over her breasts. Her nipples tightened instantly.

"You want to do it right here, don't you," Reed whispered in her ear. He moved his lips over her throat.

"Reed." Maria tried to tug his hand away, but he was forceful. She wasn't able to move it an inch. He turned her so she was in front of him and his back was to the walkway so no one passing by could see. He pushed down the bra cups, exposing her breasts, and rolled his tongue over her nipples. He unzipped his fly, took her hand and held it against his cock, hard as bone. His hand traveled provocatively up her thigh and beneath the edge of her panties to fondle her sex, already slick and wet.

"I'll stop now—yes?" he asked, his tone playful.

"No—keep going." The lingering effect of the champagne and the touch of his fingers proved irresistible.

"Are you sure?

"Yes, yes . . . keep going. Don't tease me."

"Thought so." He gave her a smile and slid first one finger, then two inside her; her pussy clenched and he gave her nub the lightest of touches. Sensations flooded, one on top of the other. She pressed her lips to his shirt to muffle her cry as she came.

He zipped up, gave her a quick kiss and grinned. "You owe me one, lady."

"Lovers never owe each other anything," she said.

CHAPTER 9

They climbed the rise to Central Park West and Seventy-second Street. When they arrived at her building, Maria offered him her most dazzlingly apologetic smile. "Afraid I can't ask you in. My friend and I have an agreement. No guys staying over." The statement sounded absurd after nearly having sex in the park, but she could think of nothing else to say.

"Feels like high school all over again," he quipped. "Kinda nice in a way." He kissed her again, this time lightly, without demanding anything in return. "I loved spending the time with you tonight. I want to see you again—very soon."

Upstairs, Lillian had stayed up. She could hardly get her words out fast enough. "How was it? How was *he*? Tell me everything."

Maria tossed her shawl and bag on the hall credenza. Ran her fingers through her hair. "The show was fantastic, the restaurant divine, but . . . I'm certain he knows."

Lillian wrinkled her brow. "Knows what?"

"That I'm Claudine. He didn't actually come out and say it, but . . ." Her voice trailed off. She suddenly felt very tired.

"So what? Most men would think you were even more of a prize."

"Not in his case. Can't say I'm surprised. A lot of men in his circles know me as Claudine. It's not destined to go anywhere, Lillian. Just as well I found out early on. You should have heard him talk about the hookers acting in a play he's staging in SoHo."

"You mean streetwalkers?" Lillian screwed up her nose in mock horror. "How could he compare you to them?"

"He didn't. Not overtly. But what's the difference, really?" she said cynically. "We're all in the same game, aren't we?" She gave Lillian a hug to show her feelings weren't hurt. "Let's just forget about it tonight. We've got a lot to do to get ready for tomorrow's trip. I'm going to bed."

"Before we leave, you should contact Detective Trainor. He left a message for you. Wants you to return his call."

Maria nodded. "Sure."

Her doctor had given her a new prescription. She got the sleeping pills from the bathroom and drank them down with water from the tap. She stripped off her dress and underwear, kicked off her shoes, climbed naked between the cool sheets and waited for the drug to work its magic.

She stared into space, wide-awake for a long time. Thanks to Andrei's connection, she knew what Trainor's news would be: the girl was a prostitute and her killing was a message. An overwhelming sadness engulfed her. She'd never felt so alone. Every aspect of her life was turning against her. Reed either knew or suspected that she was a high-class prostitute, and the police would figure that out before long too. She was being stalked by a murderer, and the sanctity of her home had been invaded.

A dream catcher she'd bought years ago at a Chippewa craft store hung on the wall over her bed. It was a large round hoop of braided sweetgrass with an elaborate net of strings knotted together like a spiderweb inside. At its center a bird carved from shell flew with outstretched wings. Her totem, the craft store manager had said. Long wild goose feathers hung from the bottom of the hoop fastened by strings of colored beads. Maria wondered why she kept it. It gave her neither sweet dreams nor restful sleep.

Her mind went back to her teenage years when her adoptive mother, Jewel, moved the family household from Providence to New York. They'd never got on well, but by the time Maria entered prep school in New York, their differences had turned into full combat. Although she naturally excelled at art, music and literature, she failed math and science dismally. Jewel filled Maria's after-school hours with tutors and stopped her from seeing her friends in a bid to ensure that she would reach top of the class in every subject. At fourteen she rebelled, sneaking out at night to go clubbing, coming home drunk and reeking of weed. She danced the night away and slept with men in their twenties. Jewel found a few tabs of ecstasy and a package of birth control pills in Maria's purse one day and threw a tantrum right on the spot. The battle lines had been drawn. At seventeen Maria declared war, fired off her missiles and moved out. Jewel cut her off without a cent.

Her life as a professional prostitute began out of need and

after a dare. A college friend who'd made good money as an escort bet Maria she didn't have the guts to do it. Her first client was a Wall Street player. Uptown boy making money hand over fist, cocaine-flushed cheeks, high sexual appetite. As it turned out, the money shot belonged to her. She worked him over for a couple of hours that night and walked away with triple the fee her friend usually made.

The months following blurred into a parade of men. She turned tricks, often a couple of them a night. She only remembered those experiences now as cum slippery on her thighs, white froth on her lips, groping hands, hazy faces. It was so easy to make cash for what many girls did—what she had done—for free. At first, the money had been sorely needed to finish her studies. A sacrifice, she told herself, for her true career. Then she became accustomed to the perks. Pretty nails, perfect hair, clothes from Bergdorf. A place to live in the hot part of town. After that another place, even larger, more upscale. She wanted to rise above the pack, make a name for herself. She left the escort world behind, knowing if she stayed in it she'd become too well-known and her more ambitious goals would never unfold. The tiny percentage of women in her price league were either film actors, porn stars or Playmates. She'd broken her way in through sheer ingenuity. Now everything was changing. And she knew that in this city your fortune could turn on a dime.

Maria turned over, facedown. Sometimes that helped her sleep. After a few minutes she rolled to her back again in exasperation, the big meal she'd been unused to eating bloating her, making it uncomfortable to lie on her stomach. A saying revolved in her mind: "What most men desire is a virgin who's a whore." Reed wouldn't go for a virgin—he'd want someone skilled in the bedroom—but neither would a high-class prostitute ever be seen as an appropriate choice for a mate. Disappointment flooded her brain. She fought it off. Fuck the double standard. She'd take whatever she could get from him. He'd get no closer to her than that.

CHAPTER 10

SAN FRANCISCO

San Francisco's Show World Live! bore little resemblance to the infamous Times Square district Show World club; the original naughty venue was long gone except for a tattered storefront on Eighth Avenue. In contrast, the new Show World Live! was aimed at upscale customers and boasted glitzy lounges with hourly strip shows. Booth babies danced naked amid blue and pink bubbles in Plexiglas boxes. A tranny bar featured top-notch talent from the Bay Area, and the porn cinema was made up to look like a grand old theater with plush upholstered seats and velvet curtains tied on either side of the screen.

Claudine was booked to perform two vignettes at the coveted Saturday night show for ticket holders in the club's famous Round Room, and after, a private performance for a select client. VIP customers accessed well-appointed and expensive private booths through a short hall leading from one of the lounges. The booths formed a wall around the circumference of the room save for a large entrance that opened onto a raised stage. Each booth had a screen with a generous viewing area allowing customers to see the show in complete privacy along with bottle service. The worst task in the club belonged to the mop boy whose job it was to clean and disinfect each booth after the VIPs had spent their load.

Matinee performances staged in the Round Room during the week were called box lunches—marketed to businessmen wanting to catch a show between meetings. Happy hour at five P.M. was for those taking in a performance before heading home to family dinner. After several warm-up acts, Claudine was scheduled to star in the finale of a full show.

The club put a stretch limousine at her disposal during her stay and footed the bill at one of San Francisco's luxury hotels. She arrived at the dressing room several hours early. Although she'd practiced her routines beforehand, the second vignette required a partner and she was anxious about working with someone she'd never met before. He turned out to be an affable, good-looking guy in his late thirties named Tyrell with curly bronze hair and warm brown skin. He was muscular and lithe, with great moves, and he quickly caught on to the routines she'd mapped out.

She'd decided on a straight old-time burlesque show for her first act, and Lillian worked wonders transforming her into a likeness of the famous burlesque queen Lili St. Cyr.

The lights dimmed. The performing area, a bare circle of blond hardwood, was illuminated by a spotlight that left the booths in shadow. A pink divan at center stage sat beside a table holding a fan of luxurious black ostrich feathers and an oversized perfume bottle, the old-fashioned kind with a rubber squeeze top. The master of ceremonies, a short sprite of a man dressed in tails and a white shirt, strode to center stage carrying a gold-topped cane.

"Ladies and gentlemen, may I present to you, from the white lights of Manhattan, for one night only, the exquisite, the infamous, Claudine."

For an instant, her stomach pitched in fear. Would her stalker be out there, watching from one of the booths? Would he be bold enough to hurt her in front of everyone, thinking to catch her off guard with a public attack? Andrei was stationed to one side of the entrance with a full view of the booths. As long as he was here she was safe. She calmed herself with that thought and the thrill that always came before a performance began to beat through her veins.

The white-blue beam of the spot swept to the performer's entrance. She heard the first notes of the music and stepped into the circle of dazzling light. Her platinum hair, styled in an updo, was cinched with a wide ribbon of black chiffon to match the flowing semitransparent fabric of her floor-length dress. It glowed under the lights.

She wore arm-length kid leather gloves that fit like a second skin and flashy high heels. Parading to the music, she shimmied, pivoted, struck various cheesecake poses. She gave her audience a sinful smile, winked and thrust out her boobs in full burlesque mode, running her hands tantalizingly over her cleavage. Turning her back to the viewers, she wiggled her ass and unhooked the skirt of her gown, tossing it aside. The pleasure and playfulness of the dance gave her extra zing and for a moment she felt as though she could vanquish her unseen enemy by the sheer force of her sensuality.

Only the long tail of chiffon and a tiny thong covered the crease of her bottom. She stepped saucily back into the spotlight, unhitched the tail and bent over so that her buttocks were on full display. With her fingers she spread the plump globes. Approving cries, muffled by the Plexiglas windows came from the booths. They sounded like hockey fans.

She kicked off her high heels, unfastened her stockings from her garters and rolled them down, slowly exposing toned thighs and shapely calves. She picked up the fan from the pink divan and, holding it in front of her with one hand, undid the eyelets of the bustier at her back with the other. She tossed the bustier to the floor, and squeezing her naked breasts together, dipped the fan down, revealing generous nipples glittering with rhinestone pasties. The audience went crazy. Smiling demurely, she grasped one pert breast in her hand, raised it to her mouth, and pushed her pink tongue against the pasty. Then, to the delight of the customers, she fanned herself as if she were too overheated to continue. She pranced around a little longer, making sure that each booth occupant got a good look at her full tits and her round tush in the tiny black thong. She returned once more to center stage, where she reclined languorously on the divan, giving herself a spray with the perfume. Every move had a comic edge but she knew the men in the audience weren't laughing. She felt their breath halt, their eyes on her—and savored every moment of it.

Her act was building up now and she slowed the pace even more to prolong the thrill. She gave a great show of tugging her gloves off with her teeth, one finger at a time. Then rolling on her stomach, breasts grazing the fabric of the divan, she slapped each ass cheek with the gloves. She rolled over onto her back and into a sitting position, her pussy concealed by only the narrowest slip of material. Slowly, slowly, in time to the crash of cymbals and a thudding drumbeat, she slipped a finger underneath the thong and pulled the material aside to show that which had been hidden. She then pulled it down over her mound, drew her knees up to her chest and kicked her legs like a Rockette, flinging the thong onto the stage floor. Her labia puffed out between her taut thighs; she licked a finger and spread her nether lips, granting a full view of her sex. Applause thundered from the booths. Their adulation emboldened her; a flush of triumph warmed her cheeks. With her legs spread wide, she stroked herself wantonly with one hand and blew kisses to each booth with the other, then delicately hopped to her feet, bowed deeply and disappeared behind the curtain.

Andrei waited for her just out of sight backstage.

"How was I?"

"Fabulous as always."

"Any psychos out there?"

"Not on my watch." He grinned.

Lillian waited nearby with a big fluffy white towel. She rubbed her down to remove the sweat beading her skin. "They loved you," Lillian said proudly. "You were electric."

"Yeah?" Claudine smiled, took a tissue from a box and wiped her forehead. The lights were so hot. It did seem to her that the club patrons' approval drew out her more salacious instincts.

Lillian helped her change her costume while Tyrell limbered up in the wings. Many of these vignettes used stock comedy themes—doctor and nurse, naughty schoolgirl and teacher, maid and butler. Tonight she'd chosen ringmaster and tiger cat with a role reversal. The music changed to a circus-themed melody.

She entered the circle of light for the second time in a red frock coat with gold piping, tight white pants, spike-heeled patent leather boots and a tiny top hat perched insolently on her head. She backed into the performance area, slashing her whip. Tyrell, in a tiger-striped leotard, long tail and a cap with tiger ears, followed her, prowling. They circled the perimeter of the room, pausing to smile and wink at the unseen VIPs, who laughed and clapped again. She popped the buttons on her frock coat slowly, revealing the inner curves of her breasts, and then thrust back her shoulders, dropping her coat to the floor, baring her full breasts sans pasties. The tight white pants fit her bottom like a glove, and she tipped her hat jauntily to the audience. At the crack of her whip, the tiger jumped on the circus drum placed in the center of the stage and crouched, muscles bulging. She gave him a lascivious smile, shook her finger and leaned into him, jiggling her breasts. She squeezed them together, and the tiger took both of her nipples into his mouth, sucking them greedily.

Another crack of the whip and the tiger obeyed her order to strip. He peeled off his leotard, revealing a thong suspended by small straps over each shoulder, the kind of getup a 1920s wrestler would wear—or Borat. She could barely hold back a laugh. He looked adorable and ridiculous. Once more the VIPs tittered in their private booths. Claudine pulled back and put a hand to her mouth in mock horror, turned away from her partner, then bowed and doffed her hat to the audience again.

The tiger, seeing his opportunity, lunged for her. He clutched her narrow waist, tumbling with her to the floor. He managed to unzip her tight white pants and pull them off, revealing red satin briefs. He stroked her through the satin until she slapped her whip on the floor, jumped to her feet and raised her right leg to give him a mock push in the chest with the heel of her big black boot. The tiger pretended to cower and shake. She ordered him to take off his thong.

He obeyed and stood before her, abs flexing with his breath, covered in a sheen of sweat. His cock was hard and fully extended. She patted it as one would a favored pet then pushed him to the floor. She turned to the audience again and slowly bent at the waist, rolling down her panties, swaying her hips as she did so. Someone in a booth whistled; she rewarded the whistler with a smile and a bob of her head.

She stalked around the tiger, naked but for her black boots and tiny top hat, cracking her whip. Then she planted both boots on either side of his head and squatted over his face, teasing him and bouncing her breasts. She straightened up, took two big steps to straddle his hips and lowered her herself onto his erect cock. The tiger roared. Except for a few intakes of breath, the booths went completely silent. Her partner's hips jerked and she matched him stroke for stroke, her breasts bouncing with his thrusts, her hair tumbling around her shoulders. After a moment or two Claudine stroked herself, simulated her orgasm and with a dramatic wink, doffed her jaunty cap once more to the audience. With a final crack of her whip the music stopped and the lights dimmed. Audience applause was muffled by the Plexiglas screens but she could still hear the cheers. Doors banged as customers exited the booths.

Tyrell flashed a smile. "Amazing, actually getting paid to do that."

"Thought you'd be used to it by now." She laughed.

"No. This is my first time . . . in public. Strictly an amateur." He pulled off the cat ears. "These ears look kind of silly, don't they?"

She tousled his bronze curls and smiled at him. "Not at all. They're cute. You'd best be off, though. I have another performance scheduled. It's a private show. A two on one. The master of ceremonies is bringing them here in just a moment."

The screen to one of the booths slid back, and before she understood what was happening, Andrei barred the entrance to the stage. But it was a woman who walked out, not a man. A tall, sharp-faced brunette. The woman had pale skin, long lacquered red nails and bright vermillion lipstick that emphasized her wide mouth. Otherwise, she was entirely naked except for a stiff nine-inch strap-on dildo.

"I'm the other half." She smirked at Andrei. "His better half, I guess you could say," she said, indicating Tyrell.

Andrei nodded at Claudine and backed away discreetly.

"You've probably cooled down by now but we'll get you heated up in no time." She gave Claudine a long critical look. "You have a sensational body. The description didn't do you justice."

Claudine gaped at the tiger. "You're her husband?"

"Married for five years," Tyrell said. "Frankie keeps things interesting."

"I'll bet she does."

Frankie moved close to Claudine and trailed her scarlet nails across her rump. "Your skin is still flushed from having my husband. You smell of him." She moved even closer. "I like that. And I love that feather brand on your wrist." Frankie grasped her hand. "Let's not waste our time," she said. "You got twice your fee for tonight and I paid half of it."

This wasn't the first time Claudine had doubled up; she had no issues with it. But she'd been expecting two men; she hated being taken by surprise and felt edgy because of it. Frankie led her to the pink divan. It had been left behind a screen after Claudine's burlesque act. She kissed Claudine on the mouth while Tyrell massaged her shoulders. He reached for her breasts from behind, raising them to Frankie's lips.

After a minute of Frankie's careful ministrations, Tyrell turned Claudine to face him, left a trail of kisses down her stomach. She tried to resist the delicious quivers his lips caused, flicked a glance back at Frankie. The woman's lips tightened, a glint of jealousy in her eyes. Claudine knew these situations were often delicate; they always risked animosity from the woman involved. She twisted away from Tyrell and ran her hands over Frankie's small perky boobs. Featherlight touches on her dark nipples solicited sighs of pleasure. "You're very attractive, and you're so hot tonight," Claudine murmured in Frankie's ear, "I'm going to have a hard time holding back."

Frankie gave her a genuine smile in response and relaxed.

Claudine gave up control to Tyrell's wife, turned around and knelt on the divan, offering herself to Frankie. She sensed Frankie approach, felt the woman reach under to lift her hips and play with the mouth of her vagina. Frankie slapped her ass and spread her wide with her fingers.

She felt the dildo press into her notch, felt its hard length slide into her up to the hilt, filling her completely. Frankie clamped her hand on Claudine's hips, forcing the dildo in deeper, rocking her with rapid motions. It was a strange, schizophrenic encounter. Claudine experienced nothing but blankness in her groin at the women's feverish assault, yet felt a lovely buzz float through her as Tyrell fondled her nipples.

"Suck my husband's cock while I do you," Frankie demanded. Claudine obeyed; she took the thick head of Tyrell's cock in her mouth and ran her tongue up and down his shaft. She grasped the base of his penis and deep throated him, knowing instinctually Frankie would want her to take all of him.

"Good," Frankie cooed, flicking her nail over Claudine's clit. The sharpness made Claudine buck, and Frankie thrust harder. After a few moments, she'd had enough and Claudine faked it by letting Frankie feel a tremble run through her body and moaning loudly.

She felt Frankie's hands on her back, pushing away, the sucking release of the dildo as it popped out. "You've really got me going," Frankie said huskily. "But now I need my man."

She moved out of the way while Frankie straddled Tyrell on the divan. He toyed with her dark ringlets, her tits and the nest of wiry black hair at her pubis. The animal in him took over for real this time. With few more preliminaries than that he pushed her on her back, pinned her arms above her head, and pushed into her. She gasped. Their bellies slapped together. After a moment, he flipped her around, pressed her head into the divan so that her tush was up in the air. He screwed her noisily from behind, his arms, abs and chest glistening with the sweat of his efforts. His wife grunted with each of his powerful thrusts, and as he came, she collapsed beneath him with a loud cry. She lay underneath her husband, his arms and legs entwined around her body. He nuzzled her and rubbed his cheek on hers.

Claudine blew them a kiss good-bye, scooped the red frock coat off the floor and Andrei, waiting in the wings, draped it around her shoulders, ready to escort her back to her dressing room.

She got a rush out of knowing her most intimate moments were shared with strangers. In a few weeks if she recalled Frankie and Tyrell at all, it would be indistinctly. It was best not to remember faces in her business. Call it professional forgetting. Clients didn't want their faces remembered. They hoped to be forgotten; that was the whole point. Sex without obligation was exhilarating. Soon, the faces of the tiger and his pale, black-haired wife would fade. That's what she loved about it. The heat of the moment dissolving to blissful forgetfulness.

But what of Frankie's compliment about her feather brand? An innocent remark or did it have a deeper meaning? She banished the thought as soon as it arose. If she wasn't careful, she'd end up paranoid, imagining every new customer an enemy.

Maria and Andrei found Lillian curled up on the cot in the dressing room, asleep. Lillian's petite, compact little body was perfectly relaxed: her mouth was slightly open, and her tiny, strong hands were tucked under her cheek. In sleep, she looked younger than her years.

Lillian had left her family in the Philippines at the age of eighteen, newly married to her cousin. She was the sacrificial lamb, earning money in America as a makeup artist to keep her parents, siblings, in-laws—fifteen people altogether—alive. She saw her husband once every three years when she went back home. He had another woman there with whom he'd fathered three children. Lillian's parents insisted on her marriage to bond her more closely to the family, the strings that kept her attached, crucial for their survival. That was the difference between Maria and Lillian. Lillian accepted her bonds; Maria refused to be tied down.

Her eyes lit on a white envelope with her name typed upon it, propped against the mirror on the dressing room table beside a white gardenia, a bow tied to its stem. She picked up the envelope and tore open the flap. Inside, on a simple piece of notepaper, were the words: *This flower is one of many but you are the finest of them all. Irreplaceable to me. A gift awaits.*

She thought immediately of Reed. It was the kind of gesture he'd make although she doubted he'd use such stilted language. But why did he think it necessary to flatter her anymore? And how on earth did he know where she was?

She woke Lillian gently. "All done. Time to go back to the hotel." Maria gestured to the table. "This note and the flower—who brought them?"

Lillian sat up and rubbed the sleep from her eyes. "One of the waiters from the lounge. He didn't get the name."

She picked up the flower and inhaled in its pungent scent. Likely one of the customers from tonight, too shy to meet her face-to-face. It was a sweet gesture.

While Lillian packed up their cases, Maria dressed in her street clothes and Andrei called down to the limo driver. In the hotel elevator on their way to their rooms, Maria held the note up between two fingers for Andrei to read. "What do you think of that?" she asked.

Andrei frowned. "From Reed Whitman?"

Ever since he saw Reed at the library a few days ago, a wall had grown up between Andrei and Maria. She'd tried to chip away at Andrei's sullen emotional distance by teasing him and sweet-talking him into a better mood, but he wasn't having any of it. All her efforts failed. He was acting like a jealous lover. It was the first time she could remember him being so difficult.

Tonight, though, she found his reaction amusing. "Don't think so. Reed wouldn't use such flowery words."

"Right," Andrei said dismissively.

Maria slipped the key card into the slot and opened the door to her hotel room. As she screamed Andrei grabbed her from behind and pulled her back into the hallway.

A blond woman lay upon thc bed, her face battered beyond recognition. Her pelvic area and genitals were saturated in blood.

CHAPTER 11

"Don't go in. Stand against the wall, both of you," Andrei ordered. "Don't move from this spot." He took out his gun, went inside and shut the door quietly. Maria scrambled through her bag for her phone. She could barely hit the keys for 911, her body shook so much. Just as the dispatcher answered, the door cracked open again. Andrei stepped into the hall, shoving his pistol back into the shoulder holster underneath his jacket. "It's not real, Maria. Hang up."

"Nine-one-one. What's your emergency?"

Maria covered her phone and whispered, "What are you talking about?"

"It's a doll. It's not real." He motioned for the two women to follow him.

"Hello? Nine-one-one. State your emergency please."

She shut off the phone. Her legs trembled so much she had trouble approaching the bed. And yes, now she could see the rubbery pink skin, the coarse doll's hair, the dimples at the knees and elbows, remarkably lifelike limbs and fingers. It was an inflatable sex doll, the kind with realistic breasts and open orifices—mouth, vagina and anus—suiting all tastes. But whether the blood that covered it was real or even human was impossible to tell. It looked to be. The doll's vacant open-mouthed smile and slack limbs spelled their own horror.

Lillian hovered outside the room, unwilling to go near it. Andrei used his phone to click pictures of the doll.

Maria went into the bathroom to splash cold water on her face. Stuck to the mirror was a photo of her posing as Lili St. Cyr at the club in midperformance. She'd just stripped off the black chiffon skirt and the bustier. The photographer snapped her as she'd lowered the ostrich feather fan, tilting her chest out to display her bare breasts, the rhinestone pasties catching the light like glittering gems. Underneath the photo were a few neatly typed lines:

> There once was a girl from Siret
> Six-year-old Maria
> Innocent angel or *suca*?
> She's a girl I won't forget.

Maria ripped down the photo. *Suca* was Russian for whore; Siret, the town near the orphanage.

She flicked a towel off the towel rack, wiped her face and stomped over to the doll, gingerly lifted it so she could see the underside of its right wrist. Printed onto the rubber skin was a feather exactly like hers.

"Look at this!" She thrust the photo at Andrei.

He raised troubled eyes to the picture, then glanced over at the blood-splattered doll. “He’s upping the ante, showing he can have access to you anytime he pleases. That he can slip in and out of your room at will with nothing to stop him. He wants to keep you in a constant state of fear.”

“Well, it’s not going to work. And why a doll this time?”

“Don’t know. Probably too risky with guests and cameras everywhere to kill a real woman.”

Maria rubbed her right wrist subconsciously, as she did whenever she felt anxious. The shrink she’d seen as a teenager said it was a kind of flashback to the times she’d been strapped to the orphanage crib. “He’s not going to turn me into a spineless victim. You have to find him, Andrei. There has to be a way.”

A hard rap on the door silenced her.

Andrei peered through the eyehole. “It’s hotel security. I called them.” He opened the door.

The security director entered the room and introduced himself. He had an air of self-importance. His eyes widened when he looked at the bed. “Jesus! Is that a sex doll?” He addressed his remark to Andrei as if Maria and Lillian were invisible.

“Yeah.”

“Any idea who did it?”

Maria interrupted the man, irritated by his attitude. “I’ve been getting threatening e-mails. Whoever’s harassing me must have done this too.”

He took in the three of them. “And what’s the relationship here? Are you all guests? I need to see some ID and your key cards.”

“We’re all hotel clients,” Andrei interjected, giving their names and individual room numbers, clearly disliking his manner as much as Maria did. "Do you have cameras in the hallways? Any chance there's video of whoever did this?"

"A very good one." He whipped out his phone and asked one of his staff to check the cameras on their floor. He suggested all three of them wait in the unoccupied room next door until the film was ready. "Have you called the police yet?"

"No need to," Andrei said. "This is vandalism, pure and simple. Believe me, I've seen hotel rooms trashed much worse than this. No one's been hurt and I imagine the hotel would prefer to avoid the negative publicity. If you don't mind, we'll wait right here until we see that camera footage."

The director hesitated for a moment, unable to make up his mind, then said, "All right, I see your point. Let's keep this a private matter."

Maria silently thanked Andrei for his quick thinking. If the local police were called and decided to dig deeply enough, an investigation would reveal that she was more than just an exotic dancer. She stood a greater chance of being arrested than the sick stalker who was messing with her.

When it finally arrived, the video proved disappointing; it showed only a heavyset male around six feet tall, wearing a knapsack, keeping his head down, approaching Maria's hotel room. A glimpse of his face shrouded by a hoodie showed he was probably Caucasian. He took a quick look around to make sure no one was in the hall, slapped on latex gloves. The time stamp for the figure's entry into her room read 12:30 A.M.—the point Maria commenced her second act with the tiger man. He used some device to unlock the door, stayed inside for twenty-two minutes, then exited the room and strode down the hall to the elevators.

"Guy's clever." The security director's eyes raked Maria's figure.

"Why do you say that?" Maria demanded.

"He's avoiding the cameras, that's why. What are you people doing in town?"

Maria had mentioned to some of the other hotel staff that she was performing at the club; he'd find out soon enough if she lied to him. "I'm a dancer. I had a gig tonight at Show World Live!"

He made a sucking sound with his lips. "Well, you girls are ripe prey for this sort of stuff. These guys can get worked up. Put a few drinks in them and a couple of hits of coke and they go a little haywire. It goes with the territory."

"You're saying staging a fake murder is *going a little haywire*?"

"Loonies are attracted to the sex stuff. I'm just being realistic."

"I'll try to remember not to go topless when I'm out shopping, then. Too bad. With the hot weather coming up and all."

He straightened up. "Listen, ma'am. I'm sorry this happened to you in our hotel. We'll put you up in one of our exclusive suites for however long you were planning to stay. I'll call a porter right now to take up your things."

"My room's across the hall," Andrei said. "I'll move to the suite as well."

He handed Andrei his card. "Here's my contact info. Hope the rest of your visit is—uneventful."

"I don't want to stay here tonight if we can help it," Maria said to Andrei on their way to the suite. "It's too late for the red-eye. Can you check and see if there's anything else available?"

She wanted to put as much distance between them and the grisly doll as possible.

Andrei looked up the flight schedules on his phone. "Everything's gone. Unless you're willing to transfer and spend a couple of delightful hours at O'Hare, we'll have to stick with the flight we've already got booked for noon tomorrow."

She sighed. "Okay. That will have to do. Thanks for keeping the cops out of this."

Andrei put his hand on her arm. "Maria, you can't take any more appointments until we find out who's doing this."

She shook him off. "No way. I'm damned if I'm going to let this stop me." Despite her bravado, in her heart she knew Andrei was right. But there were no leaves of absence in a business like hers, which was dependent on word of mouth and acutely sensitive to rumor. Taking a break would spell the end of her career. She refused to be forced into it.

As soon as they reached the suite, she ran a hot bath and sank thankfully into its foamy depths. She doubted she'd be able to sleep at all for the rest of the night and a bath was the next best thing. She set the water as hot as she could stand it, and the blood rose to the surface of her skin, turning it pink. When she reached for the soap she saw that the feather-shaped scar on her wrist had gone red with the heat. It stood out on her arm like a brand. She sat in the bath until the water cooled, then got out and toweled her hair dry. She emerged into the sitting area of the suite wrapped in one of the hotel's fluffy white terry cloth robes.

Lillian still wore her white blouse and brown slacks but Andrei had changed into lounging pants, leaving his torso bare. A glimmer of humor broke through her grim mood. She was so used to seeing Andrei in formal attire that the sight of his hard abs and broad shoulders almost seemed improper. Very enticing, she thought. She'd never cared for the bulging pecs of Schwarzenegger wannabes. Andrei was strong but sleek. Much more appealing.

He looked up and smiled when she entered the room. For a moment, she was taken aback by the sensual, gut-stirring response that simple gesture produced in her. Nonsense, she said to herself, any woman would find him appealing, half-undressed like that.

Lillian had ordered snacks from room service: cold sodas, a plate of nacho chips and a bowl brimming with popcorn. They had a movie ready to go on the Blu-ray: *The Lord of the Rings: The Fellowship of the Ring*; Tolkien was one of her favorites. Maria felt her throat catch. It was after two in the morning, and though they both must be dead tired, they'd arranged this to help get her mind off her troubles.

"What a great idea—thanks, you two." They'd left a space for her to curl up on the oversized hotel sofa. She slipped in between them. Andrei took the remote and hit Play.

Andrei hadn't seen the film before but Lillian had watched it ten times. "My dream," she said, pointing to the images of the Shire, "is to live in a little cottage with a garden, in a quaint English village."

"You can actually visit Hobbiton now, you know," Maria said. "Although you'd have to go all the way to New Zealand."

"Oh, good. I'll go there someday, then. Maybe find a boyfriend as short as me."

They all laughed; it helped to banish the earlier ugliness. Maria put her bare feet on Lillian's lap and leaned against

Andrei's shoulder as they watched Frodo and Bilbo hatch their grand plans.

Maria sat up with a jerk. She'd drifted off. Andrei's arm lay protectively around her, his hand resting on her waist. He reached over and swept her hair off her brow. "You dropped off right before they reached Rivendell."

"Did Lillian go to bed?"

"Ages ago. No doubt dreaming of little men. Good thing there's one of us to keep watch," he joked. Andrei's former sullenness seemed to have vanished and she was happy to have his goodwill back. She suddenly realized her robe had fallen open, revealing the tops of her breasts. How long had she lain that way? She grabbed the folds of terry cloth and closed them.

When he ran his hand down her hip, it felt warm, exciting. "Not to worry. Nothing I haven't seen before," he said.

And yet it was different. The two of them were alone. And against her better judgment, Maria felt turned on, wanting to feel his hands on her bare skin. "I'm going to climb into bed," she said. She got up abruptly and, still holding the lapels of her robe shut, gave him a chaste peck on the cheek. "You'll wake us in lots of time for the flight?"

"Sure thing," he said. But Maria thought she'd caught a fleeting look of disappointment on his face.

They'd been away from New York for three days. Maria now counted eleven text messages from Reed Whitman. At first they were rather sweet, then increasingly insistent, and finally demanding. Why hadn't he heard from her? Was she avoiding him? Was she no longer interested in his help? Back at home she dashed off a reply saying she'd been busy and would love to see him sometime soon. That she'd be in touch. The truth was she felt ambivalent about Reed. No question he had a magnetic draw, like a star pulling lesser planets into his sphere. And yet she found his possessiveness bordered on the claustrophobic, his self-confidence a little oppressive.

All thoughts of Reed disappeared when she picked up her voice mail messages. Trainor wanted to see her as soon as possible and this time, at his office. She left a message to say she'd see him in the morning.

CHAPTER 12

Maria chose her outfit carefully, conservative clothes that still made the most of her physical charms: a black pencil skirt and soft, dove gray sweater. She stuck her feet into low heels and donned her sunglasses. To act the part of an ingénue convincingly, she'd have to turn in one of her best Claudine performances. If you were going to outright flaunt the law as she did, you had to make sure all the appearances lined up perfectly. For this reason she was scrupulous about reporting all her earnings to the IRS under the umbrella of her event management company.

That fact gave her a little comfort as she approached the three-story redbrick building. The 110th Precinct building on Forty-third Street sat in a nondescript section of Queens, just verging on the squalid. When she gave her name at the front desk, a uniformed cop ushered her into a bland second-floor interview room with brown veneer walls and faded industrial carpeting. Five minutes later, Trainor and da Silva walked in and sat at the table across from her.

Maria's stomach was already in her throat. She kept reminding herself she'd done nothing wrong, at least insofar as their investigation was concerned. It didn't help.

"Good morning." Trainor said. "Thanks for coming."

Did the man ever smile? she wondered. "Whatever I can do to move things along—I'm glad to."

"Good. Help me with something," Trainor said.

She folded her hands in her lap, hoping he wouldn't notice her nervousness and waited for him to continue.

"I'll get straight to it. The murdered girl found with your ID was a prostitute working in the Bronx." He flipped through a notebook that he'd brought in with him. "She was very young, probably trafficked into the state, and Romanian, just like you. Interesting coincidence—don't you think?"

She had to stop herself from shrinking when he looked her straight in the eyes. She put on an engaging smile to hide how much his question had flustered her. "What? You think all Romanians know each other or something?" Trainor still didn't crack a smile, so she tried another tack. "I was six years old when I was adopted. I'm an American citizen now. Surely you're not suggesting any link between us just because we come from the same country?"

His lips tightened with his next words. "You're associated with an Andrei Baranov—that right?"

Andrei? She thought of the scrupulous records she kept for the IRS. Andrei was listed as her business manager and his salary as an expense. They must have taken out a warrant to search those records.

Da Silva spoke up. "What's Baranov's relation to you?"

"Why are you concerned about Andrei?"

"Let's just say he has ironclad ties to the Russian mafia in New York State," Trainor said. "As in, one of their right-hand men. We're talking tax evasion, contraband armaments and, what's relevant here, the sex trade. Not very nice company for a grad student, is he?"

"I had no idea."

Before she could get another word out, da Silva jumped back in. "You're running some kind of 'business enterprise'—if that's the right term. Quite a different story from the one you told us at your apartment. I hope you're not going to deny it this time."

This was beginning to feel less like an interview and more like an interrogation, as though she'd made all the wrong moves in a chess game and her queen was in peril. If they started investigating her, instead of the murder, she was finished. "I *am* a postgrad student at Yale. I can prove it." She rummaged through her purse and slapped her student ID on the table. "To support myself, I run an event management company. Andrei assists me with that. And I do performance art in that context."

Da Silva snickered. "They're calling it performance art nowadays? That's rich."

Maria ignored him and stared at Trainor. "Am I on trial or something here? I don't get why all these questions are about me."

"Smudging the truth isn't helpful, Ms. Lantos. The dead girl didn't steal your ID. It was planted on her body. We think she was targeted because she was a young, beautiful Romanian who sold sex. No accident she resembled you so closely—was it?" She was about to protest but Trainor raised a hand to silence her. "This murder was a message to you. Now, I want you to think long and hard about my next question, okay? Have you crossed someone in the past, stiffed someone?"

Da Silva sniggered and Trainor shot him a warning glance.

"Are they paying you or your friend Andrei back? If so, you've picked a dangerous guy to get on the wrong side of."

Maria cast her eyes down and said nothing for a moment, allowing a few tears to slide out. "This whole thing is terrifying. I'm afraid all the time now. If I had even the tiniest clue who it was, I'd tell you. Believe me." She bit her lip and gave Trainor a beseeching look.

His voice softened a little. "Well, I want you to think hard about it. Let's come up with some names."

"I've tried and tried. I can't think of anyone. Don't you have any leads at all? No fingerprints? No DNA?"

"We're working on it." Clearly he had no intention of sharing any information with her. He tapped his pen on his notebook. He had large, powerful hands with blunt nails. "We're going to need your computer," he said. "And your cell phone."

She blanched. "Don't you have to get a warrant for something like that?"

"Not if the person concerned is anxious to be cooperative and gives those electronics to us voluntarily. Like you just said you wanted to be," da Silva added.

She had no choice. If she insisted on a warrant, she'd just be digging herself in deeper. "All right." She opened her bag and got out her tablet, reached into a side pocket for her cell phone and handed them both to Trainor.

"This is it?" he asked. "Just this tablet and your phone?"

"I have an old desktop at home that I keep only for word processing. All my wireless goes through the tablet or the cell. I can always get a new phone but I have to have my tablet back. My research and writing's on it."

Trainor waved his large hand. The hairs stuck out on his rough knuckles. "I'll get one of our clerks to download it all. You want to stick around? Shouldn't take long, then you can have them back."

Maria followed Trainor glumly as he escorted her to the door. She tramped downstairs to the station lobby to wait. For an hour she watched the comings and goings absently, the cops casting odd glances her way. Her pulse pounded erratically. If they suspected she was a prostitute, why hadn't they arrested her? Did they want to expose her well-known clients first? The stories about Hollywood madam Heidi Fleiss flashed through her mind. While Fleiss ended up in federal prison, her male clients were given a pass. Fleiss's privileged background made her a target for the other inmates and she'd been forced to fight for her life in jail. If Maria ended up in prison, she'd fall apart with the shame of it all.

Was that her stalker's motive after all? Fleiss had been outed by rivals. Had one of Maria's clients hidden his savage side? Become spiteful and hatched this whole scheme to destroy her? She'd been so careful. But it happened. In the early days she'd known call girls who'd been ruined by vengeful clients or other prostitutes.

A female clerk interrupted her thoughts. "From Detective Trainor," she said, holding out a clear plastic bag containing her tablet and cell phone. Maria stammered her thanks and hurried out of the station.

She congratulated herself on two things. She'd been scrupulous about using her tablet only for school-related work. They'd find nothing of any interest on it. And she'd been smart enough to take her second cell phone to the interview, the one she used primarily for personal contacts. Her business cell, with a completely different server, was safe at the apartment. She rarely even looked at it. Andrei managed the client list and the correspondence. She'd wipe it clean the second she got home. She and Andrei kept their phones synced and Andrei maintained a digital file with all of their client information. He'd assured her it was deeply buried and totally inaccessible to anyone but the two of them.

Word-of-mouth recommendations were supreme in her business and not even a whiff of suspicion, whether from jealous wives or journalists, had ever touched any of her customers. She had a sterling reputation for discretion, another factor that fueled demand for her services. She could not afford to have the police on her back.

But clearly, they were on Andrei's. Maria had never inquired too deeply into his business before he came to work for her. Still, it was a shock to hear he'd been tied up that directly with the mafia. It didn't match the kind person she'd come to know. People were always full of surprises.

Her mind drifted back to the evil verse left underneath the photo by her stalker. Worm music. The words underneath the photo kept returning to her like a scratch on a record. And Siret. Only a few people knew the exact name of the town where the orphanage she'd spent those dark months was located in, or the age she'd left it at. She had a good idea where the information came from. That afternoon she meant to find out for sure.

CHAPTER 13

When Jewel Welland hit her midthirties, she was divorced and alone, so she decided to adopt a child. The idea of being able to simply select one and avoid all the pain and mess of childbirth appealed to her orderly mind. Dire conditions in Romanian orphanages has been much in the news in those days and Jewel had swooped down on one of the orphanages like an avenging angel. She paced between the filthy cots, examining the infant offerings. Most of the boys and girls were ruined by neglect and by years confined to their cots. With no stimulation, barely ever experiencing a kind human touch, many of the children waved their hands in the air as the only way they knew how to communicate. Jewel would try a tentative smile at those she thought might be interesting. The children would stare back at her with wide-open eyes and slack, dribbling mouths as if she were a cartoon character. Those who regularly burst into fits of temper or tried to clamber out of their beds had their wrists firmly clamped to the cot struts. All of them, Jewel decided, were too far gone. Impossible to mold any of these into an acceptable son or daughter, let alone one who might excel.

The stink of the place overwhelmed her from the start. Jewel's expensive heels slipped on brown floors damp with urine. She held a perfumed tissue to her nose to staunch the smell of sheets stained with mucus and feces. She'd wanted to save a child who'd endured some of the worst deprivations but now realized it had been a mistake to come.

She was about to tell the matron accompanying her that she'd changed her mind when they passed a small room. She glimpsed a cot pushed against a back wall. It was the only piece of furniture and the cement floor was pitted and soiled. In one corner she could see a nest of some kind, dozens of long, dark, slippery insect bodies swarming in and out of a crack in the cement. They were feasting on excrement. Jewel turned her head away in disgust.

Kneeling on a dirty mattress, staring at them through the high struts of the crib, a cherubic face caught Jewel's attention, matted blond hair twisting down the child's bare shoulders, and two wide eyes, a heavenly green. The worn material of the mattress was so stained that the original pattern of the fabric was barely discernible. It had split around the outside seam and the stuffing protruded.

The girl had contorted herself into a painful position, her right wrist tied securely with thin cable to the crib's top bar. She was naked. With her free hand the girl reached through the gap in the struts, opened and closed her fingers. The gesture was a parody of welcome. She was not a toddler. Jewel judged the child to be around five or six years old.

She stopped in her tracks and removed the tissue from her nose. "Who's that?"

"Older girl." The matron replied. "Trouble child. You don't want her."

"What kind of trouble? Is she mentally deficient?"

"*Da*. She has a bad mind. Screams at night. Won't keep quiet."

Jewel saw this as a positive sign. It showed the child had normal reactions to extreme deprivation. She walked closer. The girl's eyes were clear and wary. The vacant expression she'd seen on the other children's faces was missing. "How long has she been here?"

The matron held up five fingers. "Since January. Five months only."

"She must be able to talk, then." Jewel touched the small hand and the girl shrank back in fear.

She noticed a band of bruises on the girl's arm, a cluster of darker ones around the wrist secured by the rope and more bruising at the top of her thighs. "She's been beaten." Jewel said accusingly.

"I don't know that. They might have to. She tries and tries to get out."

"Why doesn't she have any clothes on?"

The matron shrugged her shoulders. "She tears them off and wets on them. Then throws them on the floor. Bad girl. Animal."

So her bed won't be drenched in pee, you idiot, she thought. That showed the child had a clear working mind. And better, a desire to keep herself clean.

"What happened to her parents?"

"Criminal people. Executed."

The girl kept her eyes glued on her visitors. Jewel thought she detected a faint glimmer of warmth. She turned to the matron. "Is there somewhere you can give her a bath? A hand wash even? And some clothes, comb her hair? Then bring her to me. I may be interested in taking her. I'm willing to be generous."

One week later Maria Lantos was on her way to Providence, Rhode Island. Jewel hired a nurse to accompany them, fearing the child might burst into the temper tantrums the matron described. It proved unnecessary. Maria was a quiet little mouse, afraid of everything. This enlivened Jewel in a different way. At the law firm, Jewel was admired for her single-mindedness. Once she'd mapped out a course of action, she was unstoppable. She managed her cases carefully, choosing only those she knew she would win. To create an intelligent, well-balanced daughter out of such deprivation presented a challenge. Jewel believed Maria was a case she could win.

Maria possessed only one tailored suit. She'd worn it exactly twice, once for an interview with the university registrar and the second time for a funeral. She felt now as if it were another funeral she was headed to; the woman she was about to see had been dead to her for a very long time.

Jewel's condo was only a few blocks away from Maria's building. Was it odd that Maria had chosen a place so close even though the emotional distance between them was fathomless? Keeping a fragile thread alive, perhaps, to her girlhood? She hoped not. That was simply too pathetic. She held her breath while the doorman called up to the apartment. There was no certainty her adoptive mother would agree to see her. So she felt both relieved and anxious when he told her to go on up after clicking off the intercom. She hit the buzzer at Jewel's door and a maid answered. The maid nodded in approval when Maria removed her shoes, and showed her into the long, elegant living room. It was the same as she remembered; not even the smallest detail had changed. Except for the kitchen and bathrooms, wall-to-wall white broadloom covered all the floors in the apartment. Jewel hated noise, said she liked it quiet enough that you could hear a pin drop. Maria had once emptied a whole box of pins on the tile kitchen floor just to see whether Jewel would notice.

Everything was spotlessly clean. The Ming dynasty china Jewel loved to collect gleamed in the glass cabinet. Tasteful antique furniture that looked attractive but felt uncomfortable was artfully arranged. The television was discreetly hidden behind cupboard doors, the fireplace long closed off. No clutter of plants or family photographs. No music playing in the background. It was as if the life had been drained out of the place. She went over to the white baby grand in front of the leaded glass windows and plunked a simple tune on the ivory keys.

She'd taken her first lessons on this piano in Providence. Jewel was at work much of the time, often not home until after dinner. Maria's nanny, a part-time college student, came from a big, boisterous African-American family in the Mount Hope district. She'd take Maria home with her and devised all kinds of games to play with her younger siblings and cousins. Afterward they'd sit in the kitchen, the main gathering spot in the house, and eat a huge meal, often with twelve at the table. More than anything else, this tempted Maria out of her cage of fear. She began to trust people again. It was her nanny who first sat beside her on the piano bench and taught her to play. Jewel was thrilled when Maria managed a complete piano score with no mistakes. It was one of the few times she could remember Jewel approving of something she did. She lifted the lid of the piano bench. She picked up the thin, browned pages of one of the music books, surprised to see Jewel had kept it through all these years. Her memories were abruptly cut off by her adoptive mother's sharp tone.

"You're lucky I was here." Jewel said. "I'm going out soon." She checked her watch even though Maria knew she had the time right down to the minute. "What did you want, Marie?"

Nothing more than that. Not even a hint of surprise at Maria materializing after a nine-year absence. And "Marie" never "Maria." Right from the start, Jewel refused to use her proper name as if it had been necessary to erase all elements of the past in order to realize her grand remodeling project.

She steeled herself, and thought, Don't rise to the bait. Be nice. "You're looking well, Jewel. I'm glad to see you."

Her invitation to call a truce was met with silence.

"How's Milne?"

"He's away. On a business trip."

Drying out somewhere, Maria thought.

Jewel checked her watch again. "I've just got time for a cocktail. Do you want one? What about a White Lady?"

"Sure, thanks." She forced a smile. White Ladies were the only cocktails Jewel ever drank.

Jewel rang for the maid and ordered the drinks. “Don’t stand on ceremony. Have a seat.” Maria lowered herself to one of the settees and Jewel sat on the other facing her, the two of them holding themselves breathlessly, like gladiators preparing for combat.

It was as if nine years had vanished in a flash. Jewel looked no older. A product of extensive surgery, she had the tight-skinned, plasticized look to prove it. Not a hair of her white-blond coif was out of place. She wore well-cut slacks and silk shirt of black, her favorite color. Pinned to her lapel, a sapphire brooch with a teardrop pearl. Milne’s wedding gift. Early on, Jewel had developed the habit of always wearing a precious gem as an acknowledgment of her name.

The maid brought their drinks and disappeared. Jewel took a sip and set her stem glass down on a coaster placed on the end table. “Well,” she said brightly, “are you still whoring?”

Maria wanted to toss her drink in Jewel’s face, smash the precious Ming china, and ruin the white broadloom. Instead she said, “Let’s not get off on the wrong foot. I know you have no desire to see me. And I wouldn’t have come if there wasn’t an urgent reason.”

“You turned out to be an extreme disappointment to me, Marie. After everything I did for you, you can’t expect me to feel charitable. All the funds spent on private schools. Your piano lessons, summer camp in the Catskills, braces. All money down the drain. What a colossal embarrassment you turned out to be.”

“And the next thing on the tip of your tongue is: I should have left you in that orphanage. I know the litany, so you can spare me the rest.”

"You were a distant child right from the start. It was unnatural."

"What did you expect? I'd just come from a torture chamber."

"I should have known that you can't make an angel out of a slut." Jewel carried on as if it had been a speech she'd been itching to give for nine years.

Maria wanted to scream at her. The same rage she'd felt as a teenager boiled up all over again. She banged her glass down on the end table.

"Look. I came because I need some information. A man has been stalking me. He's aware of things. The name of the town near the orphanage, Siret. How old I was when I came here. Very few people know about that. Have you talked about me, my origins, with anyone recently?"

"*You* are not a subject I make a habit of discussing. Why would you think I have any desire to broadcast a source of shame?" She took an angry gulp of her cocktail, draining the glass. "A man's stalking you. Do you have any idea how absurd that sounds? He probably just wants to screw you. You're not playing hard to get are you? That can't be good for business."

Maria folded her arms across her chest as if to defend herself from the river of spite pouring out of Jewel's mouth. "It's just me here. Me and you. If you don't tell me, I can send the police over if that's what you want. Wouldn't *that* ruffle your neighbors' feathers."

"The police don't waste time checking out harassment cases against prostitutes."

"Jewel, a young girl was killed because she looked like me. A child. She was only fifteen," she said flatly, making one last effort to wind the tone back down to manageable levels.

"Well, you can see how your . . . habits . . . lead to sordid endings. My advice would be to put your life back together again, seek counseling, whatever you need to do. Start afresh. Move to another city where no one knows you." It was obvious what she meant. *Far away from me.*

"Why would I do that, Jewel? I like my job. And I'm very good at it." She gave her a witchy smile.

Jewel stared at her for a moment, then pulled out her phone and checked something on the screen. Despite the tone of voice she'd used, Maria wasn't sure her adoptive mother even heard what she'd said. "Jewel! Who did you tell about me?"

Her words were met with a stony silence. Then Jewel said, "My friend's due any minute. We're off to a launch at the New Museum. You'll have to leave, I'm afraid." Her voice was cold and her waxy skin, always carefully protected from the sun, looked as white as ice.

Living in Jewel's household had left Maria with an appreciation for fine art. She kept informed about the various openings and shows. She knew there was no launch scheduled at the New Museum that evening. And likely no "friend" on the way either. Jewel had made the story up to get rid of her. For some reason this cut much deeper than the bitter words.

"I'm asking once more, pleading with you. Please tell me who you told about the orphanage."

Jewel replied with a sly smirk, touching a hand to her perfect hair. "We're finished here, I think."

Maria walked out of the room without saying another word.

One of the fedoras Milne liked to wear had been casually tossed on the Prince George table in the hall. She hadn't noticed it on her way in, distracted by the maid and preoccupied with having to face Jewel. If Milne had truly been away, the maid would have carefully tucked it away or faced Jewel's wrath at leaving things "untidy." So her adoptive mother had lied about him too.

Milne had been an attorney in Providence and Jewel married him shortly after she adopted Maria. The family moved to New York when Jewel was offered a partnership with a high-profile law firm. As a small-town lawyer, Milne quickly found himself out of his depth and when she was on the warpath, Jewel would fling his failures in his face.

As she pressed the elevator button, Maria heard the door behind her open. She glanced back and saw Milne in the hallway. If Jewel had changed little, Milne looked as though he'd aged for both of them. His hair was snowy white and wrinkles creased his face. He gave her a quick hug and stood back. "Hello, pet. You look wonderful. She doesn't know I came out here so I can't talk for long."

Maria melted at the sight of him and threw her arms around him. "I'm glad you did; it's been so long since I saw you. I didn't know you were here."

He pushed her away gently. "I know. I heard everything. That's why I came out. She was pretty upset."

"It felt like she'd just stored up nine years of rage and let it loose on me."

"Neither of us has lived up to her expectations, pet. She doesn't take that very well. But she's kept some of your things, you know. Your artwork, poems you wrote in prep school."

"I tried to get through to her, Milne. What else can I do?"

"She'll stew about your argument today. I know she will. Just give it a little time and she may come around. Don't forget. It's been years since we've heard from you. That's hurt her too—more than you might think."

Nothing had changed. Even after all these years, Milne was still trying to bridge the canyon between them, play the peacemaker. His efforts always failed. She took his hand. "Do you have any idea who Jewel might have told about my background in Romania? I need to know."

He shook his head, and Maria noticed a tremor in his movements. "We share the same living quarters. When she's home I tiptoe around, trying to stay out of her way. She wouldn't tell me." He glanced nervously at the door. "I better get back. It won't do you any good for her to see me here."

When he gave her a warm kiss on the cheek, she caught a faint whiff of whiskey on his breath. "Take care of yourself, Milne."

He padded back down the hall in his old slippers.

On her way home she thought about another mother. Her first one. Her dearly beloved. A dark-haired woman with a warm heart. How at this time of year they'd spend hours in the garden. Her mother would make little trenches in the rich brown earth; Maria would follow behind, carefully dropping seeds in place. She recalled her mother's low melodious voice, the way she laughed approvingly at how precise Maria was, making sure every seed was spaced exactly so many inches apart.

Once, a kid had bullied her and Maria ran home crying. She begged her parents not to send her to school anymore but they insisted. The next afternoon a pet kitten was waiting for her at home, a furry tabby with green eyes. "Like your beautiful ones, Maria," her mother said. "Remember. When a person tries to harm you, if you find someone else to love, the hurt will go away."

It had been a happy home until the Romanian Securitate police broke through their front door. Ceausescu kept the largest secret police force in the Eastern bloc, notorious for its brutality. Maria's father was a highly regarded officer in the Securitate. As a communist satellite, Russia and Romania were, on the surface, friends. In the last year of Ceausescu's reign, when the regime was clearly tottering, Russian intelligence kept a close eye on him. Her father, who'd despised Ceausescu, had been instrumental in passing information along to them. Predictions of Ceausescu's demise were sent back via her father. Ceausescu heard the rumors of betrayal and murdered her father and mother.

Maria was sent to the orphanage. She knew her parents had been executed but not why. On her recent visit to Romania, she'd learned the details. Her mother was raped repeatedly in front of her father. Not to make him talk. They knew everything. As punishment. It had been a bitterly cold morning when the strangers took her to the orphanage, making the bleak landscape surrounding it seem even more like a wasteland. She'd worn her little white coat with a fur hood, and the red dress and princess shoes her parents had given her for Christmas. One of the orphanage caretaker's first actions was to remove her clothing. She had no lice but they used a soap harsh with lye to scrub her and sprayed disinfectant on her hair. She resisted them in the small, ineffectual ways of a child. Shouting at her didn't work so the caretakers tied her right wrist to the crib and let her wail.

And before long the Blackbird came. Always at night, cranking down the crib railing, waking her up from a fitful sleep, putting his hands on her body in places they didn't belong.

Lillian was out on an overnight visit with a friend when she reached home. The tears she'd held back flowed the minute she walked in the door. She flung herself down on her bed and wept.

CHAPTER 14

GENEVA

She always felt freer away from home and this time, traveling to Europe would give her some much needed distance from the confrontation with Jewel a week ago and the abrasive memories it revived. What better place, she thought, than the picture postcard city of Geneva, a mountain Riviera cradled by two landmarks, Mont Blanc and Mont Salève. She loved that one of city's best-known features was ephemeral—a fountain, the world's tallest water plume. The air was crisp and clean and Lake Geneva itself had been restored to the pristine beauty of centuries ago.

Marcus Constantin had hired her to pose as La Grande Odalisque, a living reproduction of one of the most famous nudes in the world, Ingres's painting of a harem concubine. She would be featured at the launch of his new art show. In Geneva, a magnet for the global wealthy and influential, museums and galleries were as common as secret bank accounts. Constantin specialized in neoclassical art, and his gallery had earned a place among Europe's most respected establishments. After her public performance, he'd requested an after-hours session alone.

Marcus's gallery was in the old city, a gothic ramble of ancient buildings and picturesque cobbled roads. She wished she had time to wander those streets, browse through the boutiques and museums, or saunter along the waterside promenade before her assignation.

Transforming Claudine into a living Odalisque was a big creative challenge for Lillian. She could not rely on costuming or extreme makeup. The transformation called for a very subtle hand with cosmetics. She began working on Claudine at noon even though the doors to the launch wouldn't open until six P.M. She'd refused to use a print as a guide because even the better reproductions were notoriously "off" when it came to representing a painting's true colors. Instead, they'd hired a French photographer to snap a photo of the original in the Louvre and mail it to them.

"It's impossible to get your body to look like that," Lillian said, exasperated, as she bent over Claudine, who lay upon the portable massage table. "Why is the woman's figure so odd?"

Claudine regarded the photo. Pictured with her neck twisted to look over her shoulder, and painted from the rear, the concubine had an elongated back and pelvis that experts speculated would only be physically possible with five extra vertebrae. Her right arm and leg too were much longer than the limbs on her left side. The concubine's body almost seemed to flow, as if no bones supported her flesh. It reminded Claudine of the sex doll splayed on her hotel bed and she shuddered.

"It's a seductive posture, but not blatantly so. You see her bottom turned almost fully to the viewer. The artist makes you desire to see more. That's truly erotic."

"And the concubine's skin looks like it was made from moonlight," Lillian said. "I wonder how Ingres created that effect." She brushed a pearly iridescent powder over a patch of Claudine's pale skin. She stood a few feet back, squinted her eye and nodded, satisfied with the effect.

After powdering every inch of her, Lillian fitted her with dark contacts and carefully applied gray-brown shadow into the creases to deepen her eyes. Lillian checked the photo of the painting and then dipped into her palette of colors with one of her smaller brushes to adjust the look. A touch of blush on the flat of her cheeks and pastel lipstick to color and shape petallike lips completed the image. In the painting, only one baby fingernail showed, but Lillian buffed and polished all her nails anyway. It took a whole half hour to hide the feather scar. By the time she finished, the real courtesan had virtually disappeared; Lillian had created the painting anew using Claudine's body as a canvas.

Lillian adjusted the brunette wig last, then packed up the case and helped her on with a wraparound sleeveless dress while Claudine slipped her feet into a pair of flats.

"How about something to eat?" Lillian asked.

She shook her head.

"You can't go all afternoon and through the event with nothing in your stomach." She gave Claudine an energy bar packed with almonds, raisins and chocolate.

Andrei, unwilling to let Claudine out of his sight after the experience in San Francisco, stationed himself on a chair just inside the entrance of their hotel suite while Lillian worked on her in the bedroom. As an extra precaution, he paid an off-duty hotel security guard to stay in the suite while they were at the launch. He was used to seeing Claudine in dramatic costume, but she startled him when she emerged from her room. "You're a completely different woman," he said. "Lillian, you've outdone yourself this time."

Andrei drove them to the gallery. He refused to let Claudine out of his sight for a minute. She found his concern for her touching and thanked heaven she had him on her side.

Before she went in, Claudine watched people pass by. A handsome older couple, arm in arm, paused every few minutes to gaze at store windows; teenagers in private school uniforms, high on the knowledge summer break was coming soon, paraded down the sidewalk laughing loudly; businessmen, heads down, phones out, strode along determinedly.

Is he among these businessmen, incognito but in full view, laughing at me because I have no idea who he is? she wondered. She gave herself a shake and trailed Lillian through plate glass doors into the gallery. Andrei took a quick glance around at the street before following them inside.

All the threats and the violence had occurred in America, she reminded herself. It wasn't likely she'd been followed to Europe. Before they left, Andrei had installed a sophisticated hidden camera system in her apartment; it would catch anyone who tried to break in. And yet a niggling worm of doubt coiled and uncoiled in her mind. The fear of it left a trail that she tasted as surely as the raisins and chocolate chips lingering on her tongue.

Marcus Constantin greeted them effusively, with a double

kiss for Claudine. A debonair man in his early seventies, he had longish silver hair combed straight back off his forehead and wore a black jacket and pants, with a black Armani cashmere crew underneath. He ushered them over to the raised platform Claudine would occupy for the duration of the launch, while two art students arranged the rich indigo, gold and white drapery depicted in the painting. In one corner of the room, caterers set up drinks and appetizers on a long table covered with a spotless white cloth. They seemed oblivious to the small fortune in artwork surrounding them—Ingres drawings and prints, a painting by David, sculpture by Antonio Canova and Thorvaldsen.

Claudine climbed onto the platform. Lillian fixed her gold-braided and tasseled turban and slipped on the shimmering bracelets while Marcus and his assistants helped her to assume the concubine's position. She grasped the bejeweled peacock feather fan they gave her. Under Marcus's watchful eye, they moved the oversized gilt frame in place, an exact copy of the one hanging in the Louvre.

Marcus stood back to admire her. "Marvelous! What I love about this idea is that the painting is suspenseful. It toys with us, makes us wonder what the concubine looks like from the front. Ingres only gives us hints. This evening, for the first time, people will see what the painting keeps hidden."

A rather crass attempt to hog the limelight to be sure, but it worked. At six, the crowds surged in. Marcus, an adept publicist, primed the media well with sound bites and they rushed over to the tableaux like aggressive geese, snapping pictures, circling with television cameras.

By eight P.M., with all the wine gone and not even a shred of the appetizers left, "sold" stickers on the catalogue entries of almost every work of art offered, Marcus declared the evening a huge success. Claudine, who'd remained motionless for the entire two hours of the launch, clambered off the platform and nearly fell. Her muscles had locked and cramps shot up her legs when she tried to move. Lillian helped her into her wraparound, then bent down and massaged her calves rigorously.

After Lillian left and Claudine was sufficiently recovered, Marcus led her to his private apartment upstairs. A light dinner had been laid out: cold jellied salmon, white asparagus, salade Niçoise. He handed her wine, a crisp Swiss Fleurie, and tipped his glass toward her. "A toast to you, petite. You were remarkable."

"My pleasure, Marcus. It was fun. Although my legs feel like they'll be crooked for the rest of year."

"Yes, but your picture will be on the front entertainment pages of every paper in Europe tomorrow. It's fabulous publicity for you." She inclined her head to thank him. Word would spread rapidly about the performance and bring in more business for her.

Marcus set his glass down. "You're admirably suited to play the concubine; I couldn't have made a better choice. And do you know why? It is not simply your physical attractions; we have many beauties in Europe, after all." He ran his hand down her bare arm, letting it rest on her own hand. "It is a particular quality you have—elusiveness. You're very desirable, but aloof. Unobtainable. This is what really sets the fire burning. We men find that irresistible. I think Ingres had such a sentiment in mind when he painted his lady. As a concubine she was a captive, but she gives the impression it would be impossible to ever really possess her."

Claudine leaned over, her lips still glistening with wine, and kissed him on the mouth. "You're a shameless flatterer, Marcus. I love it."

He pushed his chair back and rose gracefully, took her hand. "Come petite, I wish to make the most of the brief time allotted to me."

She followed him to the door of an adjoining room. "I only show this off to my close friends," he said, punching buttons on a plate to unlock the door.

She hesitated for only a second before remembering that Andrei stood guard downstairs. "I'm honored you consider me one of them," she said graciously.

She had to stifle a gasp.

Dozens of paintings and prints adorned the walls, and marble pedestals held priceless sculpture. Here was Marcus's famed collection of erotic art. One print, unmistakably a Picasso, featured distorted male and female figures, a large penis inserted into a hairy cunt, hands holding a palette, brushes. The tangle of bodies was observed by a strange seated figure—Picasso himself perhaps? A portrayal of the artist fucking his model, literally and allegorically.

A painting of Leda and the Swan caught her eye. A naked woman reclined upon a crimson cloth as a swan inserted its sex between her legs. Judging from the brutish, masculine lines of the woman's form, it appeared to be a Michelangelo.

Marcus confirmed it was a work by the great artist. "A tempera painting," he said, waving his hand toward it. "Much copied, but this is the original. It was considered obscene and was supposedly burned in 1640 at Fontainebleau. I suspect the church fathers kept it hidden for their own titillation." He chuckled.

"And that's an engraving attributed to Jules Adolphe Chauvet." The strange picture he pointed toward showed a woman from the navel down, two cherubs pulling back her dress to expose her naked belly and sex. Out of her slit tumbled tiny figures, copulating in all kinds of imaginative positions.

But the artwork wasn't what startled Claudine most. Against one wall stood an apparatus, a bondage stand, a simple iron frame fixed to the floor and rising to a height of about seven feet. Cuffs with tensors extended from each corner. Her heart sank. She rubbed her right wrist and tried to ignore the loud pumping of her heart. "I don't do bondage, Marcus. That's clearly stated whenever I take on a client." She had nothing against BDSM and knew that was a popular venue of pleasure for some. It simply wasn't her thing. And the early memories of being tied to her crib gave her a physical aversion to being restrained.

"Of course, petite, I know. It's intended for me . . . not you." Noting the look on her face, he laughed. "Why, I'm not asking you to whip me or anything like that. I'm far too much of a coward about pain. It's the feeling of being restrained that I love. It seems to turn a switch on. After I'm bound, I want you to tease me." He patted her cheek. "With binding, the sensations are so much greater. You must try it sometime."

"I did—only once. A very wealthy client, a prominent Japanese artist. He practiced *kinbaku*."

"Ah. Japanese bondage is a high art. And you are like the *oiran*, those high-ranking courtesans who were entertainers and celebrities. I can see why he wanted you. But if you dislike bondage, why did you agree?"

"I consented because he didn't ask for sex and that made me curious. And he promised to release me if I felt any pain. He specified what I was to wear: stilettos, silk stockings with seams, a white garter belt, panties and bra. Over that, he wanted me to wear a conservative dress with a high neck and long sleeves. And no makeup. His requests were very precise—that intrigued me."

"How enticing. Tell me about it."

Claudine warmed to her subject. "He slowly took off my dress and his hands actually trembled when he unfastened my bra. He carefully removed each item of clothing until I stood only in my shoes. Holding them to his nose to seek my scent, he then folded each garment with extreme care and set them on a chair. He ran his fingers over every inch of my body as if he couldn't see, could only know me through touch. He'd hand-dyed beautiful, soft linen ropes and used them to bind me with an elaborate system of knots."

Marcus hung on her every word. "You must demonstrate, petite."

She hesitated. As long as she was directing, and the knots were not too tight, she could break her own rule of no bondage. If it would please him, she'd comply. "We'd need some rope, at least eighteen feet. Do you have anything like that?"

Marcus thought for a minute. "I have some thin cable that I use to grapple larger sculptures—just wait." He went into the other room. She could hear him rummaging in a cupboard and he returned with a length of thin blue nylon rope.

"Good. Now undress me . . . slowly."

Marcus's eyes lit up. "With great pleasure." He reached for the ties of her wrap, undid the bow and let the silky material slip through his fingers. He pulled the wings of fabric away from her naked body. The bulge in his trousers grew at the sight of her pink nipples, her supple skin and the smooth cleft between her thighs.

"Take the rope," Claudine commanded. "Slip it around my neck and make a knot so it looks like a noose. Then tie a second knot over my sternum at the top of my cleavage." After he followed her next instructions, two bands of rope circled her: one at the top of her breasts and one below. It had the effect of pushing out her breasts and making her nipples swell and harden. They looked like pink candy kisses.

"God, that's stunning," Marcus said. He took one of her nipples in his mouth and sucked gently, while tweaking the other with his thumb and index finger. The charge of his soft tongue on her breasts made her pussy throb.

"Now I'll show you another thing the artist did—but on you, not me. First, you're going to have to untie me."

Marcus did as he was told and removed the blue cable. When he disrobed she saw that he hid a myriad of flaws beneath his elegant clothes. The nest of hair on his chest and pubis was sparse and white and his skin sagged over flaccid muscles. His testicles hung low like those of an aging stud bull. He ran his hand over his noticeable paunch and smiled. "Not the body I once had. The good life has taken its toll."

Many of her customers were older men, a number elderly; that made no difference to her. Often she found them gentler, more generous. She ran her hands over his chest, his stomach and up the insides of his thighs. He tensed with pleasure. "We all focus on our flaws, Marcus. You're still a very handsome man." She kissed his neck.

He beamed at the compliment and delicately confessed that

age had caught up with him. More and more often he'd been unable to hold an erection or, at best, managed only a soft one. He detested drugs of any kind so for him the blue pill was not an option. "A harsh thing to do to one's body," he said. "I prefer physical stimulation."

"Of course, Marcus," she soothed. "I understand."

He wedged his hands and feet through the cuffs on the apparatus and she tightened the tensors until he was secured, spread-eagled inside the iron frame. She made a loop in the blue cable and tightened the noose behind his balls around the base of his penis by twisting the length of rope up his belly, then circling the two halves of rope around his waist and tying a tight knot at the small of his back.

The pressure aroused him and when she squatted and took him in her mouth, he hardened quickly. "You're very talented," he said, his breaths quickening. "Tease me. Give me more."

She sucked strongly on the head of cock and gave his balls a gentle squeeze. When she looked up to see if he liked the technique, he opened his eyes, gazed at her pink lips working his shaft and shuddered with delight.

Claudine stood up and untied the rope. She continued her story: "The Japanese artist drew me when he'd finished his binding. The act of drawing seemed to excite him even more, although it was a swift exercise, just a few expert lines. Then he bowed graciously and walked out of the room leaving me to dress. And that was all. It was the process of binding me he yearned for. No consummation was necessary. That simple act gave him great satisfaction."

"I imagine he's looked at that drawing over and over," Marcus said, still a little breathless.

"Once he'd completed his drawing, he lost interest in the muse." She let the cable drop to the floor. "Hold still; I have something else to make our evening fun."

From her bag she retrieved a tube of lubricant and a curious device, a round plastic ring crowned with short feathery fronds. She smeared lube on her palms and enclosed his penis, moving her hands vigorously up and down. She slid the elastic ring down his cock and fitted it behind his testicles, immediately enhancing the sensation. She smiled at him. "Feels good, doesn't it?"

His pelvis quivered with pleasure. "Phenomenal, petite."

She licked the length of his cock and gently rubbed his balls. She slipped the elastic ring back over his balls but kept it hugging his penis to maintain his erection.

"I want you inside me now, Marcus." She brushed her nipples against his chest, and in one swift movement, looped a leg over his bound right arm, opening her pussy wide. She guided his cock into her slit.

"God, you feel . . . amazing . . ." he mumbled. She moved her hips to match his motions, the little fronds on the cock ring brushing her clitoris with every thrust. Soon she became caught up in her own sensations, using the device to titillate her most sensitive spot. Her vagina clenched and her body rocked with myriad heavenly vibrations. Shortly after, a few short, guttural pants brought Marcus to a blissful orgasm and he slumped against her.

Rapid steps banged on the stair leading up to the adjacent room, as if the person coming toward them was taking the steps two at a time. A heavy first pounded on the door. Marcus jerked his head up in consternation, spoiling the pleasing lassitude that had stolen over him.

"Who the devil is that? Get me out of these things, Claudine!"

She struggled to get the cuffs off. Marcus wrenched his hands and feet out of them, threw on his pants and shirt. "There's a bathroom through there." He jerked his thumb to indicate the screen in the corner behind the apparatus. She grabbed her dress and bag and went in, wet a cloth, ran it over her face and hands and then wiped the wetness off her thighs. She sprayed on some perfume and wrapped her dress around her. She could hear Marcus's tones but nothing else. Her earlier fears flooded back. After a few moments of silence, she exited the gallery and shut the door behind her. Marcus was waiting for her in the reception room. Andrei stood beside him with a look of harsh determination on his face.

Her heart sank. Andrei would never barge into one of her performances without a very good reason. "What is it? What's happened?" She pressed her teeth into her lip, fearing the worst.

Andrei walked over and took her in his arms. "It's Lillian."

CHAPTER 15

Maria closed her eyes and tried to block out the terrible images flooding her brain. "The guard was supposed to stay in the room with her until we got back!" She cried, pushing away from him.

"He did. No one got into your suite, at least not while he was there."

"Then what happened? Where is she?"

"She's in the hospital. When Lillian went back to the hotel, she started to tidy up. She found a box of your . . . protective material." He'd stumbled over what to call it but she knew he meant her female condoms.

"I guess they spilled somehow," Andrei continued. "Lillian tried to put them back but the lube in one of them drained out. It got on her fingers and burned them. She tried to wash it off but the water only made it worse. According to the guard, she started screaming and her fingers bled. By the time they got her to the hospital the skin on her right hand had been seared off just as if she'd stuck it on a red-hot stove."

Her lips trembled. "Oh my God."

"The doctors treated Lillian's hand right away. Now we just have to wait and see. The security guard called me to let me know what happened. We should head over to the hospital right now."

She bid Marcus a quick good-bye and followed Andrei to the car waiting outside.

"Whatever the substance is, it was placed there deliberately. You know that, don't you?"

"Yes." She was sick at the thought of what Lillian must be suffering.

"We'll take a sample back to the U.S. and get it tested to find out what it is. Toxic as hell, that's for sure."

If it had not seeped out until she inserted the condom, it would have burned her insides and left her genitals a mass of scar tissue. "What kind of monster would do this?" What she didn't say aloud was that Lillian had paid a terrible price for her choices. "How could he have altered the lubricant, do you think?"

"My guess is he opened one of those packages back in San Francisco when he broke into your hotel room. He must have doctored it, maybe used a syringe to do it, and then resealed the box. Did you open a new one?"

"Tonight. Just before I went to the gallery." She was quiet for a moment. "We know one thing definitively. He's been a client at some point. He came to San Francisco prepared because he knew what I used for protection."

Andrei passed a taxi and slid smoothly back into his lane. “That’s right. You’ve met this pig before—that’s for sure.”

Three hours later, Lillian sat on the edge of the bed in their hotel suite, her right hand swathed in white gauze and bandages. Above the bandages, her wrist and lower arm were enflamed and swollen. Maria made tea for her and placed it on the bedside table.

“They gave me some painkillers. They’re in a bag around here somewhere.” Lillian tried to smile. It was a wan effort.

Maria put her arm around her. “I’m so sorry, sweetie. Would you like to go home? We’ll do whatever you want.” She opened the pill bottle and shook two into her palm.

“I’d rather stay with you and Andrei,” Lillian replied, swallowing the medication with a sip of tea.

Maria knew what she was thinking: *I don’t want to stay in the apartment, alone.*

Lillian got into bed. Maria pulled the covers around her and lay beside her, stroked her damp, black hair until the drug took hold and Lillian fell asleep.

Andrei thanked the guard and sent him away with a generous bonus. He poured a strong cup of coffee and took up his post in the armchair beside the door. His face looked drawn and grim; gray pouches lurked under his eyes. He seemed to have lost weight in the past couple of weeks. Maria noticed him begin to nod off, then jerk his head up. He scrolled through his cell phone idly to keep himself awake.

A phrase she once heard came back to her. *Endings come in*

their own time, not necessarily when we want them to. The phrase echoed in her brain. It was apt, nonetheless. Unless she discovered her stalker's identity very soon, a single alternative lay ahead. Let Lillian and Andrei go to keep them safe. Cut herself off from them, decisively, cleanly, permanently. She couldn't hire new staff either—as if Andrei and Lillian could ever be replaced. The horrors of the recent past would only be repeated on the new employees.

Andrei swore under his breath.

"What?" She kept her voice low to avoid waking Lillian.

"Another message." He held out his phone. She eased herself off the bed and took it from him. The screen showed a new poem.

Little girl from Siret
Name of Maria
Six-year-old.
Lani's friend
Won't keep the promises she makes,
Innocent angel?
The man in the iron mask knows
She's just another whore—soon to die.

She looked at Andre. "Do you get the allusion?"

He looked at her quizzically.

"The man in the iron mask was a famous prisoner on Île Sainte-Marguerite off the coast of Cannes," she explained. "Dumas wrote his adventure of revenge based on the prisoner's life. For thirteen brutal years, he was isolated in an impenetrable cell and his identity never revealed." The very words conjured up a dank stone-walled cell, instruments of torture, a crude metal mask that could never be removed.

"This guy has got to be hacking into my text messages. How else could he have known about San Francisco, and that we're heading to Cannes next?"

Andrei nodded grimly and tossed his phone on the table. "You're right. He must be."

For a few moments she considered canceling her appointment, then decided against it. Whether they stayed in Cannes or returned to New York wouldn't matter. Her pursuer seemed to know her location wherever she was.

CHAPTER 16

CANNES

Maria had booked them into a small, elite hotel on La Croisette near the beaches, bistros and shops. The longer stay proved a wise decision as Lillian needed more time to rest and recover. Maria insisted on being the one to change the dressings and apply antibiotic ointment to Lillian's damaged fingers. The Geneva doctor said she'd need reconstructive surgery when she got back to America.

On the second day, Lillian felt well enough to go out, so late in the morning they found a pleasant harbor-side café shaded by green palms. Andrei stretched his legs out and tipped his head back to catch the sun. His face had a hint of brown already because he tanned quickly, and with his Persol sunglasses and lithe body, Maria thought he looked like a film star himself. With amusement, she watched the group of women at a nearby table, chests puffed out like amorous birds, showing off their busts in tight low-cut dresses. They sneaked glimpses at Andrei, hoping to catch his eye, and Maria could tell they were trying to figure out which movie they'd seen him in.

Andrei removed his sunglasses and sent a few glances their way. One of the young women, with a long tumble of fawn-colored hair and delicate features, responded with a knowing smile. She shifted her chair sideways and picked up the menu as if to see it in better light, extending one leg as she did so.

Atrocious little flirt. Just an excuse, Maria suspected, to give Andrei a good look at her shapely thighs and neat ankles. Of course, he *was* quite sexy. No surprise the women were interested.

The fawn-haired girl took a pen from her purse and scribbled something on a paper napkin, tucked it under her plate. The group got up to leave. As the girl walked away she wagged her rump slightly, tossed her long hair and took a quick look behind her to see if Andrei was watching.

"Aren't you going to retrieve your message? I expect she's left you her cell number," Maria said. "She's very pretty."

"Sure I will." He laughed, reached up and ruffled a lock of her blond hair. "But my boss is so demanding, she probably wouldn't give me the time off for a date."

She watched with amusement as a busboy hurried over to clear the plates and glasses from the vacated table. The napkin with the phone number disappeared into his pocket.

During the film festival the population in Cannes swelled. People thronged to the city to party, catch a glimpse of the stars, clinch business deals or simply feed off the energy of the world's most important film festival. Among these were a small army of prostitutes. Asian and East European call girls, addicts trading fifty-dollar blow jobs for crack, agency escorts with prebooked clients, bit actors both male and female willing to screw to rub shoulders with important movie men, local street walkers. And among them, a few—models and actors—dabbled in prostitution if the money was right, even though it wasn't their primary source of income. Some commanded upward of forty thousand a night. Her client had offered fifty thousand; she couldn't turn it down.

For the last two days she'd been on a green juice fast, mindful of the need to keep her figure svelte for the evening's performance. A great sacrifice in this land of delectable food. She set down her juice glass, fanned herself with her napkin and looked at Lillian, who was gazing thoughtfully past the yachts crowding the harbor. White boats floated on the azure water; tinkling bells sent out a melody as the breeze stirred the halyards; the smell of the salt sea was thick in the air.

She scanned the yachts. Tonight she would be on one of them. Her client's boat. What would be waiting for her there? She took a sip of her juice and tried to push down the panic and worry that never left her for long.

A streamlined inboard sprayed wash against the pier. A crew member held out his hand to assist Claudine aboard while the other man kept the boat from drifting. Uninvited, Andrei jumped in after her. A quarrel in French ensued over whether Andrei could board, but she stated flatly she wouldn't leave without him, so with a roar of the motor they took off. Their destination was the *Hercules*, a 220-foot-long yacht built by Austal, with four decks and thirty-five staterooms. It could reach a cruising speed of seventeen knots and accommodate forty crew.

It had two elegant lounges, one complete with a fireplace, an adjoining dining room, spa, outdoor pool and Jacuzzi. The Middle Eastern businessman who owned it preferred flying in his private jet to yachting. He was her host for the night.

He'd not asked for any role-playing, so she wore pink Saint Laurent and Fendi stilettos with fabric straps that curled around her ankles. She'd visited a nail shop in the afternoon for her manicure and pedicure, left her blond hair natural, dipping below her shoulders, and put on her own makeup with Lillian directing, seated in a chair beside her. Once again, Andrei had arranged for hotel security to watch over Lillian.

Her client, Hassan, an impeccably attired young man, greeted them as they walked into the outdoor lounge. He spoke perfect Oxford English. Solemn faced, only a touch taller than she, he held himself erect; his serious expression gave way as he glanced approvingly at her.

It was the custom to pay escorts with envelopes stuffed with cash. Hassan motioned to one of his staff standing nearby who extracted a large Kraft envelope from his inside jacket pocket and handed it to her. She immediately passed it along to Andrei. No need to count it. Middle Eastern clients had a reputation for grand gestures. If anything, the envelope contained more than the amount agreed upon.

Drinks were poured into green cut-glass tumblers bearing the *Hercules* insignia. The guests milled around the lounge and paraded along the deck, taking in the balmy evening air. Laughter and music welled up from a boat anchored near them. The *Hercules* rocked gently with the swell of the waves. All of the men, fifteen of them she counted, appeared to be well over forty. They sized her up boldly. They knew how much Hassan had paid; it was part of the ritual and expected that as top dog, their host would trump all the others.

Of the women, in equal numbers, the oldest could not have been more than twenty. While the men were fully dressed, the women were either completely naked or wore "barely there" thongs. Claudine wondered humorously where they'd stashed their envelopes. Several girls frolicked in the Jacuzzi, two with carefully streaked hair falling to midback, one with curly locks as black as ink. She wore a diamond necklace that dangled into her cleavage. She caught the eye of the man nearest to her and playfully splashed water over her enormous breasts.

Hassan took her by the elbow and escorted her to the deck. Claudine noted how he'd kept his eyes on her from the first, as if she were his lover, not a service bought and paid for. She encouraged him by flirting with him hard. Once or twice, she caught Andrei observing this behavior with a frown. That was unusual. Normally Andrei kept his expression stiff and remote when they were on assignments. Likely just worried about security, she told herself. Working alone, with this many people on board, he couldn't be sure to cover every possibility.

She and Hassan leaned on the railing and gazed out at the lights of Cannes. "Your dress is very becoming; you have such a pretty figure. I asked you to remain clothed because you're my private pleasure. The imagination is better stirred in such a way, is it not?"

She squeezed his hand. "Like everything else in life, people want it all immediately. I prefer to take my time."

He clearly liked her reply. "I am looking forward to that. I've heard a lot about you." His smile widened to a grin. "That you bring much pleasure."

She brushed her hand lightly along the side of his thigh and she could feel his muscles tense pleasantly in response. He moved closer to her. “What is more delicious, do you think? The anticipation or the act?”

“One requires the other so that both can be enjoyed.”

“You’re clever too. Very nice.”

As she glanced at the water, Claudine’s attention was caught by a boat about thirty feet in length, not far off from the *Hercules*’s stern. It was painted black. Its sails were furled but the boat drifted through the water noiselessly. Cabin lights illuminated the figure of a lone man standing on the deck, holding a pair of binoculars, his face lost in shadow. Something about him made her uncomfortable. She couldn’t say exactly why, just that the black boat and the man’s stillness felt menacing. The vessel passed uncomfortably close to the *Hercules*. The man lifted his binoculars and trained them on her.

She touched her client’s arm. “Do you recognize the boat?”

He looked at the passing yacht. “We get many of those. They want to see the girls. It’s common around here.”

She turned her back to the railing abruptly. “It’s cool out. Do you mind if we go back to the lounge?”

“Not at all. Whatever you wish. I am glad to have your company tonight.”

They mingled with the guests for a while longer. Some began to pair off, eagerly escaping to the privacy of the guest rooms.

Claudine caught sight of Andrei, who’d trailed after them into the lounge. He nodded when she gave him a sign to let him know she’d be disappearing to spend time with her host. Along with one of Hassan’s bodyguards, he remained discreetly at the stateroom door.

The stateroom was impeccably appointed, and all the hardware had been fashioned out of gold. A little over the top, she thought, but it definitely made a statement. The king-sized bed had been stripped of its spread and covered with a fine cotton sheet. "Strip for me, please," Hassan said.

Soft lighting caught the silvery highlights in her hair and the satiny sheen of her skin as she let her dress slip to the floor. She unclasped her pink bra and slid the straps from her shoulders. Her panties, also pink, she pushed down over her hips. She stepped out of them delicately but left her heels on. Without an invitation, she sat demurely on the edge of the bed and patted the space beside her.

He grinned, approving of her boldness. "I like to watch movies first. Are you agreeable?"

"Whatever you wish."

"It's loaded already." He picked up an enormous remote and pressed buttons. A panel slid back to reveal a giant screen, a DVD player and stacks of movies on shelves underneath. The screen brightened. A porno flick started up. Two naked, dark-haired women performed cunnilingus on each other in front of a desk on a beige carpet with office plants in the background.

Claudine stretched back on the bed, amused at her client. His eyes were glued to the screen with the single-minded concentration of a teenage gamer.

Without looking away, he gestured toward the women on the screen with the remote. "Illegal in our country."

Anything goes outside it, though, for the men, at least, she thought.

The women, having reached thundering orgasms, scampered toward a well-hung man with rock-hard abs and a prize fighter's shoulders who'd just entered the office. With no preliminaries, he fucked first one, then the other. Each girl climaxed with a series of "Ohs" exactly in tandem with the guy, who managed to come twice in a total span of about five minutes. No fantasy there, she thought, laughing to herself.

Hassan clicked off the film and turned to her with eyes slightly glazed. "Let me see you," he said. He put one hand on each of her inner thighs and spread her legs. She leaned back, supporting herself with her arms extended behind her, and opened her legs wider. The cool air on her skin and the intensity of his gaze turned her on. He traced his fingers around the lips of her opening, up and down the length of her slit.

"Very nice." He moistened his finger with K-Y from a bedside table and circled her anus. She gasped when he pushed the tip of his finger inside. This was going to be intense. To slow things down she grasped his cock inside his trousers, but he gently pushed her hand away. He stood back and surveyed her. "I want you to do it to yourself first." He went over to the bedside table, pulled open the drawer and brought out a ribbed pink dildo, then handed it to her. She lay back upon the bed and placed the dildo between her breasts. She licked her fingers and smiled at him before twisting and squeezing her nipples to make herself wet. Hassan, impatient, knelt in front of her and spat on her clit. "I've seen that in pornos too," he said, laughing.

She trailed her hand down her stomach and ran her fingers lightly over her bud, slippery with his saliva. She circled her fingers around and over, moved more quickly, felt her clit firm up deliciously. She closed her eyes to savor the heat building inside and when she felt ready, with the other hand grasped the dildo. She eased it in and began a gentle pumping.

Hassan unzipped his fly and pulled out his dusky cock. He grasped the loose skin of his penis and pulled up and down with rapid movements, his body jerking slightly as he did so. Claudine took out the glistening dildo, rolled over on her stomach, and drew herself up on all fours. "Do it to me with the dildo," she ordered.

She felt a twinge of pain as he spread her bum cheeks and then soothing pressure when he pressed a wet finger into her anus. "More lube, please," she said.

Hassan squirted more K-Y onto the tip of the dildo and rubbed it around the rim of her anus, gradually pressing it inside her. A sharp twinge at first and then her muscles relaxed. The secret to avoiding pain was to push out during entry. After that, the sphincter would loosen and accept the intrusion. With the dildo halfway into her, he began a gentle stroking, pushing and pulling, while slipping his finger over and around her nub. Her buttocks clenched so tightly the dildo bobbed up and down out of his hands. She tried to hold back to no avail; she was going to come hard. She fell over the edge, a luscious tremble spreading through her groin. Her pelvis bucked. She fell upon the bed, gasping, and slid the dildo out.

"A good way to start." He grinned and sat back. She rolled over to face him, her cheeks flushed and hair mussed delectably. She noticed how his blinding white teeth contrasted with his coal black hair and brows. He poured some water from a carafe and handed her a glass. Cold and frosty. "Your turn," she said breathlessly after taking a drink, and unbuttoned his shirt to tease his curly chest hairs.

Hassan dropped his pants and moved up close to her so his

cock was level with her mouth. She ran her tongue along and around it. He firmed up quickly and pushed into her throat. She had learned long ago how to loosen her throat muscles, not fight it, and hold off the instinct to gag. Full of urgency now, he grabbed the back of her head, twined his fingers in her hair, and pressed deeper, blocking her air. She waited for the pull back so she could take a breath but instead of withdrawing, he pushed in harder. Claudine choked. She struggled and tried to move him away but he held her head tightly, preventing it. She had no choice and bit down. Not so hard as to draw blood but enough to send a sharp message. She jerked her head away and wrenched herself back. After hauling in a deep breath, she said, "Don't get so rough."

"Forgive me," he said, looking a little sheepish. "You excite me too much."

He pushed her back upon the bed, traced the flat of her belly with his palm, then grasped her hips and turned her over. He kneed her thighs to spread them. He gazed at her behind, still relaxed and open from the dildo. He inserted the tip of his cock into her rear, entering carefully. He filled her more than the dildo had and she liked the feeling of being stretched to her limit. He began a gentle rhythm, which she matched. It grew more intense. Her breasts swung back and forth with their thrusting and he captured them in his graceful hands, pinching them hard. Her ass clenched and he came fast, a hot jet of semen spraying into her, the musky odor of their sweat and sex hanging in the air. He lay on top of her until his penis went soft and slid out.

He insisted they both wash. The en suite had two sinks and he was careful not to touch the soap or towels she used. After a while, they went another round but he didn't go near her pussy. He only wanted her ass.

On the way back to the quay, the air had turned cool, and spray from the launch churning through the waves misted over Maria and Andrei sitting in the boat's rear seat.

"You cold?" Andrei asked, seeing her shiver. He shrugged his jacket off and draped it around her shoulders. She leaned into him, welcoming his body warmth. French laws forbade carrying weapons, so the calf leather shoulder holster he usually wore was missing.

"You must feel a bit naked without your gun," she said.

"Not really." He patted his ankle and gave her a little smile.

"Listen. Did you see the black yacht that crossed our path earlier this evening?"

"Yeah. Couldn't get a decent look at the guy with the binoculars, though; it was too dark."

"He seemed . . . threatening, somehow. Creepy. Maybe, though, he was just an innocent sightseer."

"That's the problem. You never know. You begin to think everyone's suspicious. It's part of a stalker's game; they count on that to ratchet up your fear."

The weight of all the tension she'd been coping with squeezed her like a vise. "I can't go on like this, Andrei."

For a moment he didn't answer but gazed at the slate black water, indistinguishable from the night sky. "I don't think we'll have to wait much longer. There'll be an end point and it's probably coming soon."

They were nearing the dock now and before she could reply,

Maria spotted the black boat at anchor, the motor silent, all its lights off. The occupants were either asleep or in town for a night of reveling. "Do you have any idea who owns that boat?" She spoke to the crew member at the wheel.

He glanced at it quickly and raised his voice over the roar of the motor. "Yes, a friend of mine. I work here all the time. Fill in as extra staff if they need it when the big yachts come in. That one's rented to an American for the festival."

"What's the American's name—do you know?" Andrei asked sharply.

"Bill Smith." The man's lips spread in a wide grin. "Not his real one, I think, eh? He's gone now, tonight was his last night. He paid my friend much cash for that boat. More than needed." He twirled his finger and pointed it at his head. "Stupid. Money here is like the air. Everyone breathing it in like they can't get enough of it."

CHAPTER 17

Andrei did all he could think of to unearth any scrap of information about the American who had rented the black yacht. He checked hotel registers, even arranged for a look at the yacht itself. In the end, he turned up nothing.

They spent the day in Cannes and flew to New York that evening. Back in the city, another avenue of exploration furnished partial results. Jewel's e-mail messages. One of Andrei's contacts hacked Jewel's personal e-mail and he sat at Maria's kitchen banquette, sifting through her messages and comparing the names and e-mail addresses to Maria's client list.

The name of one man stood out because it matched a former client—Jewel's shrink. Maria had spent an evening with him two years ago at his office in Brooklyn. He'd asked her to role-play as a pretend patient, a proposal that did not bode well for the integrity of his practice. He'd screwed her on his couch after analyzing her dreams. Otherwise, she could recall nothing abnormal; she'd had no idea at the time that he was Jewel's doctor. Andrei showed her a picture of the psychiatrist, a distinguished-looking man with fashionable glasses and a broad face. She only vaguely recognized him. He ranked high as a suspect. Of all the people Jewel may have discussed Maria's Romanian origins with, it was a slam dunk she'd told her shrink.

"The psychiatrist has a perfectly clean record," Andrei said. "A few parking tickets, a DUI eons ago—that's all. If he's your stalker, I'd expect some kind of assault charge, or a restraining order. Something that pointed to violence in his past."

"That just means he hasn't been caught yet," Maria argued.

"I don't know. The shrink probably booked you because he heard about you from your adoptive mother, but that doesn't mean he's a predator." Andrei paused. "Two years is a long time. That argues against him. He spends one night with you and waits two years to start stalking you? Doesn't make sense."

"We should be looking at recent clients, then? Over the last couple of months?"

"Definitely. Although another alternative is Jewel's husband—Milne, you said his name was? Maybe he told someone. He knew about your background too—didn't he?"

"I can't see Milne saying anything. It's just not his style. Maybe Jewel's hairdresser? Aren't they the ones we women are supposed to confess to?"

Andrei checked her contacts again. "Out of luck there. It's a woman."

"Don't see why that rules her out, necessarily." Even as she spoke, Maria knew instinctively how wrong she was. While a hairdresser could have passed along the knowledge, a male was behind this. No question. She racked her brain for a face, a conversation, a gut feeling—anything to point the way to her stalker. But he was like a snake in a hole, curled into a dark channel, marking time among a bed of brittle roots, readying himself to strike at a moment of his own choosing. She looked over to where Andrei sat, scrolling through the file on his phone. He glanced up from the screen.

"Maria, did you get under anyone's skin? Upset one of your clients? Maybe something happened you're reluctant to tell me about?"

"What's that supposed to mean?"

"I'm just saying these threats feel like some kind of payback; they're very personal. If you're holding anything back from me—don't. If you believe you know who it is, tell me. I know people who will take care of the guy permanently and discreetly."

Maria heaved a sigh. "I don't keep any secrets from you, Andrei. If I even suspected who was doing this, who hurt Lillian, I'd tell you."

He nodded and turned back to his phone, flipped to his own messages and ran his eye down the list. He frowned. "Oh shit."

"What is it?"

"My contact says Trainor's pulling back on his investigation. So far he's got nothing. They believe the Romanian hooker was a one-off. As in not related to any other attacks."

"That's so stupid," Maria cried.

"Yeah. But predictable. She was illegal. If they couldn't wrap it up fast, she was bound to drop further down on the priority list."

"Is he really pulling back or just changing his focus?"

"What do you mean?"

"I told you. He and da Silva spent most of the time questioning me about my business. I'm afraid he's going to try to nail me."

"He has to have a reason. He can't just fabricate a case and tell his superiors he wants to work on it. Besides, he's homicide, not vice. You can be sure his platter's already more than full."

Maria lowered her head. "Maybe the reason is you."

Andrei got up, put his hand underneath her chin and tilted her head, forcing her to look at him. Her skin tingled at the feel of his fingers. She had a sudden impulse to wrap her arms around him, pull him close and kiss him. Instead she turned her face away.

"Hey. I can see how upset you are. Now tell me what this is all about."

She avoided his eyes, embarrassed by her feelings. "I never inquired too much about what you did before you started working for me. I figured your past was your business and you'd tell me about it if there was any need. Trainor said you were tied up with organized crime. I pretended to be shocked. Obviously, I knew because of the Atlantic City party where we met that you had some association with the Russian mob. Trainor said you were one of their right-hand men. Is that true?"

Andrei laughed. "And you're worried I was some kind of crime kingpin? Couldn't have been a very good one. I'd be a rich man otherwise."

"He specifically mentioned the sex trade."

"That's ridiculous and you know it."

She could tell Andrei's temper rose at the last remark but he wouldn't want to confess to that, would he? And yet he'd been able to find out about the Romanian prostitute pretty fast. "So there's no basis to it?"

"I can see where his suspicions came from," Andrei said. "My parents escaped from Moscow and fled to New York right after their marriage. A year later my dad brought his kid brother over.

They didn't have two cents to rub together. My parents chose the high road, spent their life working seven days a week, running a restaurant. They never made a lot of money. My uncle saw how much they sweated for a few dollars and took a different turn in the road. He did get involved but not with prostitution."

"So you're saying Trainor just mixed the two of you up?"

"Not exactly. I was dead broke when I graduated from college. So I worked for him. No guy can grow up in Brighton Beach and be totally immune to it, you know. My uncle ran an oil distribution company, one of his legitimate enterprises. I looked after the day-to-day business for him. He was caught using the firm for tax evasion schemes. That's when I got out."

"Oh. Trainor did get it wrong, then."

Andrei grinned. "Do I still have my job?" He slipped his arm around her and gave her a squeeze. Maria found the closeness disconcerting. She liked the feel of his body against hers and wanted to respond, wanted to feel his hands on her, but a couple of months ago he would never have taken the liberty.

She picked up her tablet, glad of an excuse to shift away. "Of course. Speaking of work, time for me to hit the books."

Later in the afternoon, Lillian peeked into the study. "I'm leaving for my cousin's now." She took a long look around as if it would be the last time and gripped Maria in a tight hug. "The doctor says my hand is getting better fast. I'll be back before you know it."

She pressed her cheek to Lillian's. "Everything will be fine," she said cheerfully. "And you're not to worry. Just get better."

"Andrei's driving me to Jersey City. He said to tell you, after that he's going back to his place to get some sleep. He'll return this evening."

Maria already knew he intended to keep watch on her through the night. Lillian turned to go. She watched her assistant's small wiry figure disappear down the hallway, her swinging black hair, her hasty, energetic steps. She heard Lillian say something and Andrei answer in his deep tones. The front door opened and clicked shut. The apartment, wrapped in silence now, felt as forlorn as a ghost town with nothing left but empty houses and sad memories.

Her reaction to Andrei still disturbed her. The attack on Lillian and the threats had shaken her up a lot; on top of that, there was the police interview, and the sight of the black boat in Cannes. She needed Andrei's shoulder to lean on right now—which was probably the source of these unwelcome feelings. She dropped her head in her hands. The sight of his lean, brown body in Cannes, his arm around her in the boat, imagining what he'd be like in bed. The fantasies were starting to come unbidden and embarrassingly often. The body had a funny way of playing tricks on you. On rare occasions she'd been tempted by similar feelings for a client but those had passed quickly enough. She expected they would with Andrei too.

Maria gave herself a shake, made an effort to tidy up the lopsided stacks of books and papers on her desk, then gave up. She went to the fridge to get a Coke, thought better of it, grabbed a bottle of wine and poured herself a tumbler full. Downed it and poured a second.

For a short time she could pinch-hit without Lillian, but that was just putting off the inevitable. Nor could Andrei go without sleep night after night waiting for a phantom to materialize into a flesh-and-blood enemy. She'd have to move to a hotel or rent a full-service apartment. But whatever changes she made, they'd be nothing more than plugs in an ever-widening hole. The deluge would soon overcome her. Her stalker would destroy every last scrap of her security.

Her mind began to spin. She took a deep breath and tried to think positively. She had more than enough money to live on if she sold her place, and her studies would eventually lead to a new career. Reed promised to pave the way for her—what could be easier? Changes were good, kept you sharp, offered silver linings, new horizons. Loss was just part of life, she told herself, get used to it. The alcohol hit her empty stomach and sped into her bloodstream. When did I start drinking so much? she wondered. She ignored the voice in her head and got up to pour another. She had to lean on the table until a spell of wooziness passed.

Two weeks passed uneventfully and Maria dared to hope her stalker had lost interest, until one day when her phone trilled from the study. It cut out before she could reach it. She touched the screen and it brightened into a rectangle of light. New text, it said. Andrei, she thought hopefully. She hit the message button.

I wish to hire your services—you will be the only star and I, the only audience. It will begin on Roosevelt Avenue, the club district. Something different. A street pantomime, if you will. Dress for it like a whore. I want you to fit in. That shouldn't be hard. I'll be wearing a red Latin Kings shirt. Follow me for a time you won't forget.

CHAPTER 18

The ring of her cell phone broke the awful silence. Andrei was on the line. "Have you read it yet?" he asked.

"I just did."

"Wait, there's more. There's a second message with specific instructions about when and where to meet up. Tomorrow night at nine P.M. It's him, of course. I'm sure of it."

"How can you be so certain?"

"When's the last time a client insulted you while soliciting your services?"

"Good point. Did you get a chance to check his credentials yet?"

"Yes. I'm just pulling them up now. Calls himself Jeff Thorpe. Claims to own an Atlanta real estate firm and is up here on business. It's a shell company. Nothing but air. And since he didn't try to disguise that fact, he *wants* you to know it's him." Andrei hesitated. "Maria, we should pass this on to Trainor. Let the police track this guy."

"No! Trainor already suspects what I do, and he won't look the other way when we give him proof. I'll end up in jail. They'll seize all my assets too and claim they're proceeds of a criminal enterprise. It's out of the question."

"The police cooperate all the time with people on the shady side of legal to snag a bigger fish."

"Andrei. What if they think *I'm* the bigger fish? Or my clients? I can't risk that."

"So where does that leave us?"

"I don't know. Let me think about it. In the meantime, process the fee and tell Thorpe I accept."

Maria clicked off before Andrei could argue with her. She dashed off a text to him, repeating what she'd just said, went back into the kitchen and grabbed the wine bottle. Her fingers trembled as she pulled out the stopper and poured. She missed the glass; wine spilled onto a pile of envelopes on the counter. "Shit," she cried; her nerves felt so raw they practically bled.

She picked up the dripping envelopes and held them over the sink. Bills and flyers mostly. At the bottom, a bubble-wrapped package from an online book dealer. She hadn't ordered any books lately. The envelope's flap had been opened and then taped closed again. She tore it and pulled out the contents. A copy of *Justine* by de Sade.

How would her stalker know she had any interest in the book? Her thesis wasn't close to being published. Then Maria recalled she'd written a short article about *Justine* for an academic journal last summer. If he'd Googled "Maria Lantos" and "Yale," he would have found it easily enough.

Something had been used as a bookmark to divide the pages about three quarters of the way in. When she flipped to it, she found a miniature cropped version of the photo taken while she was dancing at Show World Live! It was the same one pasted on the bathroom mirror of her San Francisco hotel room. The scrawl at the bottom read: *This awaits you.* The passage was one of the most gruesome in de Sade's novel. She cringed at the description of the whippings the characters—young girls—endured, on their breasts and bottoms.

Reading the passage made up her mind. In a way she welcomed what was to come tomorrow evening. Warring with a ghost sapped her energy. She needed to confront the real man and destroy him.

CHAPTER 19

BOROUGH OF QUEENS, CORONA NEIGHBORHOOD, NEW YORK

Claudine leaned into the mirror at her dressing table to put the finishing touches on her makeup. For the hundredth time she wished Lillian were here. She'd had to remove and reapply her cosmetics twice and still couldn't get it right. Pale foundation, nude lipstick, heavy black eyeliner and brows, a kind of Amy Winehouse look without the dark sloe eyes. She eventually gave up on the colored contacts because she needed Lillian's help to put them in. She'd spent the afternoon at the spa getting her nails done. Tuxedo black two-inch acrylics, closer to claws than nails, like those in the pictures of old Chinese empresses. She'd also had a black wig fitted; a blunt-cut bob with a fringe of bangs, accented with a streak of magenta.

With a final lick of mascara on her lashes, she got up and walked over to the full-length mirror to check her outfit. Her breasts strained against the close-fitting, sleeveless lambskin bodysuit, so tight it made her crotch sore. It was cut high enough to show the plump rise of her buttocks. She added leather wristlets with studs, black silk stockings, knee-high platform boots. She stood back and gave herself a final, critical look, amused at the irony of a courtesan role-playing a hooker.

The club district on Roosevelt Avenue belonged to the *chicas.* Although the city had tried to put a stop to it recently, young boys still passed around flyers advertising the girls' charms. Most of the action took place inside the clubs, but a few streetwalkers lingered outside club entrances. Hostile glances greeted Claudine when she invaded their territory. Girls still in their teens with bright lipstick, small breasts jutting out from spangled tops, miniskirts barely covering their bums tottered on three-inch platforms in lime, hot pink, carmine. A woman with purple hair and thin, needle-tracked arms huddled against a wall and gave Claudine a blatant once-over. She couldn't loiter long; her presence would not be tolerated for more than a few minutes before they drove her off. A mile-deep canyon divided her privileged existence from theirs.

She scanned the street and spotted her stalker emerging from a doorway about a quarter of the way down the block. His back was turned to her. The red sweatshirt he wore with the hood pulled up had a Latin Kings insignia on the back, a five-pointed crown in black and gold and the letters *ALKQN.* He was a tall, stocky man with a barrel chest. Something about his figure struck her as familiar. She reached back into her memory and then she had it. His body type and the way he moved was the same as the man caught on video breaking into her San Francisco hotel room. They had him in their sights now.

Claudine quickly glanced around. Although she couldn't see Andrei anywhere, she trusted he had his eyes on her. She swallowed her fears and followed the hooded man.

She stayed about seventy feet behind him, but he never once glanced back. They turned the corner onto a secondary street and then another. He was drawing her farther away from the lights and activity of Roosevelt Avenue into an area most pedestrians abandoned at night. A squad car prowled past her. The cop flicked on high beams, illuminating the hunched figure of the man she was following as if a spotlight had been trained on him. She quickly turned her face away. This was Trainor's district, and although he wasn't a beat cop, she was terrified she might come face-to-face with him.

Her target stopped at a run-down building and took something out of his pocket. He allowed himself a quick backward glance to make certain Claudine was behind him, then he pushed open the door and went in.

Nervously, she checked the street again. Still no sign of Andrei. He gave her strict orders to stay visible at all times, but where was he? She didn't want to wait too long and alert Thorpe to a trap, so she stepped just inside the door to a hallway. The walls were gray with mildew, and rickety stairs rose straight ahead. The place smelled of old piss and the sweet zing of marijuana. A light glowed at the top of the stairs.

She had no intention of going any farther. She waited. Andrei should be here by now. Was he holding off until his men secured the back of the building? The door creaked open. She heard his quiet footsteps behind her. "Thank God you're here," she said, turning around.

"Not who you think, bitch." The purple-haired prostitute

with the scarred skin held a small pistol aimed straight at her head. "Your trick's waiting for you upstairs."

Claudine's stomach pitched. She didn't move.

"I said get the fuck up there." The woman gave her a hard push, and Claudine bumped into the lower step, almost falling.

She raised her hands in surrender. "All right. I'll go." She climbed the steps at a snail's pace, fear rising in her throat, the clack of her boots on the battered hardwood steps like bullets ricocheting off stone. She reached the first-floor landing and peered through the partially open door. It was pitch-black inside. She waited a moment.

"Move it," the woman said, right behind her.

She ventured a few feet inside the room. The woman was so close behind her that Claudine could smell her cloying perfume. A light clicked on. The room was bare of furniture save for a stained mattress, an old pressed-back chair and a small table. The man in the Latin Kings jersey sat cross-legged in the chair, a knife lying on the table beside him. He nodded to the purple-haired woman.

Claudine heard the door lock behind her but didn't take her eyes off the man. He'd shrugged off his sweatshirt. She was surprised to see that he looked more like he belonged in an executive boardroom than on the rough streets of the neighborhood. He wore glasses, a designer shirt and dark trousers. If he'd once been a client, she had no recollection of him. From the look on his face, she knew there was no point in pleading—nor was it in her nature to play the victim.

"Before we do anything, tell me how you knew about the orphanage."

He laughed. "That's my secret." He reached down and unzipped his fly. His cock, a fat pink worm, was repulsive, still soft; he pulled at it to make it stiffen. Without Andrei to help her, her only choice now was to find a way of turning his lust against him. She plastered on a saucy smile. "I see you're not quite ready for me." She unzipped her jerkin to show him her bare breasts, then pulled the zipper all the way down. "Well, you wanted it. What's keeping you, Mr. Thorpe?"

His eyes bugged out at the sight of her. He shuffled off his pants and got up. His penis wagged grotesquely as he approached her. She skittered away out of his reach. He lurched toward her, missed, teetered and fell on one knee. Her eyes found the knife and she launched herself at it. He rose from the floor, swaying like a dazed boxer, but he reached her in moments and slammed her into the wall. She yelped when the back of her head cracked the rough stucco. He pinned her so hard she could hardly breathe. She clawed his skin with her long nails. It had as much effect on him as a dressmaker's pin pricking an elephant's hide.

He slurped at her earlobe. "You a screamer?" She shook her head. His elbow pressed into her throat. "No? You will be when I fuck you." He bit her breast hard. Claudine yelped and flailed her body to shake him off, but he was much stronger than she'd expected. Panic began to overtake her. He ripped her stockings down to the tops of her boots, scratching her leg, and thrust his hand roughly between her legs. "Already juicy down there," he said, laughing.

He wrestled with her suit, trying to yank it down while he fumbled with his penis. She scissored her legs to stop him when he attempted to stuff it inside her.

The door burst open. In three strides Andrei crossed the room, spun the man around and punched him hard in the face. Blood spurted from his nose. Andrei rammed him up against the wall and delivered body blows in quick succession. Thorpe slumped to the floor.

Claudine staggered out of the way. She was about to chew Andrei out for not finding her sooner—until he turned and she saw his face.

CHAPTER 20

Andrei's jaw was red and swollen and his shirtsleeve ripped and bloody. He limped. Behind him, two men with iron-hard muscles and tattoos approached her attacker, who'd managed to sit up and was cowering in a corner.

"You all right?" Andrei asked, his voice gentle.

"A few scrapes, that's all." She turned her back to zip up her bodysuit. "What about you?"

But Andrei had already returned to Thorpe. He pressed the heel of his open hand against Thorpe's neck. The man swore and struggled limply. Andrei increased the pressure until Thorpe toppled over in a dead faint. He gave his friends orders in Russian and jerked his head toward the taller of the two. They heaved the man up and, supporting him between them, shuffled out the door and down the stairs.

"What are you going to do with him?"

"Take him to a secure place. Let him sweat it out until tomorrow."

"What happened to you?" Maria touched the side of his face. He winced.

"I left the other two in the van to monitor the street while I followed you. I watched you go inside, and then I got hit from behind. While I was out, someone must have gone to town on my face. A good thing I had the others with me or I'd be dead right now. The guys who attacked me ran away when they saw my men coming. They took off on motorbikes so we lost them. I was too worried about you to chase the hooker. She'll be easy enough to find later anyway."

"I'm sorry. I never should have insisted we go through with this." A wave of guilt washed over her. Her stubbornness had nearly cost Andrei his life.

Andrei gave her a wry grin. "What are you talking about? We caught him."

Maria's knees suddenly buckled; shooting stars dimmed her vision.

"You're hurt," he said propping her up.

She touched the sore spot on her scalp. "He cracked my head against the wall, that's all. I'll be okay."

"Let's get you out of here." Andrei kept his arm around her down the stairs. His two friends had dumped their quarry into the back of the van and waited, parked behind a nondescript beige rental car. Andrei gave them the thumbs-up and they pulled away from the curb. He helped Maria into the passenger side of the rental car, got behind the wheel and buckled up.

"Where are we going?" she asked, slurring her words.

"To the hospital. You've got to get checked out."

She tried to raise her voice but only managed a weak reprove. "No hospitals. We can't report this. I'll be fine."

He gave her a worried look but said nothing. Instead he pulled out his phone and punched in some numbers, keeping one hand on the wheel. He spoke a few words in Russian before he clicked off.

"I'm taking you to Brighton Beach, then—my place. A doctor will come see you there. Until we've got everything we need out of that guy, it's not safe at your apartment."

Little Odessa stretched for several miles south of the elevated subway line bisecting Brooklyn. Brighton Beach Avenue ran underneath it. Through the tinted sedan windows, she could see the bright lights of grocers, bakeries, pharmacies, clubs and restaurants. Most had signs in Russian. Even at this hour, the street hummed.

Andrei turned left off the avenue and stopped in front of a high-rise with a redbrick façade and balconies formed by ornamental white cement squares. A young man waited at the building entrance to park the car. Andrei threw him the keys and helped Maria into the building. As they walked toward the lobby elevator, she stumbled and grabbed his arm for support. "I'm all right, just a bit woozy," she said. "Don't worry."

"No, you're not." He let her rest against him as the elevator rose to the fifth floor. The adrenalin flooding through her system during the fight with Thorpe had subsided, leaving her cold and weak. Leaning close to Andrei, she began to warm up and feel safe again.

They got out of the elevator and Andrei reached into his pocket for his keys. When he opened his door she let out a little exclamation of surprise.

A vestibule opened into a spacious room with a shining floor of black oak. A large Persian carpet on it looked antique. One entire wall was lined with bookcases. At a guess, Andrei owned more books than she did. Most of the paintings, original and contemporary abstracts, were of the best gallery quality. An old upright piano of painted white wood stood against the far wall. The room was lightly scented, sandalwood or myrrh, something exotic like that.

"What do you think?" He said this a little shyly, as if he worried she might regard it as far too modest a place.

"It's lovely, Andrei. You have great taste."

That seemed to satisfy him and he eased her down on the plush sofa and arranged cushions behind her back to keep her comfortable. "Let me take off those boots," he said, his baritone a little gruff. "I don't know how you can walk in them anyway."

"Lots of practice." She giggled. Immediately the dull ache in her head ramped into searing pain. "Oh God," she pressed her hand to her temple.

"Lie still. Don't try to talk; I'll be right back." Andrei went into the adjoining kitchen and opened the fridge. He returned with an ice pack wrapped in a dish towel. "Hold this to your head."

She did as he asked. She sank back against the pillows, clamping the cold pack to her temple. "Can you hand me my bag? I have some Tylenol in there."

"You can't take anything like that. Not until the doctor's seen you." He perched at the end of the couch, unzipped her boots and slid them off. He gently massaged her feet for a few minutes. Maria watched his lean tanned hands, the tight muscles of his arms as he bent over her, and felt a tingle of desire. A dramatically different response than she had to Lillian's energetic kneading and pummeling.

She felt a cold nose on her leg, looked down and saw a large dog with rough brown fur and floppy ears. It licked her knee.

Maria reached out to pet him. "What's he called?"

"Tramp."

"You named him after the Disney cartoon?"

"No."

"Oh!" Maria laughed.

"No, it's not what you think. I found him when he was a pup, a couple of streets away, rooting around a Dumpster. He was so thin his ribs stuck out from his chest like wooden barrel staves. And he does like the ladies."

"Takes after his master, then?"

Andrei's smile must have hurt him. He touched his jaw gingerly before answering. "Certainly does. Got to get something else. Be right back." Tramp's tongue lolled with pleasure as Maria petted him. She took another look at the paintings. One resembled a Chagall. Must be a print, she thought. Coming here gave her a rare look at Andrei's private side. She liked what she saw.

He returned with a first-aid kit and a hand-embroidered quilt in bright colors. "One of the few things I have left from home. My mother made the quilt." He ordered Tramp to the kitchen.

"We just got here and now you're banishing him?" she joked.

"I set out his dinner. He won't mind at all. Stretch your leg out a bit."

He dabbed some liquid from a bottle in the first-aid kit onto gauze and wiped it over the scratch, cleaning off the crusted blood. "Sorry. It will sting for a minute or so." It did hurt, but the tingle she felt before now reappeared as a delicious sensation in her groin when his fingers brushed her thigh. After he finished, he tucked the quilt around her legs.

"Thank you. You take such good care of me." She could feel her eyes drooping. "I'm so fatigued. I'd like to sleep for a while."

He shook his head. "You can't yet. We don't know how bad your head is hurt. I've got to keep you awake until the doctor comes." As he walked over to the glass doors leading to the balcony, he was limping again, and she reminded herself that he'd been hurt too. He slid the doors open. "This is the best time to be here, when the beach has quieted down at night. Maybe the breeze will help to stave off your drowsiness."

A soft wind blew in, carrying with it the murky scent of salt water. From the light of the apartment building's windows, Maria could see a plain of golden sand stretching to the water's edge, a rim of white where the waves hit the shore and a flare of orange. "What's that light?"

"Some kids started a bonfire."

Now that he mentioned it, Maria could smell a faint hint of smoke in the air. She began to feel as though she could stay in this comfortable cocoon forever. Andrei leaned with his back against the cement squares of the balcony, ambient light from the room playing over his fit form. He'd combed his hair, changed into jeans and a sharp-looking black tee when he went to get the quilt.

"The hurricane dumped huge amounts of sand right up to our building," he said, as if from far away. "A giant piece of the boardwalk got torn out and thrown against the outside wall by the waves. There was a ton of debris. Afterward, kids used some of it to slide down the mounds like they were tobogganing. It was really treacherous here. We're one of the areas that got the worst of it. You could smell gas everywhere. At one point it felt like a tsunami, as if the storm was going to sweep the whole place away."

"I remember trying to get ahold of you through all that. You didn't answer your cell for three days. I was so worried."

"Yeah. I stayed awake the entire time. We had no power, and a lot of the older folks in this building were huddling in their apartments, terrified. Some of us got together and moved them to a community center."

They heard a quiet tap at the door. Andrei checked through the peephole and let in an older man with a full head of woolly white hair and a plump florid face. They spoke in Russian. "Dr. Levkin," Andrei said to her by way of introduction.

Andrei got a kitchen chair for the doctor to sit beside her. The doctor spent about twenty minutes checking her vision, mobility, temperature and blood pressure. Asking her questions.

"She probably has concussion but she must have X-ray, best is MRI. I can't tell much about how injured she is without that."

Andrei raised his eyebrows at her.

"I'll go tomorrow morning," she said.

The doctor clearly disapproved. "You should go right now. If you stay, you have to be waked through the night. Once every hour." He spoke to Andrei again and then bid her good-bye.

"What about you?" she said. "Shouldn't you be getting checked out too?"

"I'll do that tomorrow when we get you to the hospital. Think I'll survive tonight." He laughed.

Andrei gave her a clean white T-shirt, long enough to reach midthigh. While she changed out of her leather bodysuit, he brewed some tea in the kitchen and brought it out in a glass, piping hot. He wrapped a napkin around it and handed it to her. "An old herbal recipe; it will help the pain."

She took it gratefully. "Where's Tramp?"

"Asleep in his bed. It's long past midnight, you know."

She sniffed the aromatic tea and took a sip. It tasted bitter but had a pleasant herbal aftertaste. She sank back into the pillows and watched summer lightning flash in the sky.

"How about some music?" Andrei said.

She eyed the piano. "Sure, but only if you play for me."

He took a seat on the piano bench and lifted the cover. The yellowed ivory showed how aged the instrument was, but its tone was as pure as crystal. He ran his fingers lightly over the keys. He played effortlessly, beautifully; the music seemed to harmonize with the distant wash of the waves on the shore. The summer ocean air and his playing cast a spell over the peaceful room, imbuing the night with a sense of magic. Maria recognized songs from Prokofiev and Chopin. The sounds lulled her senses. She fought the urge to sleep because she wanted to hear every note. Again she was struck by how little she knew of the man she'd seen almost daily for the last three years.

"This next one's especially for you," he said.

It was from Rachmaninoff's Piano Concerto Number 2. She recognized it the minute she heard the first few bars. "How did you know that was my favorite?"

"You mentioned it once. I have a good memory."

It was a song her own father loved and had played often, and the melody went straight to her heart. She remembered how her mother would plunk herself on the old fat armchair with her eyes closed to concentrate on the music and Maria would curl up in her lap, listening avidly to her father play.

"What's the matter?" Andrei swung around on the bench.

She was hardly aware of the song ending; her eyes were clouded with tears. "It brings back memories of my parents, my real parents. I lost them long ago. I told you that once—didn't I?"

"I'm sorry, I didn't mean to upset you. When I play it helps me to remember as well."

"What about your parents? Are they still alive?"

"Yes. They live in a nursing home a few blocks from here. They're pretty comfortable. And still madly in love, which is a good thing because they went through so much to be together."

"How so?"

"My mother came from a Jewish family in Moscow, and my father's parents were anti-Semitic, a fact my father's been ashamed of all his life. There was blood on the floor when my parents announced their wish to marry. They ended up eloping and escaped to America. Lucky for me I was born here and not over there. That picture," he gestured toward the Chagall print, "reminds me of my parents."

"A reproduction—right?"

"No. It's an original. My grandmother gave it to my mother for her sixteenth birthday. The only family memento she took with her when she ran away."

"Oh, that's so romantic. And what about you? You were married, I think you once told me. But you never gave me any details."

"Lucia and I met at college. At the time, we were full of high hopes. I wanted to teach economics, she took science courses and planned to go into medicine. Then she became pregnant." His face darkened with the memories. "Our grand plans crashed on the rocks. I had to drop out of college to make money. That's when I went to work for my uncle. She lost the baby while I was in Mexico checking on some oil suppliers. Over that year, we grew awkward together. The harder we tried to glue our relationship together, the more it fell apart. So we divorced. Eventually, she did become a doctor."

"I'm embarrassed it's taken me so long to find out about you."

Andrei sat down on the edge of the sofa beside her. "I could have told you anytime. I just chose not to." He touched her head, lingering a little longer than was necessary. "How's the headache now?"

"Much better. What's in that tea? It's a wonder drug."

Maria raised her eyes to his and felt a sudden impulse to hold him. She put her arms around him and nestled her head on his shoulder. He smelled faintly of citron aftershave and sweat. He traced the outline of her cheek, and then kissed her gently. His lips were supple and warm. In spite of herself, she responded, kissing him back. She felt his hands on her face, his fingers twined in her hair. She opened her mouth to him, felt the shock of his tongue tasting her. She tasted him too, caressed his jaw with her hands, felt the rough stubble between her fingers.

Maria knew she should stop him. But she found herself yielding to his kiss with an urgency of her own. When she finally pulled away, his eyes drew her back in. Like a dream she didn't want to wake up from.

CHAPTER 21

Maria could feel Andrei's heart beating against her chest. He kept one arm around her and slid his other hand underneath her T-shirt. He moved it tenderly, as if her skin were a delicate piece of silk that he couldn't help but caress, causing satisfying shivers to race through her. Her lips were open, still treasuring the newness of his tongue on hers. She had no will, no desire to resist. She closed her eyes and gave herself up to the luxury of her sensations.

His hands traveled up her body, touching her waist, stomach, breasts, as if he were committing her form to his tactile memory, saving it for a time she'd no longer be with him. He touched her lightly, stroked her nipples to hard peaks. A soft moan escaped her lips. She tugged the T-shirt up to her shoulders, inviting him explore her. She gathered the strength to look at him, to confront whatever emotion she found there, but his eyes were downcast.

Andrei brushed the tips of his fingers very lightly over the red welts on her breasts. "Thorpe did this to you?"

She nodded. "If you hadn't come, I wouldn't have left that room alive. But we got him. It's over."

"You're safe. He'll never harm you again. I promise." He smoothed her hair. "I've never thought of you the way other men do. They see your beauty, but they don't see you. How smart you are, how strong." His voice was barely a whisper. He kissed her lips again, and then her jaw, and then her neck, sending waves of pleasure down her spine. She arched her back as he nuzzled her neck and murmured beautiful things to her. She ached to have him inside her. He pulled the T-shirt over her head and she fell back against the pillows. He caressed her exposed throat, and then tongued her nipples so tenderly she thought she would melt. Andrei's hands and mouth were a revelation, so different from those of her clients, whose attention to her body seemed like an afterthought.

Maria reached up and pulled his shirt over his head, arched her back to press her breasts against his powerful chest, ran her fingers down the smooth sweaty skin of his back. She trailed her lips over his Adam's apple, kissed the soft skin of his neck, loving the salty taste of his sweat. He groaned at the feeling the moist tip of her tongue produced, and placed her hand against his cock, stretched full and hard in his jeans.

A little voice inside her told her it was not too late to stop. That she could push him back, say she didn't know what had come over her, even admonish him for taking advantage of her. But her body craved him. It wanted to be wicked. A demon had taken hold of her and it was not to be denied. For once, she didn't have to pretend. Her desire was fierce; she wanted to give herself to him without holding anything back. She didn't want to be a professional tonight, didn't want to dip into her bag of tricks. Tonight she was just a regular girl making love to the man she trusted most in the world.

She resisted the urge to be the aggressor, to spread her legs for him or unzip his jeans. She didn't want to do anything to break the spell. Instead she looked into his eyes and got lost in them.

"God," he managed to say. "Slow it down. I might not be able to hold out."

She smiled. "We're just getting started."

He laughed and his gaze slid from her face to her breasts, her narrow waist and the smooth cleft between her thighs. He pressed his lips to her belly, stroking the swell of her hips with his fingers. When he got to her mound, he nudged her thighs open and breathed in her scent. For the first time in what seemed like forever, she was nervous, embarrassed, and afraid he might reject her.

He didn't. He stroked her tenderly with his fingers, liking the slippery flow, evidence of the pitch of her arousal. He gently circled her most sensitive spot, brushed over it with the softest of touches. She was used to much harder, more energetic manhandling by her clients, fingers digging roughly into her vagina, playful slaps on her bottom. This was different. This was heaven.

She pushed down gently on his shoulders. His tongue found her nub and lightly flicked over it. He tasted her, teased her, danced in and out of her most secret place. Her vagina tightened so hard, she almost cried out, then the delicious quiver began; she was almost unaware of pulling him to her, of rocking her hips. Her nails raked his back and she whispered fiercely in his ear, "Fuck me, Andrei. Please."

He searched her eyes, as if to reassure himself of what she was feeling. "I want you to be sure."

"I am." Her kiss was slow and soft, and she cradled his face in her hands. "I am."

Truth is not static, and for that moment at least, she told him the truth. Those two words seemed to lift the heaviness from the man whose face she'd seen almost every day for the last three years, whose taciturn expression she'd grown so used to.

"I'm sure," she said again. "I need you."

"I never dreamed I'd have a chance with you," he mumbled against her belly.

Andrei raised himself up, unzipped his jeans and tugged them off. His cock was rock hard, bigger than she'd imagined. She grasped it in her hands, and he jerked as though he was holding back his climax. "Whoa, whoa. Take it easy." He laughed. He reached into the coffee table drawer, got a condom and rolled it on.

With one hand tangled in her hair, he guided himself inside with the other, stretching her open. Her eyes closed in bliss, a sigh escaped her lips.

"Look at me, Maria. Open your eyes." The gaze in his own eyes spoke of vulnerability but also confidence in himself as a man.

He filled her completely, and together they watched as he moved in and out of her, his abs tensed and gleaming with sweat. The sight of him, strong and naked above her, was too much. Too beautiful. She moved her hips in time with his, felt each delicious pull and plunge of their sex. It brought an overwhelming sense of joy and abandon. A wantonness of a different kind.

With every stroke he brushed her clit with a sure, light touch, bringing her rapidly to the brink. Every time she closed her eyes, he implored her to look at him. She was powerless to resist, and that powerlessness thrilled her to her core. She gave everything she had to him. Surrendered. She cried out as the flood of orgasm consumed her, rolled through her body. And still he fucked her, moving in wider and wider circles, over and over again, grinding into her. She was molten lava inside. Everything he did to her ignited a flame. She came and came again—and didn't even feel the tremor than ran through his body when he finally climaxed.

They lay for a while in the luxurious aftermath, their bodies still entwined, still sparking. He got up and turned his back to her almost as if, having been carried away with his need, he was embarrassed to let her see him naked. He reached for a tissue on the coffee table and wrapped up the condom, tossed it in a wastebasket, swooped up his briefs and jeans and hastily tugged them on. A sheen of perspiration gleamed on his skin.

She pulled the T-shirt back on. It was as if, by donning their clothes, they were separating themselves from the intimacy that had gone before. Maria felt dazed, and became aware again of the ache in her head. Andrei sat down on the edge of the sofa and ran his fingers through her hair. "Feel better now?"

Her green eyes widened. "Oh, that's what that was—more of your medicine?"

He grinned, tucked the quilt around her and planted a light kiss on the top of her head. "Get some rest. I'll wake you up every hour like Dr. Levkin said to."

Suddenly, she felt exhausted. She snuggled down deep and welcomed the oblivion sleep brought.

An hour later, Andrei stirred her from sleep by gently stroking her arm and saying her name. She sat up with a start, not knowing at first where she was. Then she saw his kind, concerned face, sank back into the pillows and drifted off.

But her rest didn't last for long. Her old nightmare returned. She felt the lumpy, filthy mattress beneath her and a cold draft. She searched for moonlight in the high window, yet the room was pitch-black. She was frightened and stilled her own breath. She heard the softest of footfalls, and then the scraping of wood as the crib railing was slowly lowered. The Blackbird had returned, the hulking figure from the orphanage who came to her in the dead of night. He peered down at her with glittering black eyes. He had a face now. It was Thorpe's.

Maria gasped and wrenched herself awake. Andrei had left the balcony doors open. The spring breeze had turned into a chill night wind and the quilt was tangled around her legs. Her head was clear but she still shook from the aftermath of her nightmare. She sat up, reached down and gathered the folds of the cover around her. Somewhere out on the beach came the faint sound of a woman's scream. A cry of passion or violence? She couldn't tell. She shivered. The apartment was totally silent except for the steady ticking of a clock. It seemed to come from the kitchen. Maria strained to catch any sound of Andrei turning in his bed or murmuring in his sleep, yet heard nothing. The silence began to feel eerie.

The bathroom was tucked between the kitchen and Andrei's bedroom. Maria hugged the quilt around her like a cape and tiptoed toward it. She heard Tramp whine in his sleep as she passed by. She shut the bathroom door quietly and flicked on the light. Andrei's shaving things lay haphazardly on the sink counter, a wet towel lay on the floor. She peed but didn't flush, afraid the sound might wake him. Fully intending to return to her couch, she stopped when she saw his bedroom door was open and peeked in to reassure herself he was still there.

The blinds let enough light in through the window that she could see him lying on his side, the duvet down to his waist, his arm flung over a pillow. His chest rose and fell with deep, even breaths. She wanted to lie close to him. She would be quiet and take care not to wake him. Letting the quilt drop, she took off the T-shirt and slid in between the sheets. He rolled onto his back, mumbled something, then turned on his side again. Maria inched nearer, tucked her head behind his neck, nestled in a curl around him. She never slept with her clients and had forgotten the simple comfort of lying close to a man.

Andrei suddenly shifted and sat halfway up, rubbing the sleep from his eyes. "What's the matter? Are you all right?"

"I was cold. I'm sorry, I didn't mean to wake you."

He gave a low laugh. "You honestly think you could just crawl up beside me and I wouldn't notice?" He glanced at his phone on the bedside table. "It's okay. The alarm would have gone off in another ten minutes anyway for me to check on you." He played with her hair, swept a few strands off her brow. "How are you feeling?"

She snuggled closer to him. "Fine."

"Well, that's good, because I'm wide awake now and I want something."

"What?" She gave him an innocent look from under her long lashes.

"Nothing too much. Just every atom of you."

"I have a headache." Maria giggled.

"I have the antidote."

"Really? Where?"

"Where do you think?"

They laughed together, then Maria shifted down the mattress. She slipped her hand over his penis and found him already stiffening. She stroked him to full hardness, then licked his balls, moving lower to fondle the softness between his testicles and his buttocks. From experience, she knew touching a man there would electrify him, and she wanted to give Andrei every pleasure. He gasped and swore—nicely—under his breath.

Smiling to herself under the sheet, she took him in her mouth, using her tongue to explore the satiny skin of his shaft. He gently helped her fellate him, urging his rigid penis in and out of her mouth. The heat rose from him like an oil flame. When his rhythm grew too fevered, she stopped him.

"Not yet," she said, her voice muffled by the covers.

He pulled her up, gathered her in his arms and moved to the center of the bed. He made her kneel with her head down resting on her forearms. He kissed the delicate skin at the nape of her neck, and ran his tongue down the ridges of her spine. She shuddered with delight. His warm hands spanned her bottom, followed by the wet, delicious slide of his tongue down her crease. "You have a beautiful ass," he murmured before licking one finger and slipping it inside. He slid another in her vagina—a double penetration—as though he wanted nothing about her to be unknown to him. She tightened her muscles, almost swooned.

"Open your legs wider," he coaxed. "Show me how much you need me."

She obeyed, and was rewarded with the pleasure of her sex being filled slowly and completely. With one arm locked around her waist, Andrei pulled her body in to meet his thrusts. He reached beneath her and stroked her clitoris. Irresistible pressure began to build in her groin; she couldn't contain the tiny moans that rose up from deep within her. Then, suddenly, he abandoned her clit and tugged on her nipples, pinched them hard enough to make her buck voluptuously. She tried to hold back, put off the moment so they could come together, but she lost the battle. Her muscles flexed and trembled and she cried out shamelessly. Her whole body shook with the power of her orgasm. His release came in a rush on top of hers and they lay together, locked in the wet heat of a lovers' embrace.

When the morning light roused her, she could hear Andrei in the shower and smell the aroma of coffee in the air. Andrei had left her a cup steaming hot on the bedside table. She sipped at it, thick with real cream, sugar and a faint taste of mocha. She usually drank her coffee black but found Andrei's version heavenly. A demure print dress and some slip-ons lay on the chair beside the bed. She stretched, put them on, got a comb from her purse and dragged it through her tangled hair. She felt surprisingly refreshed and strong but in the clear light of day dreaded facing Andrei. Her stomach actually sank at the thought of it. She was ashamed of letting go so completely with him last night. And she rarely felt embarrassed.

Now that she was thinking rationally, Maria knew what a huge mistake she'd made. What on earth had possessed her? Residual fear from the attack? Relief that her stalker had been caught? The gratitude she felt toward Andrei for catching him? She cursed her stupidity. Just when their lives could return to normal, she screwed it up by sleeping with her best friend. It had been nothing more than a night of wild pleasure, she told herself. And that's all it would ever be. One night only—as advertised.

She could still hear the water jetting onto the tiles in Andrei's bathroom. She tiptoed into the living room and pulled open the coffee table drawer. The box of condoms was half empty. So he'd had other women here, she mused, and likely not that long ago. Maybe last night was just a blip on the radar for him too.

Maria downed the rest of her coffee and wandered into the kitchen for a refill. It was large, the kind often found in older buildings, big enough for a dining table and chairs. This too he'd renovated, with limestone counters, fancy cabinets, black enamel appliances. Tramp got up from his bed, thumping his tail when he saw her. She scratched the rough fur on his neck.

The apartment windows were old, their metal frames rusting from the salt air, but they opened easily. The sounds of early morning activity floated through the window. A few people—dog walkers, joggers and kids with their moms—were already out on the boardwalk. The water was calm and the sun already burned above the horizon. The sand looked damp. It must have rained in the night.

Maria turned from the view and saw a tiny alcove off the kitchen. Andrei's office. It was set up with a desk and a laptop. His cell phone lay beside the computer. A few papers were scattered about but he had no filing cabinet. All their business files were digitized. For the sake of privacy, hers and her clients', she and Andrei had agreed long ago to avoid the trail of hard copies. That wasn't what caught her attention.

Four photographs sat on a shelf above the desk. One of an older couple, the woman beaming into the camera, the man with his arm protectively around her. The other three were of Maria. All of them images taken on their business trips. She recognized one as being outside the Musée d'Orsay in Paris; she'd worn a simple black blouse and skirt. She remembered Andrei clicking the shutter and saying, "You look like a young Brigitte Bardot." She'd laughed at the comparison but had been secretly pleased.

The last in the row he must have shot recently in Cannes, when she'd gazed out to sea. He'd caught her in semiprofile as the breeze blew her blond hair. The kind of pictures a lover would take. Her mood plunged. He'd been nursing a fantasy about her. For how long?

Her eyes fell on the wastebasket full of crumpled paper. She picked up one of the pages; it crinkled as she unfolded it. In Andrei's handwriting was the hateful poem that had been tacked to her photo in San Francisco. The name of the town, Siret, had been crossed out and the name of the orphanage, Spital Neuropshici di Copii, written beside it.

She put down her cup without refilling it and walked back into the living room just as Andrei emerged from the hall leading to his bedroom. The water had turned his hair darker and curlier. His skin glistened with a few stray drops. The sight of him like that made Maria want nothing more than to feel his hands on her again. She lowered her eyes and fought off the impulse.

"You look much better," he said, glancing at her clothing, "although that dress isn't exactly your style. My neighbor Ana lent it to me, along with those slip-ons. They'll do for you to wear when we go to the hospital. Are you hungry? I can make you some crepes."

He leaned over to kiss her, and the attractive scent of his aftershave nearly drove her crazy; his lips were soft, and the ferocious rush of wanting him welled up in her again. She summoned all her willpower and pulled away.

He took her hand and tried to make a joke out of her response. "You don't like kissing in the morning?"

Maria stepped away from him and struggled to rid herself of the intense attraction she felt. She reminded herself that her reaction was only a physical trick her body was playing on her. It meant nothing. She held up the crumpled paper. "I found this in the wastebasket under your desk."

He ran his fingers through his wet curls and frowned. "What were you doing looking through my trash?"

"I went into the kitchen to get some more coffee and I noticed the scrunched up papers. I got curious."

"I wrote both the poems out, just trying to see if there were any patterns. Sometimes you can spot similarities in something handwritten you can't see on the screen."

Maria set her lips in a tight line. "Hardly anyone knows the actual name of the orphanage I was adopted from."

"They do if you tell them. You described your nightmare at dinner last month and the ordeal you went through there. Remember?" His eyes narrowed. "You don't think—"

"No." Maria said quickly. "I recall our conversation now. I'm sorry. Listen, there's something else we need to talk about." She lowered her eyes, not able to look him in the face. "Last night was . . . we shouldn't have let it go that far. I shouldn't have. It was just . . . the way everything ended up shaking out. I felt vulnerable. And then coming here, you looking after me, the music, talking about our families."

He was looking at her quizzically, so she blurted it out.

"Having sex with you was a mistake."

"You know that's not true."

Her heart skipped a beat. She had to shut this down now and his reaction meant only a sharp blade would do. "You're my friend. One of my dearest, *and* my business manager. We can't be lovers. And to tell the truth, I have no desire to be that for you."

He reached out and touched her chin, turned her face so she had no choice but to look at him. His eyes bored into her. "I don't believe you. You weren't pretending last night. You loved every minute of it."

Maria stepped back to gain some distance between them. "What are you talking about? What do you think I do with all those other men? I fake it for a living. You didn't pay for it, Andrei, but there's really no difference. I showed my gratitude to you. That's all. Don't read anything else into it."

His held himself rigidly. His jaw where he'd taken the punch was still swollen and bruised. He ran his hand over it as if she'd just slapped him hard.

The dog had followed Andrei into the living room. He flopped his tail, looked from one to the other as if trying to assess why the voices suddenly turned harsh.

Andrei's expression hardened. "You're right. No matter how

well you dress it up, you're still just a prostitute. Imagine me, of all people, forgetting that. You know, all this time I worked for you, I've been curious. What was worth so much money?"

Her cheeks flushed angrily. "And did you find out?"

Maria had demeaned him; his words carried an even harsher sting.

"You've got a knockout body for sure. But let's just say I'm glad I got it for free."

CHAPTER 22

Maria grabbed her bag and fumbled for her sunglasses, her cheeks still aflame. "No need to drive me anywhere, Andrei. You've done enough, I think."

She marched out of his apartment. Taxis in Brighton Beach were light on the ground anyway and this early in the morning, nonexistent. After asking directions from several shopkeepers, she climbed the stair to the subway. The platform shook when the train approached, as though a small tremor rocked it. It took her over an hour to get uptown and her headache returned with a vengeance. On the ride she phoned her doctor, who set up an immediate appointment for her at the Columbia University Medical Center, and then she phoned Lillian and asked her to meet her at the apartment later.

When Maria learned about the threatening texts, she had felt like her world was slowly disintegrating. That was nothing compared to losing Andrei. Now that they had quarreled so bitterly, it felt like a bomb had gone off. And she only had herself to blame; she'd egged him on. She was an expert on male physique, after all. She knew which sensitive areas to stroke, how to use her tongue to coax sensation. She'd plied all the tricks of the trade in some misguided attempt to make him love her. Some of her clients would deliberately hold back from climaxing, stage a sexual contest. Rarely did they last. If she had so much self-control with them, why then had she blown it so totally with Andrei? Why had she acted as if she were some infatuated groupie who couldn't control her own urges?

After being diagnosed with a mild concussion but no lasting damage, Maria left the hospital and reached home with a lighter heart. Lillian was waiting for her when she walked in the door. It had been a couple of weeks since they'd been together and the sight of her dear friend was almost too much. Maria threw her arms around her and hugged her fiercely.

Lillian pushed her back, held her at arm's length and searched her face. "My God, you look terrible. And where did you get that awful rag you're wearing? What's happened to you?"

"I have a lot to tell you. Would you mind fixing us a drink while I jump in the shower? I feel like I'm carrying around all the sweat and grime of the city on my bare back."

Lillian, Maria noted, looked wonderful in contrast. Refreshed, composed, even sporting a new hairstyle, a short pixie cut that suited her face.

The cascade of hot water and rose-scented body wash restored Maria's spirits. It would all work out, she thought as she towel-dried her hair. Ups and downs occurred in every partnership. She brushed her teeth and snuggled into comfortable jogging pants and a simple white cotton top. Lillian had gin and tonics waiting in the living room.

Maria curled up on the couch with her legs tucked underneath her and let out a deep breath. It felt good to be home again.

Lillian smiled as if she could read her thoughts. "I missed you. Staying at my cousin's was great; she has four kids and they're so much fun. But I missed our life here." She held up her hand. The swelling had subsided and the patches of raw tissue were healing nicely. "Back to work soon."

"Lillian, wait. I'm going to have to cancel on my clients next week."

"Why? You can manage without me temporarily—no?"

Maria slid her fingers under her top and pulled it up to show her breasts.

Lillian put a hand to her mouth when she saw the angry red half circles and bruises. "Oh no! What happened?"

Maria swallowed, savoring the slightly sour tang of the tonic water. "We caught the guy who's been threatening me. Andrei beat the crap out of him, but not before he roughed me up."

Lillian shook her head in sympathy when Maria told her about the attack. "He's lucky Andrei didn't kill him for that. He hides it well but he has a bad temper. I've seen it."

"Me too. Very recently."

Lillian set her drink down and leaned toward Maria. "You don't mean he's mad at you?"

"I'm afraid so."

"Why? He's devoted to you."

"That's the problem. He took me to his place last night to watch over me because of the battering I'd gone through. He was very kind and supportive and—I don't know what got into me, Lil, but we ended up making love. And this morning I found photos he'd taken of me. All this time I had no idea he had a thing for me. I'm afraid we might not be able to keep working together."

Maria did not see the expression of understanding she'd expected to on Lillian's face. Instead her smile extended from ear to ear. "You're right, things *will* change. It's about time you let some love into your life."

"Well it won't be with Andrei. We crucified each other pretty thoroughly this morning."

"Really—what happened?"

"There's no way he and I could carry on the business together if we were lovers. Emotions would keep getting in the way. He'd be insanely jealous or overprotective, or probably not want me to continue at all. Just like the other boyfriends I've had." She took a deep drink, felt the gin burn her throat. "I told him it was just a one-nighter, that we should put it behind us. He didn't take it very well. What the hell, Lillian? Why did he start daydreaming about me? Why did he have to go and ruin everything?"

Lillian swirled her drink then sipped at it thoughtfully. "You must be one of the most naive harlots in the world, my dear. Night after night you climb into your car beside him, as beautiful and seductive as can be, every last detail of your appearance designed to entice. I should know. It takes me hours to achieve the effect. For heaven's sake, Andrei is a man. How could he not want you, seeing you like that every night? And you confide in him like he's your best friend."

"He *is*, Lillian. You both are. But I've never done or said anything to lead him on."

"That just makes it worse."

"But why? We've been together for three years."

"Maybe he can see what you can't."

"What do you mean?"

"That the end of your business is near. And I'm not talking about your stalker. What do they call it for pills—shelf life? At what your men pay for you, you have a shelf life too. They are fickle. They can afford to be. I told you before, Maria. You are not a new face anymore. Andrei knows this. And maybe he thinks that now there's a chance for him."

"You're not very surprised by all of this—are you?"

Lillian paused, deciding how to frame her response. "He talked to me about it. A while ago."

"How long?"

"Couple of months."

"And what did you say?"

"I told him to forget about it."

"Well, he didn't take the advice. Why did you say that?

"Because it would lead directly to heartbreak—for him. And from what you've just been saying, I can see I was right. Much as I love you, Maria, the fact is you're haughty with men. You go through them."

"I'd appreciate you at least being on my side," she snapped. "I was counting on you to think of a way to set the clock back. Restore things between Andrei and me on a friendly basis. Your hand is almost healed. We've caught the stalker. It should be business as usual now. I don't want to stop yet. And for sure no one's going to make me do it."

"You're going to have to come to terms with it soon, Maria. Even the best treatments can't hide everything. You can't pretend to be a twenty-year-old forever. Your clients don't want a mature woman. You know that. Let Claudine go. Be Maria Lantos. Trust someone for once. Make up with Andrei. Who knows where things can lead?"

"Good Lord. I can't believe you're saying this."

"It's a hard world. Having someone on your side through it all—that's what's important. You should consider yourself lucky he's interested."

"We'd fail and end up hating each other."

"I don't see why. Isn't it odd? You can sleep with a stranger without blinking an eye but somehow falling in love with a friend is forbidden. You've got it all mixed up. You see the way women look at Andrei, you joke about it. Most women find him exciting. He's smart and cares about you. I think you're getting a twenty-carat diamond on one of those silver platters. Don't be blind to it."

"Andrei and I don't have enough in common; the sex was exciting but when that dims—and you know it does—our differences would come between us."

Lillian cocked her head to the side. "I think you're afraid. Why? Was it your childhood?"

"You mean what happened at the orphanage?"

"Maybe. You've got a—what's it called?—a shell around you. And now you don't know how to break it open."

"Don't bring that up, please. You're starting to sound like Andrei."

"That's why you don't want to give up the business. You have a nice time with a client, then you never have to see him again."

"Naturally. They're not looking for a relationship. That's

one reason they seek me out. Just fun sex. No having to call back. No strings attached."

"It's too lonely, though. No one should live like that."

"I'll find someone eventually. If I wanted a mate, Reed Whitman would be a much better choice than Andrei. He and I have a lot in common, similar interests. I could go the distance with him."

"Have you seen him lately?"

"He keeps in touch. He's been away lately on theater business."

"You don't know very much about Reed."

"I don't have to. I've seen what happened in my own home."

"How so?"

"I saw the problems between Jewel and Milne, who weren't well matched."

Lillian scrunched up her face in puzzlement. "I don't follow you."

"Jewel came from money. She inherited the spoils, became a really rich woman. She married Milne because she wanted the perfect nuclear family. Him and her, with me the adorable child. Milne was a small-town lawyer from Providence. He and Jewel both practiced law there. He took on a lot of indigent cases pro bono and didn't make much money. Then Jewel was offered a position with a top New York firm. Corporate law. We moved to Manhattan when I was eleven. On top of her inheritance, Jewel ended up making money hand over fist.

"That sabotaged their relationship. When the sore spots showed up, like they do in any marriage, she'd taunt him. Accuse him of having no ambition, complain she had to carry all the costs of their lifestyle. He stuck through it all but slowly fell apart. He's a lush, to put it frankly. The bottle comes out before noon. I've seen what a disparity like that can do to people. I'm not repeating Jewel's mistake."

"That's funny. Now we're getting closer to the truth of why you don't want Andrei."

Maria stared at her rudely, waiting for the blow.

"Because you're behaving exactly like Jewel. You two are more similar than you realize."

"Never say that to me again. We're polar opposites."

Nonplussed, Lillian finished her drink and got up. "You measure a man by how much he's worth. Some people would call that snobbery. And it sounds just like your adoptive mother. I'd hate to know what you think of a poor Filipina, who has to send all her money back home."

"That's not fair, Lillian. Jewel and Milne were torn apart by their differences. I watched it with my own eyes. Why would I want to repeat that mistake?"

Lillian opened her mouth to protest but was cut off by Maria's cell phone ringing next to her on the table. She picked it up, spoke to the caller then clapped her hand over the phone.

"It's Andrei. He's coming over. He said you'll want to hear what he has to say."

CHAPTER 23

"I'm going to change into something else," Maria said, hopping off the couch. "Be right back." In her bedroom, she slipped into an old pair of black jeans and a baggy sweatshirt. The white top was too revealing. She pulled her hair back into a ponytail. Severe, but that was the look she wanted. Nothing to suggest she'd gone out of her way to appear attractive to him. She was good at playacting. Thank God women could hide their horniness. If she got totally turned on when he walked in the room it would be her secret.

The buzzer sounded and her heart raced. He couldn't have been very far away when he called. She heard Lillian open the door and the two of them walk into the living room. Maria waited a few minutes, swallowed hard and went in.

He'd changed into one of the formal suits he wore for work and stood by the mantel holding the drink Lillian had fixed for him. His expression softened when he saw her, but only fleetingly.

Maria's stomach clutched. "Where's Lil?"

"She had to go out on some errand."

"Oh, that's right. She needed to get some new supplies for the bar," Maria said, knowing Lillian had purposely left them alone. She grabbed the glass with her half-finished drink and sat on the sofa farthest away from Andrei. "Lil makes a great gin and tonic."

"Yes, she does."

Clearly, he wasn't going to help her by smoothing the conversation out. His glance skimmed over her body, lingered on the curves poorly hidden by her sweatshirt, the skin at the dip of her throat. That one look had the force of a magnet. Maria had to fight the impulse to take him in her arms. She crossed her legs.

"Tell me your news."

"You're better now? What did the hospital say?"

"I'll be fine. The symptoms should disappear in a week or so and they gave me some painkillers."

"Good to hear." He downed his drink, set the empty glass on the mantel and moved over to the couch.

"Thorpe's real name is Charles Hock. It was a good idea to give him time overnight to think about his fate. Alone with my friends, he was all bluster to begin with. Threatening lawyers and lawsuits. By the end, he would have given us his life savings gift-wrapped if we'd wanted." Andrei allowed himself a bitter laugh.

Maria's titter in response sounded ridiculously false to her. "So was it him?"

"Yep. We found all the threatening texts on his cell phone. We persuaded him to give up his password."

"He didn't wipe them out? That was stupid."

"You can never erase messages completely, even if you think they're deleted. We discovered Hock has a thing for prostitutes. Really young ones. He seems to be under the impression that if he pays for it, that gives him carte blanche to do any degrading thing he wants. He frequents the dirtiest places imaginable. Girls and boys kept like livestock, never allowed out, drugged up to the hilt."

"I'm surprised. If that's what he's into, why did he want me?"

"That's just it. You were totally different. You were a prize he felt entitled to."

"The man is completely depraved. You're magnificent, Andrei. For catching him, I mean."

He frowned at her correction.

She filled the gap quickly. "I thought I recognized his figure from the San Francisco hotel surveillance tape. But he was never a client before last night, was he?

Andrei shook his head. "No. Not that I can see."

"Then what's the connection?"

"Are you ready for this? He's Jewel's *neighbor*. He's lived next door to her for five years. Lives alone. Been to lots of their cocktail parties. He lends an ear to her whenever she needs to rant. Apparently, Jewel told him every detail of your life."

It made sense Jewel would seek out a man for her confessor. She had no close female friends. She claimed she didn't trust other women to keep their mouths shut. She could imagine Jewel sliding next door, late in the afternoon when Milne was dizzy with alcohol, pouring her heart out about all the slings and arrows she'd suffered. What she couldn't imagine was Jewel socializing with Thorpe.

"It's hard to believe Jewel would take someone like that into her confidence."

"Well, from all outward appearances, he looked reputable and affluent."

"He must have money if he lives in Jewel's building. What does he do?"

"Sells glasses. Owns a string of optical companies. Obviously had the bucks to hire people to harass you."

"What do you mean?"

"Well, I doubt if the guy knew how to hack your e-mail account. And he hired help to beat me up last night."

"Did he kill that girl?"

"Almost positive. He admitted being a frequent visitor to the massage parlor where she worked."

"He didn't confess to the murder?"

"Well, yes. But at that point, near the end, he'd have sworn the world was flat if we'd wanted him to.

Near the end. Andrei had mentioned that twice now. "What did you do to him—afterward?" She was almost afraid to hear the answer.

"Let him go."

His words sent a shock wave through her. It was the last thing she expected. "He'll come after me again! Even if you have the evidence, I can't sue him for harassment or what I do would become known in court." Tears filled her eyes.

"Calm down," Andrei said sharply. "Let's just say he's going to have trouble getting it up for quite a long time. Besides, he's not going to be a free man for much longer."

"Why not?"

"Because I've given all this information to Trainor, who thankfully didn't inquire too deeply into how I got it. The Romanian girl tried to defend herself. Police got a DNA sample from her fingernails. If they match it to him, he's done like a roasted pig."

"Sorry. I should have realized you'd make sure."

"Nothing about you has to come out in the investigation. Trainor will focus on the physical evidence and Hock's association with the massage parlor."

She felt a rush of gratitude. "Thanks for coming over to tell me. After the way we parted this morning, you didn't have to." She cast her eyes down and tried to keep her voice as neutral as possible but it was a losing battle. She had a tearing need to feel his hands on her again.

"Look at me, Maria. I want to know if you really meant what you said this morning."

She raised her eyes reluctantly.

"Come here."

He didn't wait for her to move but took her forcefully in his arms and kissed her. His caress took her breath away. She'd managed to hold her feelings back when there was physical distance between them, but now, in his arms, her desire proved irresistible. She gave herself over to it and felt the thrill of his touch right down to her toes. She summoned her last ounce of willpower and pulled away. "Stop this, Andrei."

He sat back and loosened his tie. Maria saw the bruise on his jaw from where he'd been hit, the faint shadows under his eyes from so little sleep. "Do you really want me to stop? I don't think so. I'm not sure where your words are coming from. But your body can't lie."

She stood and walked over to the window, her form silhouetted by the golden sun. "It was just a physical reaction," she said, keeping her back to him.

"Yeah. And it came from the part of you that's most real." He rose from the sofa but didn't try to approach her again. "We were good together last night. It doesn't get any better than that."

She lifted her elegant shoulders in a shrug. She couldn't argue. He was an accomplished lover, no use denying it. Far more skilled than any she'd had before. He knew how a woman's body worked. She almost resented how easily he was able to please her. Unconsciously, she brushed her fingers against her mouth remembering the feel of his lips on hers seconds ago.

"Andrei, we're better friends and business associates. When Trainor closes his case, he'll get off my back. Everything can go back to normal. We've had a perfect partnership up till now. Let's not wreck it. I don't know why I gave in last night. I've been very weak. People do crazy things when they're feeling scared. It's completely out of character for me."

His lips clenched in frustration. "What you call your *character* is pure fiction. You know that, right?"

"I don't feel like being analyzed. I had enough of that when I was a teenager. You're a fine man and it's been a nice interlude but it has to stop."

"Is it Whitman? I hope you're not keeping a candle burning for him. I checked up on him. You should steer clear."

She turned to face him. "You did *what*?"

Andrei went on as if he hadn't heard her. "He's got one hell of a past. Married a woman who inherited loads of money. They're not together anymore, by the way."

"So what?"

"They're not together because he played around with young women. Then his wife *suddenly* died. Nothing could ever be proved but her brother accused him of killing her because she wanted a divorce."

"Probably because the brother didn't end up with any of the money. Fights over estates happen all the time. You know that." Once she got going her anger got the better of her. "You know what? Forget about him; this is about you and me." She cast around for something to say that would put an end to his romantic feelings. She found it.

"To tell you the truth, Andrei, I've had better sex with my clients. I just don't want you that way. Could we please call a halt to this?"

A moment of hurt flared in Andrei's eyes but he persisted. "Look. If you're still upset about this morning, let me apologize. I was mad, said things I shouldn't have. I know what happened to you at the orphanage. It was all documented when Ceausescu died and the new government took over. They investigated your father's death. When I started to work for you, I checked the transcripts. Children like you who are molested often end up damaged and drawn to prostitution. It's not your fault."

Maria's temper flared again. "What you're really saying is I'm a whore, but you're big enough to understand how I got so messed up."

Andrei sighed with exasperation. "That's not what I meant at all. You're turning my words inside out."

"No. You had to come up with some explanation for why I could open my legs so willingly. At the drop of the hat. For money. Men can do that any day and they boast about it. The more women they have, the more they're admired. When a woman does it, she's a slut. I saw that box of condoms in your drawer. How many women have *you* taken to bed lately? Well, I'm like a man. My clients are notches on a very tall bedpost. I take them for what I can get and don't even remember their names. Or faces. You think that's vulgar. An emotional illness. Self-destructive. But only if a woman does it."

He blanched. "What do you want from me, anyway, Maria? To watch me burn? You expect men to walk over hot coals for you. And when they do and you hear the skin on their feet sizzling, you pretend you were never interested in the first place."

"Yeah. It's a badge of honor the way a brand-new man swoons over me. I love the feel of his cock sliding into me. I enjoy a little bit of strange. Don't you?"

"That's just crude. It's beneath you to talk like that."

"I'm not ladylike enough—is that what you mean? Well maybe. But I'm never bored. I never have to turn over in bed and wish the man beside me would just go to sleep because I ceased finding him attractive about six months after the wedding. Or standing by, the faithful wife, knowing he's surreptitiously humping on his lunch hour between business meetings. I don't have that problem and I hope to God I never will."

"Tell me something. Does the idea of love ever enter into your mind?"

"Sure it does. When I find a man who doesn't judge me I'll invite you to the wedding—it could be a long wait."

She'd totally flattened him. Her warring words gave him not

an inch of room to move. He did not seem angry. Simply numb, as if his veins had just been shot full of Novocain.

He barely looked at her as he headed toward the door. "You accused me this morning of indulging in a fantasy about you, Maria. And I see now that's true. Thanks for straightening me out. Send me whatever papers you think are necessary. Our association is over."

If he'd hoped to see her relent over the prospect of losing him, he was doomed to disappointment. Instead, she gave him the haughty tones of Claudine. "Glad to. It won't be that difficult to find another chauffeur."

"A chauffeur, is it?" He emphasized his words with a cynical laugh. "Well, good luck with that."

The door clicked shut behind him, and at once Maria felt as if everything of substance inside her was dissolving. She'd spoken too sharply. His mention of childhood abuse lit a fuse inside her and she couldn't stop the chain reaction. In truth she'd often questioned whether those assaults lay at the core of her fascination with the erotic. Yes, she was a lustful woman. But the sexual power she had over men met some deep need inside her too. And the money it brought was its own reward.

But now, with Andrei gone, all she felt was a cramping, deadening melancholy.

The way she'd felt when the frightening strangers first took her to the tiny village called Siret.

CHAPTER 24

In the following days, as May faded into June, Maria and Lillian danced around one another, avoiding the topic of Andrei. Lillian kept her thoughts about it to herself. As good as his word, Andrei sent all the digital business files; she in her turn gave him a generous severance. That included her BMW.

She remembered the nights he'd take her out for a drive. They'd leave the city and find a stretch of country where Andrei could coax the car to perform to its max. She'd get a favorite music CD from the compartment and feed it into the CD player, turn up the sound. She loved the speed, the night wind whipping through her hair from the window she kept open. She couldn't imagine riding in that car again with some other man's hands on the wheel.

She bit back tears when she signed the severance check, wishing her tongue had not been so ready to fling acid, even if she'd told him the truth. She'd had no choice. Nothing could be gained by allowing him to entertain illusions about love.

She canceled all five appointments scheduled over the next two weeks, citing an urgent family matter, and was pleased when all the clients rebooked. One wanted her to role-play as Madonna. In her present mood she couldn't get worked up about it.

With grim determination, she plunged headlong into reorganizing her life, welcomed it as a way to keep her mind off Andrei. He'd left the files in good shape, although it took a lot of time to set up her own system. She hired an older, married man with a security background as driver and guard. She hit the gym early every day and pushed herself to the extreme till her muscles screamed. Mornings were devoted to business affairs and the rest of the time to her thesis, twelve-hour stretches that barely left her time to eat. She took one break a day to walk in the park at sunset when the shadows of the giant old trees stretched across the rocks and pathways, pools of darkness in the waning light. On one of these walks she found a pile of gray feathers strewn on the ground. She picked one up, running her finger over the soft down. Some little bird had ended up in the park hawk's talons.

As if he sensed an opening in her heart, Reed Whitman called daily. She agreed to have dinner with him. The air positively crackled in the apartment with Lillian's disapproval, but she said nothing and did her best to help Maria get ready for her date. It was always fun to get glammed up for a personal occasion instead of for a performance. She chose a simple but stunning dress in black georgette, given to her by a top New York designer when she'd been a featured guest model at a charity fashion show fund-raiser. She added her favorite red-soled black pumps and a pair of diamond earrings that glittered brilliantly when they swung from her earlobes. Lillian carefully painted on fire-engine red nail polish and matching lipstick, but her hand trembled as she applied the lip color. She left a smear at the corner of Maria's mouth.

"I'm so sorry," Lillian said in exasperation. "I thought I could at least manage that."

"No matter, Lil. You did fine. It will take time." She reached for some makeup remover and dabbed at the smear. It left a faint pinkish trace.

"Andrei left town." Lillian said, almost as an afterthought, while she tidied the cosmetics on the counter. "I thought you should know."

"For good?" Maria's breath stilled.

"I got the impression it's just going to be an extended vacation."

"Oh, that's great. He deserves one. I don't think he ever took more than a week off all the time we worked together. Did he ask after . . . say . . . anything else?"

"Not really. I called him to get the name of this new skin care product I'd heard about. One of his friends imports it. She's a cosmetician. But he was in a hurry. They were leaving for JFK that morning."

"He was going with someone?"

"The cosmetician. That's what I meant. I needed her e-mail address before they left."

Maria smoothed her hair. It was starting to look brittle and washed-out. "That's fine, Lil. You've been a great help—thanks." She put on a cheery smile as Lillian packed up her things and left, while raging jealousy clawed away at her insides. She stared at herself in the mirror. The dressing table lights, five bright round halogens, revealed a minuscule wrinkle at the corner of her eyelid. She touched it, then took out a bottle of skin enhancer. The retinol would puff out the skin and make the wrinkle vanish. But how long would it be before her lids turned crepey, beyond the power of the retinol to fix? Before tiny crevices permanently marred her lip line?

She imagined the Russian "friend." Young. Younger than her. Bubbly personality. Huge boobs. All Russian women were stacked—weren't they? Orgasmed easily. Probably had two or three a night.

Anger felt better than sadness. Depression drained the energy out of her. She made up her mind that nothing would interfere with her date with Reed.

The doorman called up; Reed had arrived right on time. When Maria stepped off the elevators, she saw Reed chatting with the tangle-haired woman who'd made disparaging remarks to her in the elevator a few weeks ago. She could tell by the woman's body language, the way she simpered and preened, how hard she was trying to impress him. This should be fun, Maria thought.

She walked toward them with a leisurely swing of her hips. Reed's face lit up when he spotted her. The woman turned her head to follow his gaze. Her jaw dropped. Reed put his arm around Maria and gave her a light kiss on the cheek. "You two know each other, I imagine?"

Maria tipped her sunglasses down and looked over them. "I don't remember whether we've met. I moved in recently. Do you live here?"

"On the top floor," the woman stuttered.

"Oh, how lovely." Maria gave her a fake smile and turned to Reed. "We'd best be off, then, hadn't we?"

Reed bid the woman good-bye, tightened his arm around Maria as they walked away. "Friend of yours?" he teased.

"She has an attitude," Maria said politely, and he chuckled.

She loved New York on hot summer nights. The steamy smells of overheated pavement and gutters, everyone out on the streets, hawkers pushing their merchandise until well past midnight, restaurants overflowing, the torrid burlesque of neon signs and lights—on the street, in the store windows, at the peaks of roofs, on the caps of soaring high-rises.

Reed hailed a taxi. "I had a fun idea for tonight if you're game."

"Game for anything," she said, his good spirits already lightening her mood.

"It's so nice out. Let's walk on the High Line for a while. I know an amazing place for dinner in Chelsea. New start-up. Invitation only. No walk-ins."

"Sounds brilliant."

The taxi let them out at Twentieth Street and Tenth Avenue. They climbed the flight of stairs to the old elevated rail line the city had converted to a linear park.

"These shoes weren't made for walking," she joked as they reached the top.

Reed grinned. "Well then, my lady, we'll just have to do something about that." He guided her to a bench cloaked on either side with greenery, knelt and slipped off her shoes. Then he removed his own loafers and socks. "Nothing wrong with going barefoot."

The boardwalk and patterned stonework were kept scrupulously clean by park attendants, so they had no worries about hurting their feet. Maria laughed as Reed took her hand once more. She loved catching glimpses of the city below, through gaps in the young trees and grasses bordering the walkway, the angles of building tops looming so close you could almost touch them; one was decorated with artful graffiti. A skateboarder whipped past moms and dads with kids in strollers, babies strapped to their chests, an old man with a parakeet perched on his shoulder.

Reed held her hand. "I've missed you like hell, lady. What have you been doing with yourself all this time?"

"Recovering. I fell. Ended up with a concussion. How stupid is that?"

"Oh shit. Is everything okay?"

"Fine. I still get brutal headaches but not so often."

His tone deepened. "I looked for you on campus every day."

"I've been working at home since my injury. Thank heavens I'd finished the course work before. Now it's only the thesis ahead."

"That's right. You never sent me a draft. Thought you were going to."

"I'm not there yet. It's still too raw. But I will. Thanks for remembering."

They reached the foot of the promenade, stuck their feet back into their shoes and descended the stairs. On the platform halfway down, Reed stopped, pinned her body against the railing and kissed her again. The touch of his lips spurred the memory of Andrei's mouth on hers, and she felt a painful pang of loss. She pulled back.

He raised his eyebrows. “Too public here?”

“Oh, no.” Maria recovered herself. “When you tilted my head back, it hurt a bit, that’s all.”

He hadn’t released her, his arms still held her close so her breasts pressed up against his shirt. She could feel his erection bulge into her crotch. “Damn, I’m sorry. I’ll be more considerate.”

“No worries. The ache’s already going away.”

“Right now I’d like to skip dinner and just carry you home with me.” He searched her face hoping to find the answer he wanted.

“And what are your plans once we get there?” Her lips turned up in a foxy smile.

He bent his head to whisper in her ear. “Strip you naked and fuck like there’s no tomorrow.”

She hesitated. Do it, she said to herself. It’s the only way you’ll get this crazy obsession with Andrei out of your system. “That sounds like a better deal than dinner.”

Reed owned the building where he kept his Midtown apartment. In the lobby he strode over to one of the two elevators in old-style ornamental bronze and punched in a code. He ushered her through when the doors opened. “This elevator’s reserved for my place. On the top floor.” Halfway up he pressed the Stop button. The elevator jerked to a halt.

He pulled her to him. She ran her fingers through his salt-and-pepper curls and opened her mouth to his kiss. He lifted her dress up to her waist, rolled down her skimpy black lace panties to midthigh. She spread her legs and lifted her bum as he slipped his fingers into her wetness.

She sucked in a huge breath. Felt a pleasant weakening in her limbs. He unfastened her earring and nibbled her ear lobe, kissed her neck. His breaths came faster. "Christ," he said fiercely, "the one time I don't have any protection on me." Maria was panting when he withdrew his hand and tucked her dress back down. On the rest of the ride up, his words *the one time* rolled through her mind.

The elevator opened into the apartment's main room. Lights from a nearby building were bright enough that she could make out the humped shapes of furniture, the orientation of the white walls. Reed led her to his bedroom. He flicked on the switch to the en suite. It cast a muted light into the bedroom. She leaned against the king-sized bed while he fumbled in the bathroom cabinet to find a condom. She heard the snap of the foil as he withdrew it. He unzipped his pants and rolled the latex over his penis, yanked her dress up and took her by the hips, turned her around, bent her over the bed. "I want to see you from behind," he said as he pulled down her panties. He covered her buttocks with soft kisses and inserted his fingers again into her vagina. She felt his tongue on her bottom while his fingers withdrew from her slit and rubbed over her clitoris.

She slipped over the edge. It was a sharp come, short and intense. He pushed his penis into her forcefully. Grabbed her pelvis and moved rapidly, slipped out. He swore. Maria bent her back, tilting her bottom up so he could enter her again. A shotgun series of thrusts and he climaxed. He slumped over her, then pulled out and straightened. She heard him zip up his fly.

"I knew you'd be magnificent," he said, giving her a pristine peck on the cheek. "Come into the other room. I have something for you."

With the main room lights on, Maria saw his place was

exactly what she expected it to be. Expensively furnished. Cork floor. Cool, corporate colors. The windows of the old building had been replaced by floor-to-ceiling views. Across one wall hung framed posters of Broadway plays.

Reed went into the kitchen while she stood at the window gazing out at the view of city lights. Sex with him had been a curiously static experience. Her body felt dissatisfied. The orgasm had come and gone, unremembered. Still, getting off had been enjoyable. She had no quarrel with that.

He handed her a glass of wine when he returned. "Chablis. Trust that's okay with you? It's chilled."

"More than okay."

Reed picked up his glass. "Confession. I've been intrigued by you ever since I first saw you in my undergraduate class. I couldn't do anything about it then, of course—the university frowns on such things—and I was married at the time. You're an exciting woman, Maria. And I've never forgotten you." He touched the rim of his glass to hers. "Why you haven't been claimed by some guy, I can't imagine."

"Actually, it's the reverse. It's me who hasn't claimed anyone. I've had relationships, but I don't like the thought of being tied down. You could say I'm commitment shy. And there's a lot I want to achieve before I even consider anything permanent."

"Well, I'm going to change your mind about that." He punctuated the statement with an easy laugh as if there was no doubt in his mind that he'd succeed. "I'm glad you're single. It's my good luck. Here's another confession: I'd planned a long, romantic evening to seduce you. Instead, I tripped the wire. I just wanted you so badly."

She planted a quick kiss on his lips. "And I you." A moment

of guilt came over her. She hadn't desired him as badly as she'd wanted Andrei. Not even close. But Reed was a far more logical match.

"Sit over here, lady." He gestured toward Italian leather banquettes arranged around a block of brushed steel that served as a low table. On it sat a beautifully gift-wrapped box and a tray of hors d'oeuvres from Chenwith, an upscale caterer that sold its delicacies on custom-designed china plates. He handed her the box while he removed cellophane from the plate of food.

She untied the pink bow and carefully peeled back the paper. Inside lay a gold bracelet; one of its links enclosed a diamond. The gem's facets sparkled with the cold beauty of complete purity, unique to diamonds. "Reed, this is stunning. You must be prescient, giving me a bracelet to match my earrings. I don't know what to say."

He leaned over to fasten it onto her wrist. "At first I'd thought of emeralds to match your eyes, but you're more like a diamond. You steal the show." His eyes twinkled as he took her earrings out of his pocket. She turned her head left, then right, for him to slip the fastenings into the small holes in her earlobes. "But I can't take the credit. I managed to wheedle it out of your maid. That those were your favorites."

"My maid?" Maria's brow furrowed in puzzlement. A day woman came in to do laundry and cleaning, but she couldn't imagine how the woman could have connected with Reed.

"Lillian—isn't that her name?"

"Oh, she isn't my maid, she's . . ." Maria caught herself in time. "My stylist. She comes over to do my hair and nails. It's much more convenient than hopping from one salon to another."

She quickly moved the conversation onto other topics, told

him what progress she'd made with her writing, and he listened thoughtfully as they finished the bottle of wine and snacked on the food. He made a number of solid suggestions for how she could reorder the major points. As they talked, Maria became even more convinced that she'd been right. She and Reed had something better than a fleeting infatuation. Compatibility. They were on the same level. And if they ended up sharing a future, that would become the glue to hold them together.

"You remember the rehearsal I mentioned? Of the Genet play?" Reed said, finishing the last drop of his wine. "Can you pop into the theater tomorrow afternoon for an hour or so? The director wants to review the optics and staging of one scene; make sure he's got it right."

When he saw a protest beginning to form, he put his finger against her lips. "No debate now. I'll send a car for you. If you come around three, I'll make it clear you have to be out of there by five."

"Will it just be us?"

"Us and the director. And those streetwalkers too. I mentioned them before—remember?"

Maria's face fell.

"You're okay mingling with a bit of sleaze, aren't you? I promise they won't bite."

They went to bed again. She asked that he keep the lights off, explaining this was the longest she'd stayed up since her injury and exposure to light for too many hours tended to bring on her headache. In truth she feared him noticing the marks on her breasts. They'd faded now to pale half-moons, but she was worried he'd see them.

It was a good call. He spent a long time on her breasts, nuzzling, sucking and rubbing her nipples between his fingers. "Fucking stunning tits," he murmured. "Men must go crazy when they see you."

What was that supposed to mean? Was he referring to former boyfriends or—had he let something slip? She curled around his body, ran her tongue down his stomach. He had a soft belly. She tugged gently at the curls of his pubic hair and licked the length of his penis. Took the crown in her mouth while she used both hands to stroke him. His penis firmed. She slid the condom over him, mouthed his testicles, ran her tongue around them.

He rolled on top of her. Stuck his tongue deep into her mouth and pushed his cock, full force, inside her. She wasn't ready and it hurt a little. She sucked her finger and used her saliva to ease the slide of her finger into his anus. Grabbed his buttock with her other hand and squeezed. He bucked with pleasure and pumped harder. In the end, she simulated her orgasm. The missionary position never did much for her.

Reed's penis softened and he pulled out, lay on his back. "An English guy I once knew always described the aftermath of a good screw by saying he was shattered. How apt, eh? You've left me in pieces."

She turned to kiss him on the shoulder. "I'm glad." She trailed her hand down his stomach. Within five minutes he was sound asleep.

She watched the bedside clock. Waited for twenty minutes until his deep breathing told her he was gone for the night. She slipped off the bed, taking care not to make a sound. Put on her panties and dress, padded on her bare feet to the living room. She paused to make sure he hadn't stirred and swooped up her purse. The diamond on her gold bracelet winked in the moonlight streaming through the window. She slid into her shoes and experienced a moment of panic when she thought she might not know how to work the elevator, but a simple push of the button opened the doors. She did not leave a note. In the morning she'd send over a bottle of good Chablis with a card thanking him for a lovely time.

She stepped out of the lobby into the hot dark night. The city still hummed with life. She sauntered for a while up Eighth Avenue. Two guys walked toward her, holding hands. She smiled as they passed by. Love in all its forms—she approved. With the opening of attitudes about same-sex relationships, the enclaves forming the core of the LGBT communities might one day pass into history, but for now, Chelsea was still a gay hangout.

Sex with Reed had not swept her off her feet. Pleasant, yes. Fireworks, no. Then again, she'd experienced more awkward first times with a lover. At least the absurd grip of her encounter with Andrei was starting to fade. She could nurture a relationship with Reed; she might have a future there.

She looked in a darkened restaurant window at her reflection, her figure shaped by her beautiful black dress. Took pride in her long fine legs, slim waist, voluptuous breasts, pouty lips. She was still Claudine. A gorgeous harlot. Free. In control. Nothing yet had been lost.

CHAPTER 25

True to his word, Reed sent a car around to pick her up the next afternoon. he greeted her at the playhouse doors. She loved the theater world, and a surge of anticipation ran through her as the actors—the madam, a professional who Maria recognized from a famous TV series—and Reed's streetwalkers gathered onstage. The banks of plush seats were empty except for her and Reed, sitting a few rows from the front. A young guy perched behind a video camera to film the scene. The director greeted them with a wave and walked over to sit on a stool to give him a better view of the action.

All the women playing prostitutes looked fit and healthy. In reality, Maria mused, prostitutes in the nineteenth century would have died before they'd reached her age from the curse of syphilis, toxic alcohol or the slow destruction of opium. About halfway into the scene she heard footsteps hustling down the aisle. Maria and Reed both turned to see a thin, bald man hurrying toward them. "Hell," Reed said with a frantic look in his eyes. "I didn't know *he* was coming."

"Who is it?"

"One of the play's main backers. Nate's thrown a shitload of money into this production." The director looked up from his seat, and his look of abject annoyance transformed to a beaming smile upon recognizing his executive producer. Nate looked from Maria to Reed, and seemed to make a quick mental calculation. "Well, hello, Claudine," he said brightly. "I see you two got together after all."

Maria went white. She remembered him; one of her clients from a few months ago. February, to be precise. While she didn't recall most of her clients, his face stayed with her because he'd booked a session for a threesome on Valentine's Day—a gift for his lover. She'd had the distinct impression the lover was not pleased.

A sheepish look flitted across Reed's face and he couldn't meet her eyes. She leaped up before Reed had a chance to stop her, fuming as she fled up the aisle. He *had* known all along and deliberately played with her feelings just to satisfy his own curiosity.

Reed caught up to her just as she reached the exit and held her arm. He gave her a wry grin instead of an apology. "That wasn't supposed to happen. Believe me, I didn't think Nate would be here."

She threw off his arm and pried the door half-open while he tried to hold it shut. "I should have guessed," she said acidly. "And there you were, so sympathetic about my studies requiring me having to burn the candle at both ends."

"I wasn't lying. I was intrigued. I wondered how you balanced your lives. I wanted to know what it would be like being with you."

"And you were too cheap to pay for it?" Maria taunted him.

"No. I like you. Don't misunderstand me. But—why do you do it?"

"It's a living, same as any other career. And I don't owe you any explanations."

"Career?" He raised an eyebrow. "Is that what you call it?"

"Well, fucking boring rich men *is* hard work."

"Even if they give you diamond bracelets? I woke up last night in an empty bed."

"You were sleeping peacefully; I didn't want to disturb you. I had an early . . ."

"An early meeting?" he interrupted. "Off to squeeze some other guy in before dawn?"

Her green eyes widened, incredulous. Reed clutched her arm again and held it firmly. "Hey, it's cool. I'm sorry, okay? Maria . . . Claudine. I'm not sure what to call you. Look. Maybe it's just as well. We deceived each other. Now we don't have to hide anything. It's all out in the open. We don't have to stop seeing each other, do we?"

Maria shook her head. "I should have expected this. Enough people in your circles know me in New York. I'm not obligated to tell you anything about my private life." Her voice was ice-cold. She yanked her arm away and shifted her bag over her shoulder. "And as to deception, well, I rather like it. It earns me a hell of a good living."

She left him standing at the theater entrance and blew down the street without looking back.

CHAPTER 26

Lillian shook her head the next morning when Maria told her about the exchange with Reed. "I was beginning to turn a corner on him. He was nice on the phone with me."

"He is nice. That's not the point."

"Let me make a prediction: it won't matter. You will hear from him again soon."

"I don't think so, Lil. Despite all his artsy, progressive ways, he's a prude at heart. He wanted a mad night or two of sex. He was curious about what it would be like sleeping with a high-class prostitute. Men like Reed don't bring that kind of woman home to Mom."

Maria knelt on the dressing room floor, sorting through her shoes, trying to decide which ones to bring for her next three assignments in mid-June. London again, Lyon and Monaco. Her cell rang.

"Hello?"

Trainor was on the line. "Maria Lantos?"

"It's me."

"I'm giving you a call because there's some good news and I wanted to reach you before it hits the media. I believe Baranov told you we had a suspect? We've charged Charles Hock with first-degree homicide in the death of the Romanian prostitute. While he didn't admit to harassing you, or the theft of your ID, we're confident about his involvement. I expect he'll tip to that eventually."

"Is there any chance he'll be granted bail?"

Trainor cleared his throat. "I can't make any predictions about bail. He has a good attorney, but I doubt it. He has history of abusing young prostitutes. The prosecutor thinks that will be enough to keep him inside." He paused and mumbled to someone in the room with him. "Gotta run. Just wanted you to know."

She thanked him and ended the call. She let the red shoe she still held in her hand fall to the floor and threw her arms around Lillian. "Thank God! If our luck holds they'll shut Hock away for the rest of his life."

Lillian looked at her badly scarred hand. "In the Philippines, we'd kill him."

"Word will have traveled pretty fast around Jewel's condo building. She's got to be freaking out right now." Lillian clapped a hand over her mouth. "Your mom. I forgot to tell you. Jewel's been trying to reach you. She sounded desperate. She gave me three numbers you can call her at."

Jewel answered as soon as Maria rang. "Marie, good to hear from you. Thanks for getting back to me."

Thanks? Good to hear from you? Maria gripped her cell in disbelief. "What do you want?"

"When you were here the other day, you mentioned something about a death. Of some massage parlor whor—girl. That it had a connection to a stalker you were having a little trouble with?"

"I wouldn't call it a little trouble, Jewel. More like one of the most wretched experiences you can imagine."

"Yes, I'm sorry. I didn't mean to be insensitive."

"Strange how things turn out, isn't it? I understand the man they've arrested is a close friend of yours."

"Where did you hear that? Did Milne say something?"

"I've had a few inquiries from the press asking for confirmation."

"Oh no." Jewel let out a loud sigh.

"One of them was from a big social networking site. I forget the name. Has two hundred thousand followers. Tweets compulsively."

"What did you tell them?"

She held back a snicker. "Well, my maid took the calls." Maria winked at Lillian. "I haven't had a chance to talk to them yet."

Jewel exhaled in relief. "I had no idea, Marie, I swear. Milne and I ran into Charles Hock from time to time. Of course we couldn't help that; he lived right next door. How the board ever approved him I can't imagine. I've ordered a meeting for tonight, to tighten up our rules."

Maria could just imagine what Jewel looked like now, white-faced, jiggling her leg compulsively the way she did when her nerves got the better of her. "I'm glad to hear that. I was on the point of calling one of the reporters back. Lucky I talked to you first."

"Why would you talk to the press? They're just digging for

dirt. They'll take the faintest whiff of rumor and turn it into a full-blown scandal. Surely you'd want to avoid any publicity."

The implication was obvious. Not only did Jewel wish to hide her friendship with Hock, she was afraid the spotlight would also be trained on her daughter's profession, making her doubly shamed.

"Well. I don't *have* to speak to them. I would appreciate knowing, though, what you said about me to Hock. About my origins. Like I asked before."

Jewel hesitated before she spoke. "He invited us over for cocktails once. As Milne was unwell, I went—just to be sociable. We got to talking about our children. Would you believe a man like that has progeny? Of course, he divorced years ago. Very acrimonious, apparently. I don't wonder. I did mention your adoption. You know how it is. When someone pours their heart out to you, you can hardly sit there and say nothing about your own experience. How was I to know what a monster he'd turn out to be?"

"What did you say? I want to know *exactly*, Jewel."

"Your name. The fact that your parents were killed in Romania."

"The name of the orphanage? Lani?"

"Who? Yes. I told him about that disgraceful place. How I rescued you from it."

"Anything else?"

Jewel said nothing.

"What else, Jewel?"

"I told him that you're a . . . what you do for a living. How much it hurt me when I found out."

"Not the kind of thing you'd impart to a casual acquaintance—is it?"

Another pause. "Please don't talk to the media, Marie. I didn't say anything the other day, but Milne's not in the best of health. A lot of negative publicity could affect him very badly."

She suddenly became aware she was hearing the croak of an old woman in Jewel's pleading and wheedling voice, afraid of her good name being dragged through the dirt. A surge of pity washed over Maria, followed by the sharp realization that the battle between them was finished. It had, in fact, been long over, yet she'd been blind to it, storing up the litany of Jewel's insults and small betrayals like a collection of malign family heirlooms.

She assured Jewel she wouldn't talk to the media, said good-bye and hung up.

CHAPTER 27

NEWPORT, RHODE ISLAND

All her European performances went well. Often during the trip Maria caught herself thinking about Andrei. In her mind's eye, she pictured him at some palm-fringed resort, swimming up to the pool bar, his chest bronzed by the sun, sleek with water, the Russian woman running her hands over his body. She imagined a sudden tropical cloudburst, the kind that came and went in minutes. The two of them laughing, running hand in hand back to their beach house, hot for each other. Hardly able to make it to their door before he shed his trunks, pulled off the woman's wet thong, lifted her in his lean hands and pinned her with his hard cock, her legs open to receive him.

Thankfully, those painful thoughts were fleeting and half-formed—vestiges of an immature jealousy like the empty hurts she'd stored up over Jewel. Reed monopolized her feelings now. After their argument at the theater, she'd regretted her cutting words. She shook her head when she thought of it. She'd been so self-righteous and indignant. A complete overreaction. Since then, he'd called often to say he didn't want things to end between them. He even showed up once on the spur of the moment, demanding to see her and bearing a long, heartfelt letter to say he wanted her back. She ignored his pleas, playing hard to get. Then Reed went silent. She worried her coldness had pushed him too far, that she might have overplayed her hand and lost him for good. Reed was not used to being turned down. She risked making him look like a fool.

She was on the verge of picking up the phone to call him when a text came through:

> Claudine. I wish to hire you for a unique performance
> for one night at my Newport estate.
> No special preparation will be needed. I'm prepared to
> pay double your normal fee.

The client stated his name was Lawrence Carson. He wanted to book her for Friday, June 21st, less than a week away, and on the summer solstice—doubly romantic. Maria read the message twice and smiled, remembering that Reed owned a country house on the coast northeast of New York. After the standard check on the client was carried out, the message traced back to a Yale University source. So Reed, Maria thought happily, was making the grand gesture after all. Perhaps he'd accepted who she was and, despite his recent silence, was unable to forget her. Typical of his theatrical nature, he'd conceived an over-the-top way to show it. She answered back with an enthusiastic yes.

• • •

The legendary Newport estates strung along the Rhode Island coast had originally been erected as mammoth summer homes. They echoed an age of excess. In the Vanderbilt's Marble House, sacred altarpieces from European churches had been disassembled and shipped across the Atlantic for decoration. The Newport mansions were once the locus of champagne-drenched parties, loose girls, golden boys, illegal whiskey flowing like water. Maria remembered the first time she'd ever set eyes on them when she was still a child. The garden sheds were bigger than her house. Convinced they were palaces, she'd pestered her nanny repeatedly to explain how there could be so many kings and queens.

She wondered idly whether her nanny still lived in Providence. Perhaps before she returned to New York she would try to look her up.

As before, Reed had sent a driver to collect her, a generous gesture typical of him, so she gave her new guard the night off. The limousine purred along the coast road. They passed Hammersmith Farm, the old Auchincloss estate where Jackie O spent much of her youth. As they drove by the estates, her heart lifted. She felt a lightness, new to her, and excitement over the prospect of seeing Reed again. The car slowed as it passed a white colonial fronted by a fancy pillared gate with two marble lions. Reed's home, beside the colonial, was hidden from view by two small hills and several acres of trees. A stream, glimmering like a long silver rope, wound across a meadow and slipped through a cleft between the hills. As they rounded a wide arc in the drive up to the house and climbed the rise, the estate appeared as if by magic. It was a giant house like its sisters on this section of the coast: turreted, built of warm fieldstone. The ocean rolled, blue, in the distance.

Staff greeted her when the car pulled up in front of the house. A redheaded man, big as a tank, introduced himself as Victor. Beside him stood a pale blonde named Alicia. Both were dressed in formal staff uniforms. "Welcome to Downton Abbey," Maria said under her breath.

Reed hadn't asked for any role-playing, so without the need for elaborate costumes, she brought only a suitcase. She stopped for a second to view the rotunda when they entered the house. A huge Italianate chandelier dangled from the ceiling with porcelain arms and glass bulbs fashioned to look like candle flames. She stepped onto the charcoal slate floors of the rotunda and admired its walls paneled in cherrywood. Each panel contained a niche holding a marble statuette of Grecian nymphs or satyrs, some quite sexually provocative. An interesting touch in a rich man's house.

Alicia led her up the grand staircase with Victor puffing behind her, carrying her bag. The sun flooded in through the upstairs gallery, which was clad in the same cherrywood, warming the cedar-scented wax. Their feet made little noise on the plush indigo runner offset with a design of ivory lilies.

"When is my host expected?" she asked, assuming the staff had been instructed to play along with Reed's game.

Alicia took out a key ring to unlock a door about midway down the hall, pushed it open and stood aside so Maria could enter. "Mr. Carson's been detained by business in the city. He sends his apologies. I'm afraid he won't reach here till after dinner. This is your room if you wish to change. Feel free to wander the house if you like, or the gardens. The walk by the ocean is particularly pleasant in late afternoon. Everything is at your disposal. There'll be a light supper around six P.M." The maid delivered all this in a polite but clipped tone while Victor set her bag down near the large dresser. Together they left.

The room's appointments were spotless and of good quality, yet they looked as though they'd been there since the roaring twenties. Except for the bedcoverings. Maria ran her hand over the silky sheets, soft as down and smelling of the clean powdery scent that came from being freshly laundered. Was this where Reed intended to make love to her?

In her mind's eye she saw him stretched out on the bed, nude and ready for her. Her, kneeling astride his face, taking him in her mouth, bringing all her talents to bear on pleasuring him. Her anticipation to see him again grew stronger. She changed into a simple print dress and comfortable shoes, put on lipstick and pulled her hair off her face with a clip. Nothing fancy for now. She'd eat quickly, come up and change again before he arrived.

A maze of rooms and hallways made up the second and third stories. It must have been designed to host massive weekend parties: it was equipped to accommodate legions. She wondered whether Reed had sole use of the home or if others in his family had a claim on it too. It was cool upstairs and, unlike the gallery, dark, since there were few windows. She shivered and found when she clicked on her cell, she couldn't get a signal. The remoteness of the house made her feel cut off from the world. Her phone went everywhere with her. Not being able to use it added to her sense of isolation.

Downstairs, where she expected to hear Victor and Alicia bustling about, was eerily silent. Wouldn't many staff be needed to keep a place of this size running smoothly? A huge salon occupied the west wing. Here, the updated furniture had been carefully chosen to blend in with the antiquated cornices and wall ornamentation. A massive fireplace at one end was enclosed by a carved marble mantel. Life-sized sculptures stood in each corner.

The one thing missing in this grand home was a personal touch. No family photos, books half-read lying on tables, hats tossed on chairs, umbrellas stacked in a stand. The entire place had a corporate feel. More hotel than home. Maria wondered if Reed rented it out for events as a way to defray costs. The house almost seemed to carry a pathos with it. It needed the life of a family: a Persian cat purring in a chair or a Saint Bernard stretched in front of the fireplace, tail wagging in welcome. The thought of dogs recalled Andrei's friendly mutt. She shut that memory down as quickly as it came.

Maria daydreamed about how she'd transform the place if she were ever to become its mistress. She could host amazing parties here. She imagined the guests arriving on a Friday night from New York, she and Reed greeting them arm in arm, the visitors impressed with its elegance, some casting an envious eye on what was hers. Who knew? If things went well with Reed, perhaps one day that vision would come true.

She peeked in the kitchen, found it empty too, a huge, sprawling affair modernized with black granite countertops and new cabinets. A formal dining room lay off it. Two libraries occupied the east wing; the first was a smaller, more intimate room walled by bookcases that stretched to the ceiling, with a cheerful little green tiled fireplace and antique iron mantel. Its windows looked onto a sea of grass that swept to the walk along the water's edge. If she lived here, this would be her favorite room. She imagined crystal clear morning sun flooding into it.

In the second library, a grand affair with a fresco on the ceiling, French windows had been thrown open leading to a stone terrace. The land here dropped off and her eyes were level with the crowns of maples and sycamores. To her far right she could see a beautiful walled garden. It appeared to contain a small orchard, and she could just make out the flash of color from the fruits, cherries probably, which at this time of year would be starting to ripen. Songbirds twittered and chirped in the garden. She breathed in a deep draft of clean, sweet air that carried with it a flavor of sea kelp and wet sand.

She noticed an intercom on the wall beside a large locked cabinet. The button buzzed loudly when she pressed it. "Hello . . . hello . . . Alicia, are you there?" There was no answer.

She huffed in annoyance, wondering whether the thing was even working and decided to continue reading *Justine.* A gloomy topic on such a pleasant day, but she'd fallen far behind in her studies and needed to make up the time. She'd do it in the smaller library, though. Something about this room made her uncomfortable.

When she turned to leave, Alicia stood in the doorway. The woman hadn't made a sound coming in; it was as if she'd suddenly appeared like some evil fairy. "You called, ma'am?"

Maria recovered from her surprise. "I'd like to send some texts but I can't get any cell phone service or wireless. Do you know if the servers are down?"

"Did you try it in here?"

"No. Upstairs."

Alicia offered a thin smile. The woman was so pale with her wheaten hair and colorless skin. Her black uniform only magnified the impression.

"Mr. Carson only permits cell phone and wireless usage in the libraries. He prefers his guests to think of his home as a place of leisure, away from all the pressures of cell phones and social networks."

"Oh. Good to know. I think I'll use the other library, then."

"Would you like to take your meal there?"

"Yes. That would be excellent. Then I can continue my reading. Is there any firmer idea what time Mr. . . . Carson is expected?"

"I've heard nothing more." Alicia said, then turned on her heel and left the room.

Maria settled in the small library and spent an hour or so reading, until right on cue, Victor bustled in pushing a trolley table. Clumsy and uncoordinated, his fat hands, with little red hairs springing up like coiled copper wires, grasped the trolley handle too tightly. Alicia followed him in. Victor nodded to Maria.

"Would you care to eat out on the terrace?" he asked.

"That would be lovely, thank you."

Alicia laid a cream linen cloth on the glass and wrought-iron terrace table and Victor pulled out Maria's chair to seat her. Alicia set a bottle of Evian water down along with a napkin and the place setting. "Salad greens fresh from our garden, a Mediterranean antipasto selection, saffron steamed rice and grilled quail."

"Wonderful. Thank you."

Victor uncorked a chilled rosé and poured a little in the wineglass, then handed it to her. It had a crisp, light taste with just a faint suggestion of sweetness. "Ideal choice for a perfect summer evening," Maria said as she held out her glass for him to finish filling it.

She sipped at her wine after they left. It seemed passing strange to be sitting here alone, marvelous though the setting was. But knowing Reed, she had the sense he was planning something special for the evening, teasing her with anticipation, and the more she thought about it, the more enthusiastic she became. It was a new experience for her, having someone else drawing the plotlines, making the moves, a change she welcomed. She suddenly realized how hungry she was and, finding all the dishes delectable, ate more than she had in days.

As if reading her thoughts, Alicia entered carrying a silver tray with a cup of coffee and a digestif. Alicia cleared the plates away and handed her a small white envelope. "With Mr. Carson's compliments and apologies about being so late."

Alicia dipped her head formally before leaving Maria alone on the terrace. As she turned over the envelope to open it, her eyes lit on the digestif; a lovely fluted glass containing a greenish liquid, Chartreuse probably. Something lay at the bottom of the glass. She picked it up to get a closer look. A round, perfect pearl. She took out the card. Typed inside were the words:

Pearls hide in the ocean,
Green, like your marvelous eyes.
This is the first of many.
Follow the trail for the rest.

Reed's romantic gesture touched her deeply and she regretted every minute that would pass before he came. She'd misjudged him and would find a way to make up for it. Alicia had confirmed earlier that she was expected out on the second terrace off the salon at nine P.M. Maria laughed at herself, nervous as a schoolgirl when the hour approached.

She chose a floral silk dress, smoothed her hair into an updo and took an evening purse for the pearls. Reed was nowhere to be seen when she stepped onto the terrace flagstones. The last vestiges of the sun, already dipping below the sea, cast the sky in soft peaches and violets. Dusk slowly folded into night. Flaming braziers had been set up on the terrace. She found the next pearl sitting in the center of a single water lily floating in a round glass bowl on the table.

She tripped down the long flight of steps to a pathway illuminated by solar lamps. In the warm and humid atmosphere, the night air clung to her skin. The gravel path meandered for a way through a lush grove of trees. Here, the lights had been spaced farther apart and it was much harder to see. Every now and again a small sculpture bordered the path. These were glazed ceramics and looked Chinese. Old, probably. Perhaps they'd once stood sentry at a wealthy Chinese merchant's house and, with their frightening faces, were placed to scare away intruders. Maria took her time and scrutinized each foot of the path, determined not to miss the next pearl. She came upon a flat stone about two feet high, probably put there as a seat. On it lay three more lustrous pearls. She dropped them into her purse. The path veered away from the shoreline and angled up a slope, the trees widened out and she emerged into the meadow she imagined lay behind one of the hills she'd seen on the way in, hiding the house.

Up ahead, she saw him.

She could only make out his figure moving far in the distance. His back was turned to her.

She wanted to rush to him but stilled herself. He slowed his pace almost as if he intended to make it easy for her to follow. Perched upon a broad green leaf on the grass beside the path were the next three pearls. In the dusky light she'd almost missed them. How many more would there be? Reed disappeared over the crest of the hill. She hurried to catch up.

As she reached the top of the hill, the path thinned out to a narrow track. The stream winding through the shallow valley between the hills had been dammed to create a wide pool. The moon came out, full and bright in a star-spun sky. From her elevated position, she spotted him at the far side of the pool. He'd stripped off his clothes. Moonlight shone on his powerful back, buttocks and long legs; it turned the sprays of water silver as he dove in.

She smiled to herself and hastened to the fringe of moss and delicate ferns at the pool's edge. She slipped off her shoes, stepped out of her dress and underwear, dropped them on the ground and laid her purse on top. Reed's head and shoulders broke through the surface of the water; he heaved in a deep breath and dove under again. He seemed to be enjoying his own private moment, pretending not to notice her.

She stepped gingerly into the water, testing for depth, and immediately plunged to midthigh. A soft, spongy layer of weed cushioned her feet. She pushed off and swam with long languid strokes. The water felt like velvet against her bare skin. She reached the spot she'd last seen him surface, and then tread water, her breasts bobbing on the surface, satiny in the moonlight. Where was he?

Two strong hands gripped her waist; his body bore down behind her; his lips nipped at the nape of her neck. He reached for her nipple with one hand, and a pleasing heat spread in her belly. She felt the hairy brush of his groin as he brought his knee up between her legs. He tightened his arm around her; with his other hand he fondled her cleft.

"Did you find all your pearls?" he whispered in her ear.

It was not Reed's voice.

CHAPTER 28

Maria screamed. She lashed out at the man grasping her and twisted her body, splashing furiously in her panic to get away. It did no good. One or two powerful strokes and he had her again. He pulled her pelvis against him and she felt the stiff bone of his erection. "You don't remember me?" The moonlight fell upon his face. It was Claude Ferrer, her client from the Victorian dinner.

"Get away from me." She tried again to push away from him.

He released her. She swam as if a shark were on her tail and reached solid ground at the pool edge, found her footing, sloshed over to where she'd left her clothes. She threw on her dress, raced barefoot down the path. Despite the temperate air, she shivered, and willed herself not to cry.

He caught up to her as she reached the safety of the terrace steps. She'd stopped finally, panting at the exertion of running, and nursed her feet, hurt by the shards of gravel on the path.

"There should be some warm towels for us in that bag," he

said, pointing to a canvas gym bag near one of the French doors. He retrieved two white terry bathrobes from the bag, stripped off his wet clothes without making any effort to hide his nakedness, and wrapped the robe around him. She hesitated for a minute, then turned her back and did the same.

"Would you rather go inside?" he asked gently.

She shook her head and sat down at the table where she'd eaten dinner. He slumped in the opposite chair. Alicia had left an ice bucket with champagne and two glasses on the table.

He handed her a face towel. She wiped pond water off her face and ran her fingers through her hair to get the tangles out.

"I'm sorry," Ferrer said. "I planned what I thought would be a very romantic evening. It looks like I miscalculated."

She patted her face dry with a corner of the towel. "I'm the one who should be sorry. It *was* romantic. It's just . . . you startled me. I was expecting someone else."

"Who?"

She swallowed hard, unwilling to mention Reed's name. Her fear had subsided completely now and she felt like a fool. Shame colored her cheeks. "His name doesn't matter. It was just someone who . . ." She waved her hand around. "The pearls, the mystery—he loves drama, and it was the kind of thing he'd do. And he owns a house on the coast. I wasn't sure exactly where."

"Well, my dear, there are a good number of houses on the Rhode Island seaside, you know." It was a mild reproof. She should have known better.

"Yes, there are. I made the wrong assumption. Why did you use the Carson alias?"

"Your rules. They specified you'd spend only one night with a client. I was afraid you'd reject my request out of hand."

She looked up at him, puzzlement in her eyes. "But how . . . ? We always check clients out beforehand. Your text traced back to an IP address on the Yale servers."

He shook his head. "No idea. I have no connection with the university at all."

As he spoke, the answer came to her. She'd trusted her new guard to check the profile. He had her entire contact list. Somehow he must have mixed them up; tracing the message to Yale had been an error.

"Oh. No harm done." She made a mental note to have her client profiles checked much more carefully.

"Listen, my dear. I think it's safe to say our evening has not turned out as either of us wished. But the night is yet young. Would you like to retire upstairs for a while? And then if you're up to it, we could regroup in the small library. Alicia tells me you like it there." He tapped the bottle of champagne from the ice bucket and said, "I'd hate to drink all this by myself."

She came to her senses and gave his hand a squeeze. "That's very kind. I'm the one who made the error. I'll meet you in the library in an hour."

After a shower and a change of clothes, she felt more like herself. She was in a different frame of mind too. She readied herself, physically and mentally, to entertain Claude Ferrer. He'd paid a substantial sum for her company and she wouldn't disappoint him. She'd do her best to reward him for his efforts. That was her job, after all.

She felt embarrassed for letting her fantasies about Reed overcome her good judgment. Her interest in him had completely deflated once she realized he no longer wanted her. Irrational though she knew it was, she hated the thought of him now.

Ferrer had a fire burning in the library grate when Claudine came back downstairs. It made for a cheerful atmosphere and he'd thoughtfully turned the air-conditioning up to compensate.

He handed her a glass of champagne. She curled up beside him on the settee and they toasted their misadventure. They talked for a while; he was quite knowledgeable about the history of Newport and explained he used the house primarily as a corporate retreat.

She observed him as he talked. A fine gray gristle lined his jaw and he had small, dark eyes, a narrow face and prominent nose. He didn't look much like Reed. And he was older. Still, his height and girth were almost identical to Whitman's. He was well muscled and his stomach still flat. And he had the same languid movements as Reed. At the side of the pool in the dark, anyone could have made the same mistake.

The eight pearls she'd collected sat in splendor on the coffee table. Beside them, another row of four. "You missed them," he said, "but I'll add them to the collection anyway. And in between each will sit one of these." He opened a small drawer in the table and took out a velvet drawstring bag. Fourteen small platinum cylinders spilled out. "Twelve pearls are hardly enough to make up a necklace."

"They're stunning." Claudine reached for one of the cylinders, admiring the way the firelight glinted off it.

He bent over and kissed her cheek. "I have a favor to ask. Would you consider staying for one more night? I know it's not in keeping with your rules but I'm hoping since this evening hasn't worked out, you'll take pity on me. Of course I'll pay for the pleasure."

She could still see the faint pink line where she scratched his face. He had been cheated out of a good part of the evening through no fault of his own and the additional money was welcome. "Of course. It will be my pleasure."

Ferrer beamed and patted her knee. "I'm delighted. Now, you must be exhausted after my shenanigans tonight, my dear, let's get you up to bed."

The covers in her room had been turned down. She let the wrap slide off her. Underneath she wore a translucent nylon negligee. Like a veil over a bride's face, it gave a tantalizing hint of her rosy nipples, the creamy length of her torso and hips, her belly button and the crease between her legs. Ferrer lifted the gown up to her shoulders. "As lovely as I remembered. And tonight I don't have to share you."

He began at the dip in her throat and slowly licked his way down her breasts and belly. The feel of his tongue and breath on her skin excited her and she was wet by the time he reached her mound. He opened her, and explored her with his tongue. She moved her hips to meet his rhythm when suddenly, he pushed two fingers into her vagina, felt along the delicate rim of the condom she wore. "A very clever contraption," he murmured. "I almost missed noticing it the night of our Victorian dinner."

Ferrer stood and brushed Claudine's hair to the side, licked the delicate skin of her neck and swirled his fingers inside her. Each time he pulled his fingers out he lightly rubbed her bud, giving her spurts of pleasure.

He asked her to squat with her back against the headboard.

He moved the skin of his penis rapidly up and down to achieve a full erection and pushed inside her. She gripped his shoulders and moved in concert with him. He came in a rush between her tanned legs, growling with the strength of his orgasm. "I apologize," he said turning his eyes away from her. "I have that problem. I climax too fast. That has always been an issue with me."

She stroked his chest. "You're able to get hard again quickly—no? That compensates." She smiled and caressed his cheek.

"You're good at calming insecurities, my girl." he said, a penetrating look in his dark eyes. "We'll make up for it tomorrow."

CHAPTER 29

The benign end to their evening hadn't settled Maria's nerves. After Ferrer left, her disappointment over Reed resurfaced, making her insomnia worse than usual. Although she popped enough sleeping pills to stun a horse, they only resulted in an unsatisfying, restless doze. Sometime later a noise roused her, a loud rustling outside her window. Three hoots, followed by a sharp cry from some creature's throat. It unnerved her and she sat up. Her eiderdown and sheets were mangled from her tossing and turning. She threw them off and moved over to the window that she'd left open, thinking the fresh air might help her sleep.

A giant sycamore branch spread outside the window. In the bright moonlight she could see the flush of the sycamore's pointed leaves, the strange scales of light and dark on the bark that looked like lizard skin. An owl sat in a crotch of the branch; it had trapped a little songbird in its curved beak. The owl's head turned from right to left and then the ferocious yellow circles of its eyes stared directly at her.

Maria slammed the window shut and it flew off with a flap of its great wings. She picked up the eiderdown at the foot of her bed but found no comfort in its warmth. She finally drifted off, waking an hour later to the nightmare of the Romanian orphanage. Hock's face had vanished; this time her molester wore an owl mask. Yet the eyes staring at her were not yellow but black and glittering. The human hands reaching for her were covered with scales and in place of fingernails were sharp yellow talons.

Why could she never remember her tormentor's face? He'd only come to her at night but it was never so dark that she couldn't make out the walls and rails of her crib. Her counselor believed she'd deliberately pushed the image far into the unreachable depths of her memory. "One day, you'll remember," the counselor had said. "It won't come by trying to force it."

She stayed in bed until midmorning when Alicia brought in a breakfast tray. "Mr. Ferrer is working in the main library today. He'd prefer not to be disturbed. The small one is at your disposal, of course. He'll see you at teatime." Alicia paused. "Are you unwell?" she asked.

"No, I'm fine. I just didn't sleep well. An owl outside my window last night disturbed me."

Alicia frowned. "Odd. We rarely see owls around here. They're more common in the woods, inland."

She'd brought a delicious breakfast: an omelet filled with Brie and basil, and thin slices of buttered whole wheat toast. Maria hadn't the stomach to eat and left most of it on her plate. She laced her coffee with real cream and drank two cups before getting out of bed. She filled the tub with hot water and added foam bath, turned on the Jacuzzi jets and had a good, invigorating soak. No matter how understanding Ferrer had been, she wanted desperately to go home and lick the wounds that her misreading of Reed caused.

There'd been no further messages from him. He'd truly given up on her. Perhaps that was all to the good. It wasn't likely Reed would ever be able to let go of his prejudices about her past, even if she gave it up to be with him.

At the bottom of her heart she'd always suspected love would pass her by. The happy dream of a loving husband had been spoiled by too many clients wanting escorts younger than their own daughters, serial wife cheaters and fiancés booking a final fling before the wedding. Once, a client had phoned his intended to discuss their upcoming nuptials. The man cooed to his fiancée while sitting on the hotel bed, his penis stiff, stroking her naked sex.

Claudine dried her hair and tried to make it look presentable, but it was a far cry from Lillian's efforts. Alicia had hung her dresses up in the closet. She riffled through them, unhappy with the choices. Exasperated, she chose a navy outfit. She picked up the earrings Andrei had given her long ago when they first began to work together, hesitated about whether to put them on, but concluded she should and felt comforted. She poured a third cup of coffee, grabbed her tablet and went to the small library to read.

Her mind wandered. She kept thinking about the last poem she'd received from Hock. Something about it bothered her.

Not the allusion to the man in the iron mask, although his foreknowledge of her itinerary was troubling enough. Nor was it the death threat. It was something she hadn't paid enough heed to at the time. Suddenly, she had it. Lani, the boy she'd shared a cot with when she first came to the orphanage. Her adoptive mother hadn't known Lani's name because the boy died before Jewel visited the orphanage. Therefore she couldn't have passed that information on to her neighbor, Charles Hock. Hock hadn't written the second poem. Someone else had.

A tap at the door distracted her. It opened before she could answer and Ferrer entered. "This seems to be your home away from home," he joked. "Alicia tells me you've closeted yourself here most of the afternoon."

Claudine shut off her tablet and stood up, smoothing her dress with her hands.

Ferrer frowned. "Navy doesn't suit you, my dear. It's too severe.

"Shall I change, then?" she asked good-humoredly.

"Of course not. Soon enough the dress will be off you anyway." He winked and took her hand. "Let's go for a walk. I've asked for an early dinner so we can make the most of our evening."

"That sounds lovely. I was thinking. Once you feel we've . . . finished for the evening, I'd like to return to the city. It's been a marvelous treat staying here, but I have an important appointment early tomorrow morning."

"By all means. You've been good enough to grant me the extra day."

"I'll just call my driver to make arrangements."

Ferrer took her arm. "No need for that, my dear. Victor will escort you back."

She left her cell phone and tablet on the table and accompanied him to the salon, out onto the terrace and along the path they'd taken last night. Instead of following the route to the pool, he veered onto another trail running through the grove of trees. They soon came upon a round stone building roofed with a dome. Graceful Corinthian pillars circled the building.

"The original owner built this summerhouse," Ferrer explained. "Legend has it he hosted incredible debaucheries and used this place as a kind of Dionysian retreat. It was a temple, open to the air. Later he added the stonework you can see between the pillars, leaving only that wooden door. A woman died during one his revelries and he never used it again. He blocked it up and abandoned it."

She shivered. The tall trees surrounding it ensured the building lay in perpetual shadow; she'd already sensed malevolence about the place. The path ended at the shoreline where the surf jetted plumes of spray. They talked amiably about not much in particular, then turned around and retraced their steps.

"I saw a garden from the library," she said. "I imagine it would be especially beautiful this late in the afternoon—may we walk through it?"

"Certainly. I'm glad to show it off."

The garden was protected by a high stone wall. As they neared it, she heard the twittering of birds again. "The birds are attracted to the scent of the fruit, I imagine?"

"In a manner of speaking," Ferrer replied as he opened an iron gate fixed into the garden wall. They entered a small orchard. He let her through and the gate clanged shut after him. The fruit trees were gnarled and overgrown and gave off a strong, cloying odor.

"What kind are they?" Yesterday she'd thought she'd seen orange and red fruit hanging from the branches and assumed they were varieties of sweet and sour cherries.

"Mostly peaches and pears, some apples."

"It's too early for those to be ripe—no?"

"Most of them—yes." Ferrer said.

His answer puzzled her. What were the colors she saw, then? A ladder leaned against one of the trees farther off and she could make out Victor balanced upon it, a basket propped on one of the ladder steps, picking what must have been the early pears. White dots of bird excrement littered the sparse grassy ground. The lower leafy canopies seemed alive with fluttering birds. She craned her neck, trying to catch sight of them.

"How beautiful," she was on the point of saying when it dawned on her what she was looking at. Dozens of songbirds—robins, chickadees, goldfinches—hung upside down from the branches by their spindly legs, twisting, trembling and flapping their wings in a frenzy to get free.

She understood now what Victor was dropping into his basket. Dead birds. After he gathered them, Victor would pluck and gut them, throwing the leavings—organs and entrails—onto the ground.

She swung around to face Ferrer. "What in God's name are you doing here? This is terrible!"

"They feel nothing," he said flatly. "Victor slits their throats quickly and efficiently."

Her breath stopped. Ferrer went on as if his words had no effect on her. "It's an old Cypriot custom. From my homeland. We paint the tree branches with a lime-scented syrup. The bird's legs stick to it. They can't get away. It's a perfect time to harvest them while they're trying to fatten up over summer. They're a delicacy in most Mediterranean countries. We make a tasty dish with them called Ambelopoulia." He acknowledged the look of horror on her face. "You seemed to like it well enough."

"What are you talking about?"

"Alicia served it to you for supper last night."

Her throat convulsed. "She said it was quail."

"Ah," he chuckled. "Perhaps she thought you'd be sensitive about it. You see, my dear, if it *had* been quail—how is that any better? They're dear little birds too. Frankly, I don't see much difference."

"I'm going in. I don't want to stay here any longer."

He took her arm again. This time, the pressure of his hand was a little too hard. "We can enter the house through here," he said. "Dinner should be laid out by now."

Eating was the last thing she wanted to do. "I'm afraid I'm not very hungry." She changed the subject. "You know, I thought you were American. You don't have any trace of an accent."

"The very first thing I did when I came here was to work like hell to erase it. I hired a voice coach. I wanted to fit in."

When they reached the small library, a fire had been set in the grate, the terrace table brought inside and placed in front of the fire. Dinner and drinks were already laid out. Red wine, rare roast beef with fries and fresh garden vegetables. It would have been appetizing if her stomach wasn't still lurching from the sight in the orchard. Her gaze fell upon the desk. "Where's my tablet and cell phone?"

"Quite safe and sound. Alicia removed them to your room before she left."

"She's not here?" She felt a flicker of panic in her gut.

"It's her night off."

"Let's sit down, then. My appetite is back." The lie slipped easily from her lips; she wanted to get the evening over with as soon as possible. She tried to make small talk. "Tell me about Cyprus."

A hint of irritation showed in his features, which he quickly covered up. "Even though I spent my childhood there, my memories of it are not happy ones. I grew up under the thumb of a tyrant, my father. If you don't mind, I prefer not to spoil our evening by recalling those days." He uncorked the wine and poured each of them a glass. "To my beauty," he said, holding up his glass. She took a couple of hearty swallows to steady her nerves.

"You look under the weather today, my girl. Alicia said you spent a restless night."

"Yes, I did," she admitted. "Because of a nightmare. A recurring nightmare I've had since my childhood."

"Did that occur because of some dreadful experience when you were young? Some form of abuse? Sadly it's common enough."

Her fingers worried the scar on her wrist. How strange that he would pinpoint the reason so accurately. Her vision seemed to grow foggy momentarily; she blinked to clear it.

Ferrer spoke before she had a chance to reply. "Your reluctance to talk about it confirms my thoughts. I suspect abuse *was* involved. Most people would think such acts absolutely vile. That would be the predictable view. And yet perhaps you reached the wrong conclusion. It might help to come to terms with it if you saw it from a different perspective."

"What do you mean?"

His face grew serious. "You're a beautiful woman and no doubt were an adorable child. A little blond angel. Isn't that why your adoptive mother chose you out of all those other dismal children?"

"How did you . . ."

"Perhaps the man involved loved you. You only see the harm because you don't have the full picture. You have no idea what his feelings were."

"When did you find out about me? Who told you?"

He smiled sympathetically. "The past is not so easily hidden my dear. What do you recall about that man?"

She had difficulty forming her next words. "Only his terrible eyes."

"There may be an explanation for that. He wore a surgical mask. He had to. Tuberculosis was rife among the children."

The years fell away. She stared at his black eyes, and remembered. Her stomach convulsed in fear. The man who offered her pearl necklaces, who chatted about Newport history, whose fingers had probed her most private parts—was her torturer. Her gaze fell on his wineglass. He hadn't tasted so much as a drop.

Her chair tipped over as she lurched to her feet. She grabbed her glass by the stem. The remnants of her wine spattered the white tablecloth like drops of blood. She smashed the rim.

Her reaction caught him by surprise. He'd only half risen when she came at him with the spear of glass. He threw his hands up and the shard sliced the fleshy base of his thumb. She jabbed again and cut into his upper arm. He swore and grabbed a napkin to staunch the welling blood.

She ran for the door.

She'd almost reached it when her legs turned to sponge and she fell heavily to the floor. Her heart felt tight; her lips numb. She tried to crawl on her hands and knees but only moved a few inches before she flopped on her stomach. Ferrer stood over her. She craned her neck; gaped at him. His figure seemed to enlarge and then blend slowly with all the other objects in the room into wavering strands of color. The color modified, became one flat screen of gray. He said something to her. She had no idea what the sounds meant.

CHAPTER 30

Maria felt as though she were being carried through water in slow motion. She thought she heard doors opening and shutting, had a sense of descending. She entered a sphere of bright white light. She wondered idly whether she'd died and this was the entrance to heaven.

She was much closer to hell. Her arms and legs were jerked roughly away from her sides, her hands and feet tethered to some structure that kept her upright, with her toes barely touching the floor. It took all her strength to raise her head. She heard heavy footsteps receding; a door bang closed.

Her stomach cramped as the drug wore off, scorching her throat with wine and bile. Hardened leather straps bit at her wrists and ankles as she tried to twist away from them. When her vision cleared and she could focus better, she saw a tiled floor and windowless walls. Another apparatus sat directly in her line of vision; a scaffold with diagonal braces called a Saint

Augustine's cross; chains and straps hung from it. Beside it an assortment of sexual aids, a variety of dildos, anal balls, harnesses and rings lay on a counter. Placed near a sink was a trolley with a groove running around its circumference, reminding her of the morgue tables she'd seen on TV. Piled in one corner on the counter were her tablet, bag and suitcase. Ferrer had removed all evidence to show she'd ever been upstairs.

She tried to scream. It came out more like a croak. Her legs were so tightly bound she could only shift them a few inches, and she realized her dress was ripped along the side seam to the waist in order to allow her legs to be pried apart. From somewhere behind her she heard a key turning in the lock. She let her head droop again and feigned unconsciousness.

"She's still out." Victor's voice.

"Shouldn't be," Ferrer replied. "Get the needle and stick it in her pubis; that will rouse her."

Maria opened her eyes. Ferrer stood before her naked and smiling. He wore only boots. A crude bandage was wrapped around his hand and upper arm.

He dropped something metallic on the counter and walked closer to her. "Ah," Ferrer said. "I presumed you were faking. You're good at that sort of thing, aren't you?"

"Where am I?" Her speech was slurred a little from the drug.

"Still in Newport. I must confess to a little lie. The original owner who built the summerhouse I showed you earlier did not cease his orgies. He took them underground. My establishment here is a kind of gentlemen's club for men who seek clandestine pleasures and require complete discretion. They are connoisseurs of sexuality. Little is forbidden these days, but some practices still require secrecy. I make a fine bit of money off their proclivities. Not very much different from your source of income."

"I don't hurt people."

"If there's hurt, as you call it, only the lewd and immoral need fear it. Degraded women who have only themselves to blame."

"Like me, you mean?" She stared at him defiantly.

"Yes, my dear, exactly like you."

"How did you find me after all these years?"

"When I came to this country eighteen years ago, I tried to find you but I didn't know your adoptive mother's surname—your adoption records were sealed. At Siret you were listed simply as Maria, so neither did I know your birth name, Lantos. It was only when one of the members of our club befriended his next-door neighbor that I learned where you were and what had become of you."

Maria shivered with fear. Keep him talking and distracted, she thought. Try to buy some time. "You mean Charles Hock. He's sitting in jail now for assault and first-degree murder."

Ferrer laughed. "Oh yes! The *other* Romanian prostitute. Her resemblance to you was remarkable. When he brought her here we had a delightful time. Hock is a man of awful appetites; but that just makes him easy to manipulate. He was quite willing to do anything I asked. All he demanded in return was a tiny taste of the infamous Claudine he'd heard so much about. How could I deny him that? Now the police have him in custody and I'm not even on their radar. It's ended very well, I think."

"And what makes you believe he hasn't told the police about your dungeon here? Tried to bargain with them? That's the first thing I'd do."

Ferrer pulled up a high stool and dragged it toward her. He stopped about five feet away and perched on it. His flaccid penis drooped between his thighs. "He has two daughters, one at Cornell, the other at Berkeley. Apparently he does have some redeeming features, because he places a higher value on their lives than revealing anything about me or our club."

"And how did you escape having any redeeming features at all?"

He chuckled. "My girl, the time for idle talk is over. You were kind enough to stay for an additional evening. It's wasting away. Victor wants a sample before I send him upstairs. You see, I'm not so far gone that I'm not willing to share."

Maria retched at the thought of Victor's fat fingers touching her. She twisted her right wrist, made her hand as narrow as possible to see if she could wriggle out of the bindings. The bonds held firm.

"There's no point in squirming. It's not attractive." Ferrer looked past her and beckoned with a crooked finger.

She could hear Victor approach her from behind: the slap of his bare feet on the tile, and the sound of his fat thighs rubbing together as he waddled toward her. He yanked her dress up to her shoulders. A cold blade brushed her hip. Victor used shears to cut through one leg of her panties, then yanked the tattered briefs down to her ankle. Ferrer's eyes glittered at the sight.

Victor's fingers, plush like sausages, examined every inch of her, every hollow, every orifice. His tongue followed the trail of his fingers. She shuddered every time his fingers and mouth touched her skin.

He moved around to her front. She spit in his face. Ferrer laughed at her feeble attempt to defend herself. Victor rubbed his face on her stomach to wipe the spit off. He sucked first one, then the other nipple. She tried to twist her body away, but that only excited him more. He raised his head and sucked the flesh underneath her jaw, leaving an angry red mark on her skin.

He opened his mouth to flick his red tongue over her lips. Maria kept her lips firmly closed, and wrenched her head sideways. She bit the top of his ear. He shook his head like a wet dog and yelled. She clamped down even harder and tasted blood. He plowed his fist into her stomach. Her belly crumpled with the pain. Maria shrieked; it felt as though something had broken inside her.

"That's enough, Victor; you've had your taste. Give us some privacy now."

When the door closed behind Victor, Ferrer continued: "I'd have left you alone, you know, if only I'd discovered that my little angel had grown to become an honest woman. Married perhaps, with children to her credit. Not a whore."

"Get your disgusting carcass away from me!" She panted in an effort to recover her breath after the blow.

"You find me repugnant, my dear, but surely you've endured others you don't care for. I understand you'll take anyone. You only have one measure for your partners—dollar bills."

He selected one of the glass dildos with wicked-looking spines and ridges that was lying on the counter. He kicked away the stool and approached her, gripping her neck and jaw with his left hand, pressing them painfully to the side. She struggled for air. It felt as though he was crushing her windpipe.

With his right hand he shoved his fore and middle fingers into her anus. The delicate tissue burned. Maria tried furiously to shake him off but the restraints held her fast. Ferrer took his hand from her neck and, grasping the glass dildo, stuck it into her slit, roughly pushing it all the way up. Her belly, still aching from the blow, spasmed.

"You're a pig. A pedophile."

He ignored her taunts. Instead, he focused on her reaction to the molestation with the dildo; it made him hard. "It's my desire to relive the memory of our early encounters. I was your first, Maria. Nothing matched your purity. And I shall be your last as well. Alpha and Omega, an act of perfect harmony."

Maria's heart seized. She knew perfectly well what he meant. She would die in this room. One slight hope remained. She fought through her panic and tried to concentrate. "This isn't how it was at all. You were masked so I couldn't see your face. Just your eyes. You're old. You're getting senile and your memory's failing you."

The flush in his face told her that her words had bruised him. She was desperate to shake him up, keep him off-kilter.

"Well, we shall have to make do with less than perfect circumstances, won't we?"

She tried one more time. "I had only one hand tied to the crib, not two, and nothing on. They'd taken my clothes away from me."

"We can easily rectify that." Ferrer scooped up the shears from the mat where Victor had dropped them and cut off the rest of her dress, letting it and the scissors fall back to the mat. He undid the buckle securing her right hand to the leather bond. She shook it furiously to regain some feeling.

"It couldn't be you want that hand free to do some damage to me?" he said. "How transparent your thoughts are." He gripped her lower arm and squeezed. Maria clenched her teeth, tried to mentally move away from the blazing pain. A fine bone snapped. A fire roared up her arm and she screamed. She was barely able to see for the stars of pain in her eyes.

"I am not too old to forget that we loved," he said.

"It was torture, not love."

"And one last touch." He picked up the scissors, walked over to the counter behind the trolley, opened a drawer, extracted a roll of gauze and cut off a long length. He returned to her side and began wrapping it around her head to bind her mouth. "I fear those teeth," he said.

He bent his head and caught her breast in his mouth, rubbed himself up against her sex, his breath becoming jerky with his arousal.

It took a supreme effort of will to raise her hand. Tears coursed down her face as the grating edges of broken bone sent out a volley of hurt with every move. She tried to flex her fingers and found she could. Another agonizing jolt of pain hit her as she forced her hand higher, praying that Ferrer, so intent on molesting her, would not notice. With great effort, she pinched her earring, slipped it from her earlobe and, using her index finger, loosed the tiny clasp to extend the thin gold shaft it concealed.

When Ferrer began to force himself inside her, she urinated on him. "You bitch," he swore, jerking his head up to glare at her. For an instant, as he tilted his head back to glare at her, his neck was fully exposed. She plunged the needle point of the gold shaft into the throbbing vein at his throat. The earring dangled absurdly from his neck.

His brittle eyes turned black with shock. He put a hand up to his throat, took it away and stared at the smears of blood on his fingertips. "What did you do?"

She whimpered beneath the gauze. "Paid you back."

She didn't know whether the words registered in his brain, for his blood had already carried the drug to every organ, infiltrating every cell like a hidden enemy. He crumpled to the floor.

With waning strength she managed to free her good hand. She used it to release the leather straps binding her ankles and rip off the gauze binding her mouth. Ferrer had collapsed on top of her torn dress. She kicked him over and pulled the garment away, wrapped it around her as best she could, swept her shoes up from where they'd fallen. She pulled the earring from his neck and folded it inside the crumpled gauze, then ran to get her cell phone from her bag. She frantically punched in 911 and swore when she saw there was no connection. She threw her cell phone and tablet into her bag, grabbed the shears. Not a very effective weapon but all she had. She yanked the door handle and almost cried in frustration. It was locked.

CHAPTER 31

Maria glanced around the room wildly. She recalled Ferrer stopping near the counter when he came in for the second time. He'd put his keys down. She rushed over and snatched them up. Her entire body quaked at the thought that Victor might walk in at any moment. She had no defense this time. When they first began working together, Andrei had given the earring to her as a final fail-safe if her life was ever in danger. The tiny spear on her earring carried only one lethal dose; it couldn't be used again.

She cracked the door open and braced herself, listening for the sound of Victor's heavy tread. Nothing. A staircase spiraled up to her right, likely leading to the summerhouse. Straight ahead stretched a stone-walled passageway that she guessed went back to the main house. She chose the stairs. The wood surrounding the summerhouse would offer her good cover and protection.

At the top of the stairs she entered a room with a slippery wooden floor. The light from the chamber downstairs was so weak here she could only just make out the round shape of the room. She worked her way around the circumference of the wall, feeling for the door. It smelled of mold and was slimy to the touch. In the silence she heard the staccato beating of her heart. Her fingers brushed a frame. She hadn't remembered any padlock on the outside and when she groped along the vertical edge of the door, her hand touched metal. Ferrer had at least ten keys on the ring. She felt for the keyhole and began testing keys.

Footsteps sounded in the passageway below. Victor returning. She listened to him enter the chamber where Ferrer lay, pause and rush out of the room. He halted at the bottom of the stairs. She held her breath. The ring of his footsteps sounded on the iron steps and her heart plummeted. In seconds his large body blocked the entrance to the round room, plunging the space into greater darkness. She sensed him hesitate, heard him sniff the air like a predator. As quietly as possible, and holding her breath she tried the keys again. After the third painstaking attempt, the lock snapped open. Victor lunged at the sound. Using her full body weight she threw herself against the door and forced it open. She ran outside, slammed it shut, heard the lock click back into place and stumbled toward the trees.

Victor used his body as a battering ram to split the door. From the sound of the blows, it wouldn't take him long. She melted into the cover of the trees. Ocean waves crashed ashore in the distance. The sound would serve as a guide to take her to the beach, where she could walk to the nearest residence.

After she made it about fifty feet into the grove, she heard the summerhouse door burst open. She didn't look back. The wood here was dense enough that she couldn't avoid making noise as she pushed her way through. Maria quickly dropped down into the bracken, stifling a cry when her broken arm brushed against a mossy log. She inched underneath a fir tree; its lower branches sweeping to the ground screened her body. She lay there, breathless with fear.

After a while, she eased herself out from underneath the fir, her stomach and arm protesting with every movement. She made her way through the wood and stopped where the grove gave way to meadow grass. On the rise of one of the hills she could see Victor's hulking silhouette, black against the night sky. He was using the higher elevation to try to spot her.

After a short time his figure disappeared behind the hill. She prayed he was giving up the chase and going home. She sat down gingerly, whimpering with the pain, and searched through her bag for her phone. When the screen lit up and showed a connection, a giant sigh of relief escaped her lips.

Without stopping to think, she called Andrei. His sleepy voice came on the line and she remembered he was in the Caribbean somewhere, much too far to help even if he was willing to.

"It's me," she said, her words tumbling out. "Where are you?"

"Home."

"In Brighton Beach?" Her heart leaped.

"Yeah. It's almost three in the morning. What's going on?"

"Andrei. You've got to come and get me. Claude Ferrer tried to murder me. We were wrong about Hock. It was Ferrer all along." She broke down and sobbed.

"Ferrer? Get ahold of yourself. Just calm down and listen to me. Call the police *right* now, Maria."

She swallowed in an effort to stop crying. "I can't."

"Why?"

"Because I killed him. It's a total disaster, Andrei. You've *got* to come."

"Where are you?"

"In Newport. I can't remember the address. It's on the coast road. I'd have to cut off our call to check it on my e-mail and I'm afraid to. I might lose the connection again. You remember the password to my business e-mail?"

"Of course. It hasn't been that long."

"The address is on there. The invitation was for one night at his Newport estate. He gave the name of Lawrence . . . Lawrence . . . God. I can't remember it. It wasn't his real name."

"Listen to me. You're not thinking straight. It will take me more than two hours to get there. You have to call the police."

"No! I want you to come. Andrei, I'm out here in the middle of the night, my arm's broken, it hurts so much, I . . ." she moaned and cried again. "There's another man, named Victor. He's looking for me. He's going to hurt me."

"All right. All right, I'll get there. I'll find the address. Are you still in that house?"

"I'm outside. But I think I'm still on the estate." She looked over at the neighboring home in the distance. "There's a place right beside the one I was in on the road that runs along the ocean. It's white; it has pillars I think and lions out front. That's all I can recall. I'll go there and get help."

"Okay. I'm leaving now."

"Andrei? There's something else."

"What?"

She ceased speaking for a minute, overcome by the sight of blackbirds, unaware they were simply a product of her delirium.

"Andrei," she said, "there are so many blackbirds here you wouldn't believe it. They're roosting in all the trees around me, making so much noise I can hardly hear. I can't get away from them."

Andrei's voice was tight, though she could tell he was trying to keep it calm. "Get to that house. Do it right now."

Maria left the shelter of the trees and reached a fence she couldn't cross without using both her hands. She'd have to dip down to the beach. Her arm was hot with pain; her hand had no feeling left. Her belly ached and felt bloated where Victor had punched her. Her breaths were short, and little pains stabbed her when she inhaled. She touched her stomach. It was hard and swollen. She wondered vaguely whether she could be bleeding inside. But the worst were the birds. When she left the wood they flew off in one vast black cloud. There must be thousands of them, she thought as they hovered over her. They followed her every step with their strange chittering and clacking cries.

She dragged herself up the last slope to the white colonial, every step of the way she felt on the point of fainting. A dense cedar hedge surrounded the house. She couldn't see any lights. That didn't surprise her given the late hour. She circled around the hedge to the front drive, struggled up to the door and leaned on the doorbell. Waited. No one came. She tried a few more times with the same result. She pounded on the door, weeping with frustration.

She found the small gatehouse beside the two mammoth stone entrance pillars about thirty feet from the road. It was locked. She sank down on the damp grass beside it, sat with her back propped up against its wall. She drifted off, then snapped her head up as the flock of blackbirds settled on the ground and spread around her. The birds seemed to vanish and then magically reappear. Each time they descended near her, she squeezed her eyes shut.

While he drove, Andrei frantically searched for the text Maria described but could find nothing on either her personal or business mail. He pushed the BMW to 130 mph on I-95, praying radar wouldn't catch him. He called the Newport police, told them his friend was gravely injured and delirious. He gave them the description of the pillars and lions she mentioned. They said they'd send a car along Ocean Avenue but without better directions held out little hope of locating her.

He drove the length of Ocean Avenue and had to double back again. He found her just after five thirty A.M. She'd fallen, unconscious, over her bag, one arm crooked awkwardly under her head, the strands of her hair, gold in the early dawn, hiding her face.

Andrei left the car door open and the motor running. He lifted Maria gently and put her on the seat beside him. Her dress barely covered her, and he tucked his jacket around her. When he got behind the wheel he cradled her head and shoulders on his lap. He kept one hand on the wheel and the other on the soft part of her cheek where her skin was still warm. A breeze had sprung up. He left the window open to feel the cool air on his face and tore down the road.

CHAPTER 32

Maria spent a week in intensive care at Newport Hospital. Victor's blow broke a vein in her abdomen and caused a life-threatening hemorrhage. Her only memories during that time were of Andrei's and Lillian's faces. They seemed to come and go, magnify and fade, dreamlike. Once, when a doctor wearing a face mask leaned over her, she became hysterical. After transferring to the Columbia University Medical Center in New York, where her own doctor could see her, she'd improved enough to breathe on her own and take a few halting steps.

One morning, after the nurse had finished checking Maria's stats and doling out her medication, Jewel walked into the room. She carried a mammoth bouquet of lilacs in a vase. She placed it on the windowsill, then settled into the bedside chair uneasily. The floral scent immediately swelled through the room. "How are you doing, Marie?"

She tried to swallow her shock. "I'll live. So they tell me," she said, her voice weak.

"Well, thank heavens. I've been so worried about you. I thought perhaps . . . it might be better for me not to intrude. But Milne insisted."

"I'm glad he did. Thanks for the flowers. They're lovely."

Jewel waved her hand. "Just a token. I thought they'd cheer you up." An uncomfortable silence followed. Jewel tried to fill it. "You and I haven't had the easiest time. I am not one to make a display of my emotions, but I wanted to tell you that when I took you into my home, I was very happy. I . . . loved my little girl."

Maria stared at the tears forming in Jewel's eyes. Jewel quickly took a tissue from her purse and blotted them away, gave her head a shake and sighed. "I don't know how things got so off track between us. I'm sorry, Marie, for the way things turned out."

"Me as well," she said. "I'm happy you told me." Jewel was sitting close enough that Maria could reach over and touch her hand. "Sometimes two different natures just collide."

They chatted for another ten minutes about Maria's studies, Jewel's charity work—safe topics. A fragile bridge had been constructed and both of them were cautious about testing it too much. Jewel did not linger and soon left her alone to rest.

Around noon, Detective Trainor arrived. He came alone, without da Silva. He leaned against the wall and gave her a nod. "You've had a rough time of it," he said.

"We agree on that," she replied hoarsely and put her hand to her neck. "I'm sorry. I can barely talk. They intubated me."

"I'll go easy on you, then."

She detected a surprising glimmer of a smile.

"Just nod or shake your head if you want. Can you write? Use a keyboard?"

"Yes. Although even that tires me out."

"Well, do your best. You have a tablet or a laptop or something?"

"Yes."

"Good. As soon as possible, I want you to write as full a statement about the attack on you as you can. Every detail about what occurred in Newport. Include anything you remember Ferrer or his staff saying during your stay there. Send it to me as an e-mail attachment. When you're back on your feet, we'll have you come into the precinct office to witness the report and add anything more you can think of. We're working with the Newport police and the FBI on this." He dug into his pocket, pulled out his card and set it on the bedside table. "My e-mail address is on that."

"Okay. What about Victor? Did you find him?"

He shook his head. "No sign of him. He's probably left the state."

"And Alicia?"

"She claims she knew nothing of what went on. Said she was only domestic help."

"She's lying."

Trainor raised his big shoulders and let them drop again. "We can't prove any differently. She wasn't present during the attack—correct?"

"No."

Trainor glanced around the room. His eyes came back to hers. "Charles Hock's attorney urged him to cooperate with us. Hock maintains that all of this—the threats, the stalking—was just a game Ferrer created to scare you. He explained that Ferrer was obsessed with you. That when Hock told him what you do for a living, Ferrer lost it. Hock says that he doesn't know anything about the Romanian prostitute's murder. We don't believe him. We found his DNA under her fingernails. We've confirmed he was the man who followed you to San Francisco and broke into your hotel room. Because their crimes crossed state lines, the FBI are involved. They've agreed to let us wrap the case up in cooperation with the Newport police."

Maria grew paler; the shadows underneath her eyes, dark as bruises, seemed to deepen.

"I won't be much longer," he said hastily. "The FBI medical examiner tells me a pretty vicious chemical cocktail killed Ferrer. Where did you get it from?"

She'd anticipated the question and had already put some thought into what she'd say. "Ferrer had it in a syringe. He was going to use it to kill me after he raped me. He'd untied my right hand. I saw which pocket he put the needle in. I pulled it out and jabbed it into him." She held her breath, hoping he'd believe her.

"You did all that without his noticing? With a broken arm?"

"I managed." She paused and swallowed. "His mind was on other things."

"What did you do with the syringe?"

"I was afraid Victor would come back and try to use it on me so I took it. I threw it away when I ran through the woods."

She could tell from his expression he doubted her explanation, but he let it go. "You won't be charged with murder. The DA agrees it was clearly self-defense."

She waited, expecting to hear the other penny drop. That she'd be charged with criminal solicitation and prostitution. He shifted his shoulders as though his jacket was uncomfortable. "Because Ferrer carried out a sexual crime, as the victim, your name won't be released to the media."

Tears sprang to her eyes. "Thank you." She would have kissed him if she'd been able to.

He started to leave, then hesitated and said, "One other thing. A word to the wise. You're in the wrong business, Maria. I hope that's apparent to you now."

She had one more visitor that day, late in the afternoon. Andrei stepped into the room quietly. She noticed his look of surprise and imagined he barely recognized her without the jumble of catheters, tubes and wires. Now only a single IV trailed from her arm.

He eased his lanky frame into the hospital chair. "How are things going?"

Maria didn't smile in welcome, only raised her heavy lids, her eyes dull and flat from all the drugs saturating her system. "I've felt better."

"Are you okay to talk?"

She tried to sit up. "Can you put a pillow behind my back? It's hard for me to speak lying down."

Andrei supported her back while he tucked a pillow behind it. His hands were gentle, different from the nurse's efficient but brusque motions. "Do you remember anything?" he asked.

"I remember you. We were on our way home. You were driving so fast. Even faster than you usually do. My head was in your lap and I didn't know why."

"I had to speed. It was touch and go."

"I know that now. Thank you."

"Is there anything I can do for you?"

She raised her hand as if to wave his question away. "I'm being well looked after here." Her words masked the way she really felt. Any hint of the way she used to be, her old sparkle, the sly way she had sometimes of smiling, had totally vanished. She struggled to fill the silence. "How's Tramp?"

"He's great. He told me he misses you."

She closed her eyes for a second and then said, "Could you get me a drink? The water carafe is on the stand there."

Andrei poured some water into a glass. Her hand shook as she reached out for it. "Do you want me to hold it for you?"

"I can manage. Just give it to me."

He sat back down. "Are you up to hearing how it all turned out?"

She drank and held the glass out for him to take. "I know some of it. Trainor came to see me a few hours ago. He's not going to charge me with anything."

"They haven't got the DNA results back yet but suspicions are high that chamber links to a couple of killings, including the Romanian girl's. My police contact told me they found no membership lists for Ferrer's 'club,' though. He hid that very well."

He looked weary, Maria thought. He was no longer limping but the mark on his face hadn't fully healed. "I really screwed up," he admitted.

"How so?" She shifted uncomfortably, pulled the blanket closer around her.

"You have to understand. I wanted to kill Hock after what he did to you in Queens. Had to hold myself back. I threatened him—way too hard. It wasn't strategic. He spewed out what he thought I wanted to hear. Had he told us the truth about Ferrer, you wouldn't be lying there right now."

"It's too late for regrets," she said expressionlessly. "You did what you had to do."

Andrei shrugged. "Hock did San Francisco, including planting that toxic chemical that burned Lillian's hand; Ferrer rented the black boat in Cannes. Ferrer was the architect of the whole thing. He had enough money to hire the best and used hackers to send the texts and plant them on Hock's phone. None of the messages you got could be traced back to him, including the invitation to his Newport house. He wiped that off your phone. But I was able to find out something."

"What?"

"Ferrer grew up in a Greek Cypriot family. Dad ran a private investment bank, mostly to hide illicit funds for foreign politicians and businesses. That's how he came to know Ceausescu. His father sent him to Romania to assist Ceausescu with getting money out of the country. They became fast friends."

"How old would he have been then?"

"Early twenties. In those days, it was easy for him to indulge his passion for young females with no consequences. When his father died, he left for America with the family fortune, and invented a whole new life for himself."

Andrei met her gaze and for a moment Maria felt a softness for him. It quickly vanished and she let her head fall back on the pillow. "Have you decided what you'll be doing next?" She asked this again in a disinterested voice, the way someone would fill in the gaps in an awkward conversation with a stranger.

He rose from the chair. "I'm moving to Los Angeles. A friend runs a cosmetics import company. I'll be helping her to set up a branch out there." He made a halfhearted effort to smile.

"That's good. You never did like our East Coast winters."

He took a few steps toward the door. "I should be on my way. Don't want to tire you out. What will you do when you get out of here? Carry on with the business?"

"I have a plan," she said.

"I'm glad to hear that. It'll help you to get well faster. If you have a goal, I mean."

"Yes. I don't have much to do here, day after day. So I've been thinking about little else."

"I'm sure it will work out fine once you regain your strength."

"Oh, it will."

"What is it, then?"

"My plan? To disappear. One day someone will try to call, or book an appointment. But they'll be too late, because I'll be long gone." Her voice was faint. "Andrei?"

"What?" He stopped on the threshold of the door but didn't turn around.

"I know you hoped things would turn out differently between us. It wouldn't have worked. I was never what you needed."

He gave the merest hint of a nod, straightened his shoulders and walked away.

CHAPTER 33

Maria left New York in the waning days of August. Although the sun shone steadily, the winds already carried a hint of autumn chill and the light was slowly dying. She wrote Jewel a hasty note to say she'd be going away for some time, stowed her jewelry and other valuables in secure storage and took nothing more than a carry-on bag for the plane. All her clothes, costumes, racks of shoes went to charity. She told her Realtor to list her place at under market value. It sold in one day. A portion of the money went to Lillian, who'd decided to go back to school. They hugged each other good-bye and promised to keep in touch.

Maria grieved for Claudine and the life she'd led. She didn't try to push those emotions into the background; she'd been numb for far too long. She experienced the sadness of that life ending, acutely. She'd never felt shame over her profession. Most of the time, it had been glamorous, exhilarating and fun. But she was no longer that person.

Before she left New York, she ran into Reed Whitman when she went to Yale to sign some forms. He gave her a collegial pat on the shoulder as if she'd been nothing more than an acquaintance. "I've missed you around here," he said brightly, "although I'm glad our paths crossed. Where have you been hiding?"

Maria was suddenly aware of the wide gap in their ages. He looked much older than she remembered. And the insipid smile he'd plastered on was patently false. *In a very dark place*, she was tempted to answer. Instead she said, "An urgent family matter came up—totally unexpected."

"Sorry to hear that. Everything all right, I hope?"

"Yes. It worked out okay in the end."

She tried to walk on but he reached for her arm. "Look. I realize there were a few loose ends we neglected to tie up." His face flushed a little. "You wanted me to mentor you, give you some assistance to get ahead around here."

"*You* offered to help me, you mean," she said with a pointed stare.

"Well, I've given it some thought and I made a mistake by continuing to pursue you after we quarreled at the theater. Even though I'm not supervising you in any way, under the circumstances, it's best we let things drop. Since we had a relationship of sorts, I'm concerned about appearances. It's a small world around here. What others think they know can sometimes do more damage than the truth. I wouldn't want to do anything to hold you back."

She grinned. "I know exactly what you mean, Reed, and I'm glad you brought this up. In this small world, you're regarded as a two-bit jerk who hits on women. A guy who's way past his prime. People laugh about it. Being associated with you would have been a bad move for me."

Maria was an emotional refugee. One without a home or destination. One who wanted only to drift like a corked bottle, blown about by the sea. She had no ambition, no passion and no desire. She went first to Paris, a place close to her heart. The moody autumn atmosphere suited her frame of mind. She spent eight weeks there; found a small, inexpensive, family-run hotel, watched television, lay awake at night, thinking of nothing, listening to the sounds of traffic outside and the steady beat of her heart. She slept most of the day. When she did venture out, it was always late in the evening. She walked for hours until her feet felt heavy as lead. Got lost in the enchanting maze of Parisian streets and didn't care.

Andrei came often into her thoughts. She missed him terribly. How strange, that when she finally realized how much he meant to her, he'd chosen another woman. Love has no mercy, she thought bitterly.

One evening at a wine bar, a man came up to her. An American. He slipped onto the stool beside her, elbowed into her space in an overly familiar way. "I know you," he gave her a wink. "Claudine, right? We spent a night together."

"My name's Maria. You've mistaken me for someone else. Take off." She shifted farther away from him.

The man's face reddened in annoyance. "For a hooker, you're pretty unfriendly, aren't you? I *should* remember, I paid you enough."

She threw some euros on the counter to pay for her drink, slid off the stool and marched out.

In Geneva she decided to look up Marcus Constantin. She made it to his gallery door but couldn't bring herself to go in, and at the last minute, turned away. She left the city the next day, took the train to Bern, went on to Italy. Like a phantom, she floated through cities, invisible. If she experienced any joy, it was in knowing she mattered to no one.

One night in Turin she stood on the bridge named Ponte Mosca with her hands in her pockets, the breeze ruffling her blond hair. She mused about how easy it would be to leap off, let the black water slip over her, peacefully and permanently. Although she eventually turned away, she wasn't sure why.

After Italy, Maria traveled to Prague, Sofia and Belgrade. The weather over the past weeks had turned rainy and gray and she found herself craving sunshine. She decided to stay in Crete for a time, sleepy now that the tourist season was finished. Its bleached white landscape and azure sea lifted her spirits.

A long letter to her supervisor at Yale had gained her a substantial extension to the deadline for her thesis. It would be a waste to turn her back on her MA. Every afternoon she left her modest rental apartment and walked half an hour to a café, where she ordered brutally strong coffee and a bite to eat, and set up her tablet to write.

When she'd first started going to the café, men wouldn't leave her alone. Her allure had diminished, not disappeared. Many of the locals seated at the tables, smoking, trading stories and jokes, cast hungry glances at her. A beautiful woman sitting alone day after day was a mystery to them. A swarthy fellow wearing a lot of flash, gold rings and chains around his neck, pestered her constantly. She'd decided she'd have to choose another spot for her regular hangout, but then the café owner intervened. After that she was left in relative peace.

Physically she felt almost back to normal. She'd put on weight and all the walking strengthened her. And there were other changes. Except to tidy her hair or brush her teeth, she never looked in a mirror. On the occasions she did, she barely recognized her own reflection. She'd stopped the waxing and laser treatments and now had a silky golden fringe around her pubis. She changed her birth control prescription and it felt strange to have her monthlies again after years without them.

But her interior life had not caught up. Inside she felt empty, like an old tree with beautiful bark that hid a rotted-out core. She'd stayed in Crete too long. Perhaps that was it. Boredom was setting in.

She made plans to leave. The day of her departure she went to the café for a quick coffee and to say good-bye to the owner. It was warm out, sunny for November. She sat outside.

As she got up to pay her bill, she noticed the figure of a man down the street. Something struck her as familiar about him. His easy stride, the confident way he carried himself. She gave her head a shake. Her mind was playing tricks on her. She'd almost succeeded in erasing Andrei's memory. And now here she was again, imagining the impossible. She'd have to hurry to make her flight.

He called out to her.

It might be possible to mistake a figure, but not a voice. Maria's heart leaped. For a moment she was unable to speak.

He took off his sunglasses and gave her his old familiar grin. Instantly his smile swept her back, to the dinners, the drives, the laughter over drinks, the magical night at his place in Brighton Beach. "Glad I caught up with you," he said. "Were you just heading off somewhere?"

She hoped her voice wouldn't betray the emotion that overcame her at the sight of him. "I have to be at the airport by six P.M. for my flight. Why are *you* here?"

"I've been wondering how you're doing. Lillian told me you'd come to Crete and gave me your address. You neighbor told me you liked to come to this café."

"I thought you were in California . . . with your girlfriend."

The ring of his laughter sent her spinning. It was so good to hear his voice again. "You've got the California part right. If you're talking about the woman I helped with her business, she's married to a good friend of mine. Very happily," he added.

"Oh!" Her face flushed in embarrassment.

His eyes searched hers. "You look much better; I'm happy to see that."

She glanced away, unable to trust her reaction to the scorching impact of his gaze. "Yes. Going away was a good move for me."

"It wasn't for me. I've missed you like hell, Maria." He moved closer, took her hand. She felt the gentle strength in his grip and melted. "I wasn't going to say this right off. But there's no point in pretending. If you'd rather I leave you alone, I will. I just thought . . . it was worth a try."

It would be so easy to step away, return to the safe cocoon she'd spun in the weeks since she'd left New York. All she had to say was no and she knew Andrei would accept that as final. As Claudine, she'd always had power. Her wanderings through Europe had not altered that. Asking Andrei to stay would change that equation and she feared the uncertainty of it. She swallowed hard, the words he didn't want to hear on the tip of her tongue.

But when she looked up at him, she knew she couldn't deny the decision her body had already made. "I could ask you to go away and I'd be fine, but you'd take half of me with you."

Andrei pulled her to him; the top of her head just brushed his chin. She could feel the heat of his skin through the thin fabric of his shirt, his strong arms around her. She touched his throat with her lips and drank in his warm familiar scent. He captured her face in his hands and kissed her fully, passionately. When at last their kisses cooled, a round of applause from the men seated at a table behind them made them laugh.

They sauntered arm in arm back to his hotel room, a short walk from the café, saying little, basking in the luxury of their nearness. A moment of sheer fear struck her. What if when they got into bed, the intimacy they'd experienced before failed to come again? What if after all that had happened, the harsh words they'd exchanged had taken their toll? Having found him again, she couldn't bear the thought. She was more open now than any time she could remember in her life. The realization frightened her.

As if he could read her thoughts, Andrei slowed his place and looked at her. "I love you. After we quarreled I could barely think straight." He stopped and drew her closer. "Promise me you'll never leave me again."

His words brought tears to her eyes and her fears slipped away. "I couldn't imagine being without you again. I belong with you, Andrei."

As the day had been warm, Maria wore only a light shirt and skirt. In the privacy of his room, Andrei undid her shirt buttons, spread the wings of the fabric apart, reached around her back, unclasped her bra, and pulled down the straps. His gaze swept her naked breasts. Maria read his deep hunger for her in his eyes. "I can't believe I'm holding you again," he whispered. "I almost didn't come to Crete; I was so sure you wouldn't want to see me."

Without a word, Maria opened the buttons of his shirt, pressed herself against his broad chest. Felt their hearts beating in tandem. She put her hand on the dark hair at the nape of his neck, twined the curls in her fingers. She touched her lips to the cleft of his chin.

He kissed her lips again, softly, softly, while his fingers brushed along her ribs and found the exquisite heat of her breasts. He bent his head low and captured a tender nipple in his mouth. She undid his jeans, let them fall to the floor. He unzipped her skirt and it fell too. Holding each other for balance, they slipped off their shoes. They moved to the bed and lay facing each other.

With the lightest of touches, Maria ran her hand down his lean chest, his taut stomach and his cock. His crown grew moist and she felt a slight tremble in his body. He pulled her panties down and she raised her hips to help him. "I like it better this way," he said, brushing the golden hairs.

They gazed at each other for a long time, a shaft of light from between the curtains burnishing their skin. Maria pressed her hips against Andrei's. She raised herself on one elbow and pushed him back on the bed. He helped her straddle him, and she swallowed him slowly with her tight heat. She moved up and down with languorous movements, drawing him deeper into her until he filled her completely. Her hair tumbled around her shoulders, and he buried his hands in it, as though luxuriating in her beauty. She rolled her hips, circled round and round upon him, squeezing and releasing until his breath grew short and he made tiny moans in his throat. She rode him harder now, and clasped his hands for balance. With their hot palms pressed together, she started to grind against him. The delicious pressure upon her nub caused ripples to flutter deep through her pelvis, roll and spread into her abdomen. She cried sharply at the moment his seed emptied inside her and savored his gruff groan of bliss. Her whole body vibrated with pleasure as she came. The world stopped spinning for a moment, and she lay upon him. He began to soften. She wiggled her rump closer so he wouldn't slip out. "Just stay inside me forever," she murmured.

He laughed and ruffled her hair, gave her a kiss. "Happy to. I always did obey your orders, can't see stopping now."

After a time, he rolled her onto her side and cradled her in his arms.

They barely left his room for the next five days. Fucking gloriously, learning the landscape of each other's bodies, telling their secrets, making promises, some of which they kept, some not.

On their last night in Crete they went to a club, a crowded, smoky cubbyhole. The four-piece band played American pop. "Dance with me?" she asked after watching the other couples. She held out her arms.

"I'm not great at it," Andrei admitted.

She smiled and touched her lips to his. "Finally I've discovered something you're not good at. Just hold me and move to the music. It's easy."

They waited until a slow song came on and elbowed through the gyrating bodies on the dance floor. She slipped her hands underneath his top to feel his bare, sweaty skin. He hugged her close. His dark hair brushed her cheek. "I've been thinking," he said.

"Hmmm? About what?" she murmured, swaying to the rhythm.

"What we'll do—in the future. I've saved all the money I need to buy a house in Brighton Beach. You liked it there—didn't you?"

Andrei felt her head nod against his jaw but her shoulders tensed. He continued, "It's a nice place to raise kids. Maybe two . . . or three. I've got enough connections to get a good job . . ."

Her heart sank. She tilted her head back and looked at him.

"Andrei, that's not my idea of . . ." His wicked smile stopped her short. She gave him a playful slap. "You almost had me there."

He burst out laughing. "Oh, I don't know. You'd look pretty good in high heels and an apron—no?"

She laughed.

He pulled her to him. They danced a few turns around the floor before she spoke again. "I want to finish my MA. After that I have no idea, no plans."

He brought her closer and his voice grew serious. "I have a plan."

"Tell me."

"To spend the rest of my life, however long it is, with you."

The author is a bestselling, international award-winning Canadian novelist whose work has been published in many countries. She's writing under the pen name **Barbara Palmer**, inspired by the famous seventeenth-century English courtesan and royal mistress.